"He could be the one, dear."

"Mother!" Alex hushed her as she shut the door. "What if he sensed you were here?"

"Dr. Michael Duffy—what a nice name," her mother mused aloud, oblivious of Alex's warning. "I always dreamed you'd marry a doctor. And he has lovely eyes...."

Alex threw her hands up in surrender. "Fine, he has bedroom eyes. But he's probably married with six kids."

"He wasn't wearing a wedding ring and he lives in an apartment. Six children and an apartment don't mix. Besides, he's an improvement over the other men—"

"Mother, please!"

This can't be happening, Alex thought to herself. *I can see it all now—she'll put a spell on him and it'll explode right in my face.* She groaned. *If this is what turning thirty is like, forty is going to be hell!*

ABOUT THE AUTHOR

Linda Randall Wisdom is a well-known name to readers of romance fiction. A background in marketing and public relations gives her a wealth of experience on which to draw when creating characters. Linda knew she was destined to write romance novels when her first sale came on her wedding anniversary. She lives in Southern California with her husband and a houseful of exotic birds.

Books by Linda Randall Wisdom
HARLEQUIN AMERICAN ROMANCE

Don't miss any of our special offers. Write to us at the following address for information on our newest releases.

Harlequin Reader Service
P.O. Box 1397, Buffalo, NY 14240
Canadian address: P.O. Box 603,
Fort Erie, Ont. L2A 5X3

LINDA
RANDALL
WISDOM

FREE SPIRITS

Harlequin Books

TORONTO • NEW YORK • LONDON
AMSTERDAM • PARIS • SYDNEY • HAMBURG
STOCKHOLM • ATHENS • TOKYO • MILAN

Chuck-It-All Tours motto,
"We send you where you don't want to go,"
is another word for "The trip from hell."

Many thanks to Susan James, C.I.A.'s best
customer, who has traveled the world over and
thanks to Chuck-It-All now refuses to leave that dark
spot under her bed. We had no idea your Halloween
weekend at Dracula's castle would end up with your
blood pouring instead of blood pressure soaring with
excitement. The least we could do was cover all
charges from the blood bank. It's clients like you
who make the travel business fun, fun, fun!

Published August 1991

ISBN 0-373-16401-7

FREE SPIRITS

Prologue

Cartoonist Talks About The "Trip From Hell"

The newest cartoon strip to come to the Sunday comics section is "Chuck-It-All Tours," with the whimsical motto, "We send you where you don't want to go." That is just what cartoonist Alex Cassidy and her alter ego, Fritzi, a frizzy-haired tour operator have done. Shown us the kind of vacations we could have ended up with! From a trip to the Himalayas to a hike with the Abominable Snowman (with the caution to bring enough food for yourself *and* your leader, since his carnivorous appetite is well known!). My favorite is the U.S. gourmet tour which involves visiting all well-known truck stops along the highways. For an extra fee, the client can also work there!

Alex Cassidy prefers the quiet life, staying close to her San Marino apartment where her strip comes to life under the watchful eye of her Siamese cat, Suzi Q. Divorced, the lovely cartoonist enjoys playing softball with friends and creating new tours to alternately shock and send the readers into gales of laughter. If you want to discover which trip to miss when vacation time rolls around, read "Chuck-It-All Tours." *Los Angeles Times*

Chapter One

"I'm very worried about her, Patrick. She should have awakened hours ago." The woman's voice was soft and normally soothing to the ear, unless said ear felt as if it would fall off at any moment. "Do you think something could be wrong? I wish we could call a doctor for her."

"There's nothing wrong with her, Marian. Considering her condition when Beth brought her in last night, she's better off sleeping as long as possible." The male voice was equally intrusive to the delicate eardrum. "Remember when she rolled in after her all-night party when she graduated from high school? Of course, she hadn't imbibed then. At least, that's what she tried to tell us, although a hangover is something that's easily recognizable. I guess she figured her birthday was another reason to tie one on."

The object of the whispered conversation moaned and slowly rolled over onto her back, her arm flung across her closed eyes. Unintelligible words left lips still colored with a trace of deep red lipstick.

"Alex does not look well."

"You wouldn't either if you had come rolling in at 4:00 a.m. singing 'Happy Birthday to Me' at the top of your lungs. She still has a tin ear when it comes to music." The masculine chuckle pounded through the sensitive brain encased in cement. "She's going to wake up with a hell of a hangover."

"Please, stop," Alex begged, her cement-encased eyelids fluttering. "And turn out those psychedelic lights before they blind me."

"Alex, please wake up. We've come a long way to see you." The woman's voice coaxed.

Alex's brow furrowed. Something didn't seem right. For the life of her, she couldn't figure out what it could be. She carefully drew her arm away and slowly raised one eyelid. Two shadowy figures stood at the foot of her bed with blinding smiles on their faces.

"Mom? Dad?" she croaked, wincing as the sound of her words reverberated through her pounding head.

"You've got one beauty of a hangover, sweetheart," her father told her. "You must have celebrated your birthday in style last night."

"Yeah, I guess I did. You know, it's really funny. I thought you two were dead. Isn't that . . . ?" Reality may have been slow in sinking in, but when it arrived, it arrived like a proverbial freight train. "No!" She shot up in bed, eyes the color of blue ice widening until she looked bug-eyed. One look was enough to convince her she wasn't having your normal, everyday hangover dream. She did the only logical thing. She screamed.

The couple stepped back a pace, startled by the shrill sound escaping her lungs. The scream turned into a moan of pain as her head separated from her body while the sound bounced around inside her tender brain. "Oh, my God." She squinted at the figures standing before her. "But you're . . . and I . . . then, if you're . . . I must be . . ." She held up her hand in front of her, fully expecting to see it disappear in a wisp of smoke before her very eyes. "I'm dead!" Alex wailed, her bloodshot eyes widened in horror at the idea that she had died and didn't even know how.

"Oh no, my dear!" Marian Cassidy, sitting next to Alex's hip, moved to put her arms around her daughter's shoulders, but Alex shrank from her touch. "Alex, you are not dead. You're very much alive. We're the ones who are dead," she informed her with a broad smile that indicated that everything should be all right now.

Alex didn't see it that way. She watched Marian with a wary gaze. "This has got to be somebody's idea of a sick joke."

"No joke, and you're still hung over and very much alive," Patrick Cassidy said dryly.

She would have shaken her head, but she knew better than to make any movement that might destroy the fragile threads holding her skull together. "This doesn't make any sense. How can I be alive and see you, when you're dead?" she insisted, her voice rising in pitch. "I should know you're dead. I was at your funeral ten months ago!" She whimpered as she placed her hands against the side of her head. She greatly feared it was going to shatter into millions of tiny pieces any moment now. "This is all a bad dream. It's just part of my hangover," she assured herself, but not sounding very convincing. After all, how could a person sound convincing when she was whimpering like a lost puppy?

"You got any tomato juice in the kitchen?" Patrick questioned.

"Yes. There's a can in the cabinet over the refrigerator," Alex answered without thinking. She stared at the two people standing in the middle of her room. Two people who most definitely did not belong there. She wasn't sure what to believe anymore.

"I'm going to fix her my infamous hangover cure," he told Marian. "Once she drinks that, she'll be fine."

Alex stared at the man leaving her bedroom and shifted her apprehensive gaze back to the woman smiling at her. The woman who looked like her mother, sounded like her mother, but who couldn't be her mother. She wondered if she wouldn't be better playing along with this crazy vision until her dream stopped and she fully woke up. "Look, it's very nice to see you again, but luckily I'm intelligent enough to know you're nothing more than a figment of my hangover. Once I wake up, you'll be gone and I'll be able to suffer this torture in peace."

"No, dear, we're not a figment of your hangover or your imagination. We've come back to be with you for a very important reason."

Alex opened her mouth to ask what reason would bring them back from the dead, when her father walked in carrying a tall glass of red liquid with strange specks floating on top. "Drink this down in one gulp and then take a long hot shower," he advised. "You'll feel loads better afterward."

"This can't be real," Alex chanted, cautiously accepting the glass. She grimaced at the first taste. "It's amazing something that doesn't exist can taste so horrible."

"You go take that shower while I fix you some breakfast." Marian patted Alex's hand as she stood up on wobbly legs. "You'll feel even better after you put something in your stomach."

Patrick grimaced. "Marian, please, don't cook. She feels bad enough without having to eat your cooking."

"Wait a minute," Alex begged their backs as they left the room. "I have questions. This is my dream, I should be allowed to find out what's going on before I wake up."

"We'll answer them while you eat." The door closed after them.

Alex looked around the room, wondering if that had also changed. Nope, her decorating efforts of four months ago were still intact. The quilted bedspread with the hand-painted irises fluttering across the soft cream background lay in a tangle at the end of the bed. Matching shams were tossed onto the nearby soft turquoise chair. Even the vertical blinds with the same design remained closed against the bright morning light that she knew would sear her tender eyeballs if she dared open them.

She practically crawled into the bathroom. The same design was echoed in the embroidered design on the towels and in the stormy blues, purples and hints of pink in the shadow pattern on the rug and shower curtain.

"It appears the only thing that changed overnight was the number of occupants in this apartment," she muttered, closing the door behind her. "At least that imaginary concoction helped my head. It's amazing how real dreams are getting nowadays." With a critical eye, she examined herself in the mirror over the sink, then wished she hadn't. Thick, dark brown hair hanging in limp tangles framed a pale face blotchy with hectic color, once-clear blue eyes were bloodshot and sore-looking. Even her teeth hurt.

"This is it. No more hangovers. My system can't handle this. Freddie Krueger looks better than I do right about now." She turned on the shower and adjusted the temperature before stepping behind the curtain.

Alex turned on the massage unit on her shower head and stood under the hot pulsating jets for as long as she could handle it. Once she began to feel a bit more human, she set about washing her hair and soaping her body.

"It was all a dream," she reassured herself, as she briskly toweled herself off and wrapped another towel turban-style around her hair. "It was just wishful thinking on my part. And perfectly natural. I thought about Mom and Dad last night during my party. I was wishing they could be there, so naturally I would dream about them suddenly appearing before me." She loaded toothpaste on her brush, in hopes a good brushing would banish the green fuzzy things she was certain resided inside her mouth. "You'll go into the living room and you'll see that there's no one there." She kept up her speech as she emerged from the steam-filled bathroom, her robe now wrapped tightly around her body. She froze in the doorway, her head uplifted, nose quivering from a scent she never thought she'd inhale again. There was no mistake. Burned French toast.

"No, it can't be." She hurried out of her bedroom and through the living room to the kitchen, where she found a scene from her past; her mother stood at the counter overseeing blackened pieces of bread while a sleek Siamese cat yowled her way around her ankles and her father sat at the table reading the paper. "Oh, no," she moaned, collapsing against the doorway. "It's got to be a dream."

Patrick looked up from the sports page. "You look much better, kiddo. Of course, you haven't eaten your mother's cooking yet."

"Patrick," Marian remonstrated, turning from her task.

"Marian, we've been married for thirty-four years and you still can't cook worth a damn." He blew her a kiss. "But I love you, anyway."

Alex clutched the doorway to keep from falling to the floor. When would she wake up from this crazy dream? "I still don't understand what is going on here." Her normally husky voice sounded rough.

Patrick put the paper aside. "Come and sit down, Alex. Have some coffee. We'll try to explain this to you as best we can."

Marian handed Alex a cup filled with the dark brew as she hesitantly took a chair across from her father.

"You—ah—you look well. For being dead, that is," she said for lack of anything better. "Someone must have put some kind of drug in the champagne last night. That's the only way I could sit here with you." She beamed, pleased that finally she had come up with an appropriate reason.

Patrick chuckled. "No such luck, kiddo. I know this is a shock for you, Alex. This is a bit of a surprise for us, too. We didn't think this was possible. We're very glad it is."

"Oh, Patrick, tell it to her straight," Marian urged, taking a chair next to Alex. "You see, dear, we've come back to see you properly married."

Alex choked on her coffee for two reasons. One, because of her mother's announcement; two, because her mother's coffee was always strong enough to float the entire U.S. Navy. No, it was all some drug-induced dream, and she only thought she was sitting here drinking coffee when she was actually still in bed. She held on to that thought and sat back to enjoy her dream.

"Jason hasn't proposed yet," she explained.

Patrick grimaced. "Jason Patterson? You're still seeing that stuffed shirt? I thought you would have more sense by now."

"Jason *Palmer* is a wonderful man. He has an excellent position with Trainor and Associates. And most of all, he's nothing at all like Craig." Her face twisted with distaste as she mentioned her ex-husband's name.

"The man is boring."

"You only met him once!"

"Once was all it took to tell he was more boring than an insurance salesman!"

"Now listen, you two, time to stop before you end up in a shouting match," Marian announced, as she placed a plate in front of each of them, then returned with a bottle of warmed syrup. "The two of you have never agreed on Jason. And I doubt either of you will change your mind now."

Alex stared at the black squares of bread her mother called French toast. She looked up at her mother. Amazing how dreams were so real, she marveled to herself. "Mom, didn't they have cooking classes in...on...wherever you were?"

Patrick chuckled. "I think it's too late for that."

"This from the daughter who dared to have me buried in this horrible dress," Marian grumbled, placing a dish of cat food in a corner. "Here you are, Suzi Q. At least someone appreciates my cooking."

"She doesn't need to worry. You only opened a can for her," Patrick murmured.

Alex sat back, amazed at the familiar banter floating around her. She felt as if she had fallen back in time. Her father, dressed in his favorite blue suit and white shirt with a blue-and-gray striped tie. She remembered the tears she shed as she pulled the suit from the closet to take over to the funeral home. His thick silver hair was brushed back from his forehead in the style she well remembered. Her mother wore a deep rose silk dress, her hair, tinted to a lighter brown than Alex's own dark tresses, was pulled back in the French twist she'd worn for years. Her mind, still befuddled from the events of the night before and what she'd seen this morning, could only come up with one conclusion.

"I don't want to believe you two are ghosts."

They looked up, both smiling at her.

"Too bad, daughter of mine, because we are," Patrick assured her.

Alex's laugh was a bit shaky. "No, you're not." She studied each of them long and hard. "Ghosts wear long white robes or look transparent or walk through walls or something. This is just a dream that I'll wake up from in the morning." She smiled brightly, pleased with her decision.

Marian sighed. "Myrna said her grandson said the exact same thing. Alex, we're real ghosts, not the kind from books or movies. Due to special circumstances we were able to return here to make sure you're married properly."

"As long as it isn't that Potter idiot," Patrick muttered, into his coffee.

"*Palmer!*" Alex was astounded she could argue so easily with a figment of her imagination. "I'm curious. If you two are real ghosts, can just anyone see and hear you? Or just members of the family? I mean, are there special rules?''

The couple shared a long look that said they were going to have a long haul convincing Alex.

''Just you,'' Patrick replied. ''You're the only one who can see and hear us. To you, we're as real as any three-dimensional object. That means you can also touch us. Anyone else would just walk right through us as if we weren't there, and they wouldn't feel anything nor would we.''

''And Suzi Q.'' Marian looked down at the Siamese prowling around her ankles. ''She also sees us.''

Alex looked off in space as she blindly reached for the pack of cigarettes and lighter on the table.

Marian fixed her with a steely glare. ''You told me a year ago you gave up that nasty habit. You even said something about going to one of those stop-smoking clinics.''

Alex lit the cigarette. ''I lied,'' she admitted without apology. After all, she wasn't actually talking to her mother, right?

The older woman straightened her shoulders. ''Then I'll just have to convince you to give up the filthy habit.''

Alex shook her head. Her argument with her mother about her smoking had gone on for a long time, and Alex wasn't about to give in just because her mother came back in a dream to hound her about it. ''This is an incredible dream. My friends give me a surprise party last night to celebrate my thirtieth birthday, I have a bit more fun than usual, and I wake up to find my dead parents in my bedroom telling me they've come back to see me properly married. I once read somewhere that dreams are a part of a person's subconscious. It's amazing what I'm learning is in mine. I only hope I remember all of this in the morning.'' She frowned in thought. ''My dream hangover is bad enough. I hate to think what the real one will be like.''

Marian sighed heavily. "She'll never believe us," she told her husband.

"Yes, she will. Once she's gotten her hangover out of the way and is willing to listen to reason." Patrick patted her hand.

Alex chuckled. "Oh, I'm very reasonable. This is all a dream."

"If you're such a reasonable woman, why did you choose this dress for me?" Marian inserted, looking down at herself with distaste. "This color makes me look sallow."

Alex looked at her dream mother. "But I thought that was one of your favorite dresses."

"This was never a favorite. I always hated it. In fact, I meant to get rid of it. Now I'm doomed to wear it forever." Marian plucked the silk folds with open distaste.

Alex frowned. This was starting to get a little out of hand. *Maybe it's a nightmare,* she silently told herself. "Aunt Irene thought it would be appropriate."

"You allowed Irene to choose the dress I was buried in? That explains everything. She wanted me to go to my grave looking sallow. That sister of mine never forgave me for stealing Patrick out from under her nose. She couldn't understand that Patrick really wasn't interested in her when we first met him at Jane Simpson's birthday party. Darling, you must eat before your food gets cold." Patrick and Alex exchanged a telling look. They'd established a long time ago that Marian must not have any taste buds where her own cooking was concerned. "Was it a nice funeral, dear? Were there a lot of people there? How was the weather?" she asked brightly.

Alex's eyes widened in shock. "I can't believe I would have a dream allowing you to ask such morbid questions?" she squeaked. "I'm having enough trouble understanding why I haven't woken up yet and I'm listening to you ask

about your own funeral in such a blasé way! I'm still trying
to figure out how you got in my dream!''

"Alex, honey, we keep telling you we aren't part of a
dream, but I guess it's just going to take time convincing
you. As for your mother, you know her well enough to
know that she wants every little detail,'' Patrick cut in. "As
for how we got here, that's a trade secret. The one thing I
can tell you is that we received this chance because we died
before our time.''

She stared at him over the rim of her cup. She was well-
known for her creative mind, but even she couldn't have
come up with an idea this outrageous. This was one dream
she just had to remember when she finally woke up! "I beg
your pardon?''

"We weren't supposed to be on that road that night. Because we took a wrong turn, we were wiped out by an eigh-
teen-wheeler that wasn't supposed to be there either,'' he
explained. "Ironically, when all this happened your mother
and I were talking about you and Peterson and how we
hoped you'd get smart and throw him out of your life.''

"Palmer," she stressed the name. "You do this deliberately, Dad.''

"It's Freudian,'' Marian spoke up. "Patrick figures, if he
doesn't remember Jason's name, you'll soon forget the
man.''

Alex chewed on her lower lip as something else came back
to her. "This is incredible. I have you talking about seeing
me properly married. How much more properly married can
I get than with Jason?'' She held up a forefinger. "Aha!
See, now I know you're a dream. Otherwise, you'd admit I
was right. I'm remembering you two the way you were. Believe me, by now you both would realize just how right
Jason is for me,'' she concluded happily.

Patrick exhaled a breath of frustration. "This dream
business is beginning to annoy me. He's not right for you,

Alex. The man has his life so strictly controlled that he not only knows where he's taking his vacation five years from now, but he's probably already made his reservations! Why, I bet his suits are lined up in the closet according to color and season and his shirts kept in the same order. Of course, there's not much you can do with an entire wardrobe of white shirts. Why, I bet he even has his underwear starched.''

"So what? At least I can count on Jason a lot more than I could ever count on Craig!" she argued. "When I thought Craig was performing noble works at the hospital it turned out he was hidden away at the No Tell Motel with his latest conquest. Who knows how long that would have gone on if one of those bimbos hadn't decided she wanted to be the next Mrs. Dr. Craig Summers and showed up on the doorstep. Her stunt might have lost her chance of being a doctor's wife, but that didn't stop him from marrying someone else two weeks after our divorce was final. She caught on to his flings a lot sooner than I did and her ultimatum worked just as well as mine did. Their marriage lasted an entire four months." There was no bitterness in her voice, only resignation. "Marriage to Craig taught me one thing. Being married to a doctor is bad for one's mental health."

"Not all doctors are like Craig," Marian protested. "Look at Doctor Fletcher. He and Lena have been married for more than forty years."

"He's one of the rare ones," Alex conceded. "But if the two of you are worried about my unmarried state, don't be. I'm very happy with my life as it is and I'll take the next step when Jason and I decide it's time. And the way he's been talking lately, I'm sure he'll be proposing soon. Will you stop that!" She glared at her father, who was bending over the side of his chair, pretending to stick his finger down his throat. "You never gave him a chance."

"Fine, I'll give him one now," he quipped, a twinkle in his eye.

"You can't, because you're nothing more than a dream!" She'd had enough. Alex jumped up and carried her dishes over to the sink. "Look, it's been nice seeing you two again, but this dream is not going well. So, no offense, but I'm going to wake up now. Why don't you two return to wherever you came from, and we'll all be happy. I've got a deadline for my next batch of strips staring me in the face and a ton of work ahead of me."

"Dear, we can't leave."

She turned at her mother's words, with panic etched on her face. There was something in the older woman's voice that smacked too much of the truth. What if this wasn't a dream? What if . . . no, she stoutly assured herself. This had to be a dream, right? *Right?* "What do you mean you can't leave?" She felt suffocated.

"Just that," Marian replied. "We're here until you're married to the right person."

Horror filled Alex's mind. She had a dreaded thought. If this wasn't a hangover-induced dream, she was actually sitting here with her parents who had died ten months earlier! "And if I don't marry the person you two deem right for me?" she whispered between stiff lips.

Marian's smile grew even broader. "Then we stay until you do."

Alex spun around, bracing her hands on the sink. "I can't handle this," she muttered, turning away and running out of the room.

"I don't think she believes us yet." Patrick's words followed her out.

Alex first escaped to her bedroom, where she quickly dressed in a pair of loose white cotton drawstring pants and a bright, hot pink oversized cotton T-shirt. One long look in the mirror convinced her this was no dream. This was about as real as it could get, and she wasn't too sure she could handle it. After ascertaining her hair was dry enough, she brushed it out and pulled it back in a ponytail high on her head before heading for the second bedroom that she had set up as her office and workroom. Right now the drawing table and bottles of ink and pens waiting for her offered a welcome retreat into reality. Right now she needed that heady dose of reality. Before settling down to work, she turned on the portable television she kept there for company.

"And now we'll return to our morning movie, Bob Hope in *The Ghost Breakers*," a disembodied voice announced.

"Oh, no, you don't." Alex snatched up the remote control and punched a button with more force than was necessary. She wasn't fond of game shows, but she decided she could always change her choice in programs.

"And now for our next question. What famous ghost—"

"Augh!" The channel button was punched again.

"If you're not careful, you'll punch your finger right through the control." Patrick stood in the doorway.

She set the control down. "I still can't take all this in. This isn't a dream, is it?" She sounded hopeful that he might say differently.

"I'm afraid not." He walked in and looked at the cork board on one wall, decorated with colorful cartoon strips, stopping to read each one. "These are wonderful, Alex." He chuckled over one. "A tour of the North Pole where the Abominable Snowman can take you on a one-way hike? And be sure to bring enough food for both of you? That's good."

"A friend complained about the heat last summer and asked why 'Chuck-It-All Tours' couldn't have some trips to cooler places. That was one of the ideas I came up with," Alex replied, still watching him with a suspicious gaze. "The strip is doing so well that I'm featured in another twenty-five papers.'' Her mind was spinning with dozens of questions. If they were really ghosts, how could this have come about? She wanted to go back to the belief that it was a dream.

Patrick beamed. ''I'm proud of you, baby. Who knew that your love for doodling would grow into a syndicated comic strip featuring a crazy tour operator?''

'''Chuck-It-All Tours'—motto, *We send you where you don't want to go,*'' she quoted, still watching him as if he might disappear in a puff of smoke at any minute. ''It has turned out to be a surprise success. I don't think Fritzi will ever be as popular a character as 'Cathy,' but she's holding her own.''

Patrick nodded. ''Your mother and I knew our appearing like this would startle you and you would have trouble taking all of this in, but the last thing we want to do is frighten you or make you feel harassed. It's just that we love you, and like any parents, dead or alive,'' he flashed a grin, ''we want what's best for you. Can I help it if I don't think Jason is good enough for you?''

''I still can't believe this is happening. But if it is, you have to understand that Jason is very good for me. He isn't threatened by my success nor the idea that I draw a comic strip,'' she explained, tamping down that one niggling memory of Jason explaining to people she was an artist and not mentioning the cartoon strip at all. ''If you want me to be happy, then let it go at that, because ghosts can't properly matchmake when no one else can see them. Ghosts,'' she groaned. ''I can't believe I'm actually using that word!''

He smiled. ''You'll have to, I'm afraid. As for matchmaking, we have ways you'd never dream of. I'll let you get to work. Do you still have cable?'' She slowly nodded. ''ESPN?'' She nodded again. ''Good, maybe I'll get lucky and find a golf match on. And maybe I'll talk your mother out of cooking lunch for you.''

Alex watched her father leave. "Dad?" He turned his head, a questioning look on his face. "Can you and Mom disappear? You know, go up in smoke or something?"

He grinned. "I'm sure the time will come for you to find that out."

"That's what I'm afraid of," she muttered, turning back to her drawing board.

It wasn't surprising that two hours later Alex remained seated there, her mind a complete blank.

"None of this can be real. Unless it's to help me think up some new ideas for the strip. Maybe 'Chuck-It-All' should offer tours of haunted houses," she mused, staring at the heavy white paper with its neatly drawn-in large black squares taped to the slightly slanted board. "Ride with the headless horseman, float along with the lady in the lake, fly with the ghosts of Orville and Wilbur Wright, eat dinner with Henry the Eighth." She nodded to herself as she jotted down notes on a lined pad she kept nearby. She'd learned long ago that it helped to write down her ideas before she sketched them out. "Maybe something good will come from this, after all." With the idea quickly growing in her mind, she took up the heavy-duty felt-tip pen she used for her rough drafts. Within moments she was hard at work, her unexpected guests forgotten as she brought her idea to life.

"SO WHAT ARE WE going to do?" Marian plopped herself down on the couch next to Patrick, who was concentrating on a football game since he hadn't been lucky enough to find a golf match on.

"Hmm?" He didn't look up as his eyes remained trained on the television. "Do about what?"

"Patrick, I'm talking to you about Alexis, your loving daughter." She grew exasperated. "What are we going to do?"

He frowned. "What about Alex?"

Marian sighed. "About her assumption that Jason Palmer will make a perfect husband, when we both know she would be bored to tears with him within a week. Not to mention those suspicions that he's involved in something illegal. I'm just grateful they haven't moved in together. It would make things that much more difficult."

"The easiest thing to do would be to find her someone better suited for her." Patrick's attention was still centered on the television screen. "Will you look at that? I forgot how brutal Australian football was."

"Patrick Thomas Cassidy, forget the football game," she scolded, snatching the remote control out of his hand. "We have some serious plotting to do. And we don't have any time to waste. I looked in Alex's appointment book and she has a dinner engagement with Jason tomorrow night."

"There's no need to do anything right away," he argued, his eyes trained on the television screen. "Not if he isn't coming around until tomorrow."

"What if he decided to give her an engagement ring for a birthday gift? From all that she's said, she'll accept his proposal."

That caught his attention. He frowned at the idea. "I hadn't thought of that."

"You should have. You proposed to me on my birthday," she reminded him.

He reached over and kissed her cheek. "May seventeenth. A day I'll never forget, my love. I guess I didn't think he would have that much imagination. I figure his idea of an important day is whenever he closes a deal."

"Then we should come up with a distraction, just in case."

"Alex isn't too happy with this, as it is. Let's take it step by step. We'll play tomorrow by ear," he decided. "If we're not subtle about this, she'll never forgive us."

"Meaning you don't have any idea what to do."

"Meaning I want our plan to be foolproof. We need something she can't blame on us. You know what kind of temper our darling daughter has, and just because we're ghosts doesn't mean she won't blow her stack at us." Patrick's features lightened in speculation. "Don't worry. When the time comes, I'll have something more than appropriate." He patted her hand. "We didn't go to all this trouble to fail right off the bat, did we?"

BY THE TIME ALEX CLOSED her bedroom door that night, she felt as if she had survived four lifetimes in twenty-four hours. She reminded her parents the couch pulled out into a bed—if they had the ability to sleep, that is. Then she retired to her room for a long, hot soak in the tub and snuggled under the covers with her small television set perched on the bed.

"Maybe I'll get lucky and wake up in the morning to discover I was right and this was nothing more than a crazy dream," she murmured, leafing through the television listings. "'Ghost and Mrs. Muir.' Hey, just the thing to watch in my situation." She looked up at the ceiling. "If you wanted to send me a ghost, did you have to send me my parents? My mother still can't cook, and she's already started hiding my cigarettes. My father has never approved of my taste in men." Her attention was diverted by her cat stalking the air-filled hills in her covers until she finally pounced on Alex's lap. "You can see them too, Suzi Q, can't you? Either that, or you're having this dream right along with me." She didn't expect an answer, as the cat curled up against her chest. "And you've always loved to talk to Mom. Well, it's got to stop now, because I don't want any of my friends to see you talking to thin air. That is, if Mom and Dad are right and no one else can see them." She flopped back, groaning loudly. "Oh, come on, this can't be happening! And if it is, why did it have to happen *now?* Something's going to go wrong, I just know it. And before too long it's going to explode in my face. I can see it all now. The world is going to find out my parents are haunting my apartment and Bill Murray and Dan Aykroyd are going to come in and rout them out. If this is what happens when I turn thirty, I can see that forty is going to be hell!''

Chapter Two

"It was nothing more than wishful thinking," were Alex's first words when she bolted upright in bed. "That and a dream that would make a wonderful movie of the week."

Normally not the type of human being to wake up feeling cheerful and ready to face the big bad world, she was surprised to take stock and find herself mentally alert without her usual frantic need for caffeine first thing in the morning.

Pacing back and forth in front of the closed bedroom door, Suzi Q yowled her plea for it to be opened.

Alex frowned. She never closed her door unless she had overnight guests. "Okay, Suzi, I get the message."

She crept out of bed and cautiously opened the door. Silence greeted her. She heaved a sigh of relief. She was right. It was nothing more than a dream, a result of her spoken wish at her party that her parents could have been there to celebrate her birthday.

"Come on, let's find some breakfast." She padded barefoot into the kitchen and set up her coffee maker, then sneaked out the front door to grab the morning newspaper lying on her doorstep. Within ten minutes, she was seated at the table with her paper, a cup of coffee and two slices of toast topped with strawberry preserves. When the phone rang she kept her eyes on "Dear Abby" while reaching for the receiver, raising the antenna to the cordless model. "'Lo?"

"My, what a lovely greeting first thing in the morning." The male voice was well modulated and confident. "Honestly, Alexis, I thought you were more articulate than that."

Alex smiled. "Good morning, Jason. And to what do I owe this surprise call?" During business hours Jason Palmer avoided personal phone calls, which he considered frivolous. Much as he told her he adored her, she was not business.

"First of all, I hope you enjoyed your evening out with your friends two nights ago. I'm sorry I couldn't make your party, but I knew you would understand that I couldn't cancel my trip." As far as he was concerned, that was apology enough.

She frowned. Two nights ago? Had she drunk so much champagne she'd lost track of an entire day? Still, this wasn't the time to figure it out. "Of course, Jason, I understand. Besides, we have this evening for our celebration." She lowered her voice to a seductive purr.

"Actually, that's why I'm calling. Ronald Bishop and his wife are in town for today and tomorrow only," he explained. Alex winced. She already knew what was coming. "I realize I promised you an intimate dinner for two this evening, but I really do need to get together with him and…"

"And why couldn't the four of us go out, so I could keep Mrs. Bishop entertained while you dazzle Mr. Bishop with your financial expertise," she finished for him, tamping down the feelings of disappointment in her soul. When was the last time they had had a dinner out, just the two of them?

"That's it exactly." There was no mistaking the smile in his voice. "You did so well when we took the Burnses to dinner and later on the Edwardses that I know this will be much easier for you. And I do want to talk to Mr. Bishop about a very important investment.''

She managed a tight smile it was just as well he couldn't see. ''Of course. What time will you pick me up?''

''That's another problem. Since their hotel is on the other side of town, I hope you won't mind meeting us at the restaurant. I thought we'd dine at that new French place you and I tried two weeks ago. I made our reservations for eight o'clock and why don't you wear that black dress with the sequined jacket? And why don't you try your hair in an up-swept style?''

Her smile froze. She wasn't as fond of that dress as he was. She thought it made her look like one of those mannequin wives she met at Jason's get-togethers. ''Of course. I'll see you then.''

''Alexis, you're a dream. There goes my other line. I'll see you this evening, then.''

''Do you mean to say he even tells you what to wear and how to do your hair?'' Patrick spoke from behind. ''I knew it, the man doesn't have one romantic bone in his body.''

Alex shrieked, the phone flying from her hand. Only her father's quick reflexes kept it from falling to the floor. She turned around, gripping the back of her chair. ''I thought you were a dream,'' she gasped.

Patrick shrugged and shook his head. ''Far from it, sweetheart. We're about as real as ghosts can get. I thought you finally accepted that yesterday.''

Alex breathed deeply several times to slow down her rapidly pounding heart. Then, fearing hyperventilation, she forced herself to relax.

''This can't be happening.''

''You said that yesterday,'' Marian spoke up, understanding warming her features. ''Alex, we're here for the duration.''

"Oh, no, then I didn't just dream you?" she groaned. "You really showed up, and my birthday was two days ago instead of yesterday?"

Patrick nodded his head. "No dream. And judging from the conversation you just had with Potter, we got here in time to save you from a nasty mistake."

A moan escaped Alex's lips. "Palmer. Just once, get his name right!"

"Can you truthfully say you enjoy helping him entertain his clients, who are probably as boring as he is?" Patrick quizzed.

She tried to remain as calm as a person could in this kind of situation. Answering questions was the easiest way to begin. "I haven't done all that much in the way of entertaining, but it's interesting. Besides, sometimes the wives talk about their trips and I get ideas for my strip from their stories."

"I bet that would go over real well, if what's-his-name knew you were pumping his clients' wives for your cartoon strip."

"Patrick, you promised me you'd behave." Marian stood in one corner of the kitchen cooing to an excited Suzi Q who let out her earsplitting Siamese yowls as she waited for the dish of food Marian was holding.

"That cat is completely nuts," Alex muttered, watching Suzi Q's antics. Something then occurred to her. "How did you know what Jason said to me on the phone?"

Marian flashed her an apologetic smile. "Trade secret. Dear, surely you mean to eat more than that toast for breakfast? Would you like me to fix you some nice scrambled eggs or an omelet?"

"No!" Alex held out her hands as if to ward her off. There were too many memories of scrambled eggs as hard as baseballs. Marian's idea of an omelet was too horrifying to even contemplate. She still wasn't sure what was happening, but she couldn't accept this as a dream any longer. As difficult as it was to accept, she had to admit that her ghostly parents were right there before her! "Honest, Mom, this is all I want." She turned to her father. "Is there a reason why you two don't eat? Or is that another trade secret?

"We don't need to, and I'm very glad of it," he replied.

"Yes, I can understand why."

Alex still wasn't convinced that her ghostly parents intended to stay with her until they were satisfied she had married properly.

"I can't get any more proper than marriage to Jason," she reiterated.

"Proper." Patrick formed the word as if it was an obscenity. "He carries a clean, neatly pressed handkerchief in his pocket. He has a fire extinguisher and emergency roadside kit in the trunk of his car, although he hasn't used either once in the last fifteen years. And don't say he doesn't, because that one time I met him he suggested it would be a good idea for me to carry one. I'm sure he's added an earthquake survival kit to it. Has he even tried to get you into bed?"

"Dad!" Alex pretended to be shocked. "That is not something I am going to discuss with my parents. Why, I'm your virginal daughter."

"Not for a long time, you haven't been. And your statement means he hasn't. And you've been dating for how long? Two years?" He shook his head. "The man is clearly not as enamored of you as you think he is. Or he's gay and doesn't want the business world to know it—or he just doesn't give a damn about sex."

"He believes in respecting a woman," she said stiffly. "And he knows my marriage didn't go well. I think it's wonderful of him to be willing to give me time."

"Time, yes. Forever, no."

Alex looked at her father, the one person she always felt understood her. The one person who understood the wildness that sometimes surfaced in her. How could she explain that she hoped Jason could help her tamp down that wildness? She'd opted for excitement when she married Craig after a whirlwind courtship. She got anger, bitterness and self-disgust by the time it ended in a messy divorce.

"Jason keeps me calm, Dad," she explained. "He keeps me on a steady plane and I desperately need that. I already have a somewhat crazy job. And now I'm looking for a home life that will bring me back down to earth. He can give me that. And children."

"And if he decides your work isn't proper for an investment banker's wife?" he prodded. "Does he talk about your own work to his clients? And are you honestly sure he won't see children as a hindrance to his eternal entertaining of clients?"

She shifted her weight. "Those kind of dinners are strictly business." She felt obliged to defend Jason. "And of course he would want children to carry on his name."

Patrick looked sad. "Then, my darling, I feel very sorry for you, because marriage to him will cause you to miss out on a great deal." He walked away to join his wife, who was still conversing with Suzi Q in her own special language.

Alex jumped up. "This is getting crazy again." She left the kitchen for her bedroom. By the time she dressed, washed her face and brushed her hair, she felt more like herself. She still took the precaution of taking two aspirin.

When she walked out of her bedroom she found her parents with their heads together, whispering. She dreaded hearing their next brainstorm.

"This is a definite improvement over yesterday," Marian smiled.

"Yes, well, I decided one hangover in my lifetime was more than enough." She pulled open the drawer of a lamp table and drew out a pack of cigarettes. She couldn't miss her mother's look of disapproval. "Please, Mom, not one word. I have very few bad habits. I don't live on coffee or eat much junk food, I rarely drink alcohol, except on my birthday," she added dryly, "and I'm not a heavy smoker." She paused to light her cigarette and set the lighter down.

Patrick sighed. "I have to admit I miss my cigars."

Marian eyed her husband. "I don't."

Alex stiffened when a knock sounded at the door. "Who is it?" she called out, forgetting about the peephole set in the door.

"It's me," a feminine voice replied, muffled by the heavy door. Laughter filtered through. "Hey, do I get to come in?"

Alex swore under her breath, earning a censuring gaze from her mother. "It's Beth." A look of panic crossed her face.

"She can't see us, Alex," Patrick assured her.

"Yes, but she'll know I'm not acting my usual self." She headed for the door. Before opening it she pasted a stiff smile on her lips. "Hi, Beth."

"Hi. I'm sorry I didn't get to come by yesterday to see how you survived your party. I ended up pulling a back-to-back shift at the hospital since we're so shorthanded." The tall blond woman breezed by her. With shoulder-length curls, emerald-green eyes and a model's figure encased in a soft pink jumpsuit, she looked nothing like the competent pediatric nurse she was known to be. She turned around, her hands braced on slim hips, a teasing smile on her rose-glossed lips. "You were feeling no pain when Todd and I brought you home that night—or should I say that morning. I can imagine you'd prefer to forget yesterday altogether," she teased.

Alex winced under her teasing. "Something like that," she said dryly.

"I bet you looked like hell," she said frankly. Beth Grant was one of the few people who could get away with saying that to Alex. Probably because they had forged their friendship over finger paints in kindergarten twenty-five years earlier. During those years they had suffered through Girl Scouts, first love, a marriage and divorce each.

"Yes, well, the hangover was more than memorable," she murmured, cast a quick look around the room and gasped when she noticed her parents standing by the window.

Beth stared at her quizzically. "Are you all right?"

"Fine," she squeaked, then coughed. "Just fine." She ran a hand through her hair as she tried to look nonchalant, and failed miserably.

Beth narrowed her eyes and studied Alex carefully. "You look pale. Are you sure you're all right?"

"Remnants of the night before last," she said smoothly. "I didn't expect it to go away in twenty-four hours." Her eyes widened when she saw Suzi Q sitting at Marian's feet, the tawny face lifted upward as she batted one paw at Marian's leg. A garbled sound left Alex's throat.

Beth looked puzzled as she followed the direction of her friend's gaze. "What is with that cat?"

Alex's smile felt as if it had been pasted on her face. "She's chasing dust motes. It's become her latest hobby."

Beth continued studying the cat. "She's always been strange, but this is something new." Shrugging it off, she turned back to her friend, a look of expectancy on her face. "So what did Jason get you for your birthday?"

"He hasn't given it to me yet. He probably will tonight. Unless he feels uncomfortable giving it to me in front of his clients."

Beth was stunned.

"Wait a minute. He's taking you out for your birthday, two days late, and he's bringing clients with him?"

"They're only going to be here for two days and they're very important to him," Alex explained, getting more than a little put out that she'd had to be on the defensive all morning.

Beth wasn't convinced. "Alex, don't try to defend the man. How many times have you looked forward to a nice dinner out, just the two of you, and he's sprung clients on you? You, who hated any kind of business political games, now have to play them with a vengeance. Alex, this isn't you."

"Amen to that," Patrick murmured, looking all too innocent when his daughter shot him a warning look. "I told you she couldn't see or hear us."

"That really relieves my mind," she said under her breath.

"What?" Beth gazed at her.

She smiled, the motion more than a little strained. "Nothing."

She looked suspicious. "You're acting strangely, Alex. Not at all like yourself."

"It's been a crazy week."

"It didn't start out crazy until your party," she chuckled. "You definitely partied hearty that night, my girl. When Lynn, Cheryl and I decided to give you a surprise party, we didn't know you'd suddenly turn into the all-time party animal. You must have drunk enough champagne to equal your body weight and you danced with every guy there, including two of the waiters. One of them asked for your phone number."

Alex winced. "I only regret I don't remember more of it."

"Don't worry, Todd videotaped the whole thing, including the male stripper." Beth rolled her eyes. "He was something else!"

Fragments of the evening came back to Alex in horrifying detail. "Oh, God."

Beth patted her shoulder. "Don't worry, I won't tell Jason and we'll keep the only copy of the videotape locked up to watch when we're eighty and want to recall our misspent youth."

"You just wait until your thirtieth birthday."

"At least you have six months to come up with something memorable." She glanced at Suzi Q still batting at invisible air and shook her head. "There is most definitely something wrong with that cat. What does she see over there that we don't?"

"Actually, she can see a lot more than we can," Alex blurted out, ignoring her parents' gasp.

"Don't do it, Alex," Patrick warned, sensing her intent.

"Alex, she won't believe you," Marian told her. "You'll only look a fool."

Alex picked up her pack of cigarettes and lighter. She had just applied the tip of the cigarette to the flame when it blew out, courtesy of her mother, now standing next to her.

"I told you I'd find a way to stop you."

Beth laughed uneasily. "That's funny. There's no breeze, and it was as if someone blew it out."

Alex took a deep breath. "Something strange happened the day after my birthday," she began. "I know you won't believe this, but, Beth, this isn't a story I could make up—" Her eyes widened as she felt her body lose its balance. To keep from falling backward she twisted to one side, fell against the coffee table and felt her head connect with a hard object. Just as darkness descended she heard her mother's admonishment.

"Patrick, now look what you've done! Did you honestly have to trip her?"

"ALEX, ALEX, you want to try to wake up now?"

The words were low and soothing to her fuzzy brain. Except the last thing she wanted to do was open her eyes.

"Come on, Alex, open up those great big eyes of yours so I can see what color they are."

The portion of her brain still functioning tagged the voice as male, slightly husky, with a trace of amusement running through it. And not one bit familiar. If he wanted her to wake up and she was lying prone, who was he? And where was *she*? She lifted an eyelid that felt as if it weighed a ton and found herself looking into a pair of dark blue eyes. She hazily decided it wouldn't be all that difficult to look into those warm eyes all day long. He smelled good, too, if you liked the sharp tang of disinfectant.

"Where am I?" she croaked, disconcerted to find herself flat on her back on a surface that was more hard than soft and in surroundings that were too white for her taste. Horror widened her eyes as the memories flooded back. "Oh, my God, I died, after all! Dad didn't just trip me. He killed me!"

The man leaning over her smiled. "No, Alex, you're still very much alive, although I'm sure you're going to end up with a nasty headache. Let me take a look at those pupils." He shone a pencil flashlight in her eyes briefly, then whipped it to one side to check the reaction. "Looks good. Can you tell me your full name?"

"Alexis Marie Cassidy." She winced at the light.

"Age?"

"Thirty."

"Know where you are?"

"If I'm not dead, it must be a place that's too cheap to spring for a bit of color on the walls. What happened?"

He smiled. "Beth Grant had you brought in. She said you lost your balance and fell, striking your head against a figurine on your coffee table. When you wouldn't come to right away, she got worried. I'd say you have a concussion."

The meaning to her surroundings sunk in. "I'm in a hospital," she said with distaste.

"'Fraid so." His fingers carefully moved over her head until he found a raised bump along the back.

"Ouch!"

"Sorry." He turned away to jot something down in her chart. "It might be a good idea to keep you here overnight. Just to make sure there's no complications, I want to get an X ray taken."

And risk the chance of running into dear old Craig? No way! "No, thanks. A bit of aspirin and I'll be just fine," she assured him.

He frowned. "I don't think you realize the gravity of this, Ms. Cassidy. You need someone to check on you through the night."

"I have someone at home who can do that." She squinted to read the badge attached to the pocket of his white lab coat. "Duffy. A good Irish name."

He eyed the thick dark brown hair that resisted any attempt at taming, icy blue eyes that tilted up slightly, lush mouth and exotic features. "This coming from a Cassidy?"

"See, I'm coherent. I know all about concussions and I know the warning signs. I'll be fine."

He folded the chart under one arm, resting it against his hip. "You've had one before?"

"No, but I was a faithful viewer of 'St. Elsewhere' and I watch the reruns of 'Marcus Welby, M.D.' Honest, Dr. Duffy, I'll be just fine if you'll sign me out."

He hesitated. "You really don't want to stay here, do you?"

"Would you, if you didn't have to?" She sat up slowly so her head wouldn't spin. Now that she had him believing she would be fine on her own, she didn't want to spoil all her fine words by sitting up too quickly and falling on her face in front of him.

He shook his head. "I still advise against it, Ms. Cassidy. You took a pretty hard blow to the head. Your friend is a nurse and she wouldn't have brought you in here if she wasn't worried it could turn out to be more serious."

"I told you. There's someone who can keep an eye on me, and I promise if I start to see double and forget my name I'll come right back and ask for you personally." She flashed her most winning smile. The same one that got her out of her last parking ticket. If it could work on the local police force, there was no reason why it couldn't work on the medical community, too.

Dr. Duffy slowly shook his head. "I'm sorry, Ms. Cassidy. I don't feel right in releasing you."

She swallowed words of exasperation. "Then I'll just have to sign myself out."

"Tell you what, you remain here for a half hour, and when I come back we'll talk about it," he compromised.

"Dr. Duffy, we need you over here," a nurse called out, urgency strong in her voice. "Now!"

He studied her. "Promise you'll stay."

"I promise."

He looked at her another moment before leaving the cubicle. It wasn't until he was out of sight that Alex lifted the hand that had been hidden behind her back, fingers crossed.

By the time Alex signed herself out, grateful a major emergency kept Dr. Duffy too busy to argue with her, and found a cab to drive her home, she felt as if her head was ready to fly off at any moment. And here she thought a hangover was bad. Glad Beth had had the foresight to bring along her purse, she paid the driver and climbed the steps to her second-floor apartment.

When she walked in, she found her parents seated on the couch, worry etched on their faces.

"I have to say that when you decide to take matters into your own hands, you do it up big," she announced, throwing her purse on the table.

"Are you all right?" Marian stood up. "We were so worried about you, and there was no way for us to find out how you were."

She collapsed on the couch, her head flopping against the back. "Oh, yeah, I'm just fine. My friends give me a party to end all parties, where I end up feeling no pain until the next morning when reality sets in in the form of a killer hangover. My dead parents come back to inform me they're not leaving until I'm married to someone they deem right for me. And because I'm going to tell my closest friend about said parents, my father trips me and I almost get killed. Yep, I'm doing great. What are you going to do for an encore? Bring Elvis home for dinner?"

"I only meant to trip you up a little, Alex. I would never hurt you." Patrick sighed. "It appears our visit wasn't such a good idea, after all."

Alex closed her eyes against the hammers striking against her skull.

"I know that. Besides, Beth would have thought my story was just that—a story." She couldn't remember ever feeling so tired. She closed her eyes. A cool hand covered her forehead, pushing her hair away.

"Should you be home?"

"Dr. Duffy wanted me to stay overnight, but there was no way I was going to be under the same roof as Craig," she answered her mother's question. "I practically swore a blood oath that I would be all right, but Dr. Duffy wasn't about to believe me. He had the prettiest eyes." Her voice slurred.

Marian and Patrick exchanged telling looks.

"Who did, dear?" Marian asked softly.

"Dr. Duffy." She yawned widely. "A very deep blue. Beth would call them bedroom-blue eyes. You know what a sucker she is for blue eyes."

Marian's fingers moved gently over Alex's face. "Was he nice-looking?"

"Uh-huh." She could see a soft mist closing in around her. Sleep never seemed more welcome.

"Should she sleep?" Patrick spoke up.

"As long as we wake her every hour or so to make sure she's still alert, she'll be fine." Marian giggled softly. "Do you realize she forgot all about her important dinner tonight?"

He winced. "She'll accuse us of doing this deliberately."

"Since it caused her to meet someone who caught her attention, I won't worry one little bit."

DR. MICHAEL DUFFY was worn out. For a few doctors the practice of medicine meant regular office hours, perhaps a few late-night calls. For him, it meant stitching up a kid who had been hit by a baseball bat one afternoon and stitching up another kid who had been in a knife fight that night. Today was no different. After treating the victims of a car accident that wouldn't have happened if two teenagers hadn't been drinking heavily, he retired to the doctor's lounge in hopes of catching a few minutes' sleep.

"Dr. Duffy?" A tall, blond nurse appeared in the doorway.

He groaned. "What's the bad news this time?"

"Oh, no. I'm Beth Grant. I work in Pediatrics. I just came down to check on Alex Cassidy. They said you treated her."

He swore under his breath as he looked at his watch. The half hour he'd promised to return by had stretched into four hours.

"I wanted her admitted overnight for observation." He rubbed his hands over his eyes. "I'm sure she's settled in upstairs."

"No, she's not."

He opened his eyes. "She's not?"

Beth shook her head. "They told me she signed herself out. Which sounds like something Alex would do. I couldn't check on her sooner because I had to go on duty, and since we're so shorthanded I couldn't get away."

Michael forced his mind to function as he recalled the dark-haired woman with the intriguing eyes who he'd treated what seemed like a lifetime ago. A woman he couldn't easily forget. "She did say that there was someone to look after her, so I guess she figured she could be taken care of at home. She said something about her father accidentally tripping her, so I assumed she lived with her family." He noticed the look of alarm cross Beth's face. "She doesn't live with her family." It was a statement, not a question.

"Her parents died almost a year ago and all she has waiting at home for her is her cat."

Chapter Three

"I didn't realize doctors still made house calls."

"I wouldn't have made this one if you'd listened to reason. Is it all right if I come in?"

Alex stepped back, suddenly conscious of her tangled hair falling into her face, and her robe, comfortable but far from fashionable, and the white-knuckled fingers that gripped it. One of the times her mother woke her up earlier she had stumbled into the bedroom long enough to slip on a nightgown and the robe before falling into bed. When she roused herself long enough to realize someone was knocking on her door, she considered ignoring it until a familiar voice insisted she open up or he would find the manager to let him in. She didn't doubt his determination to do just that. It was easier to let him in than cause an embarrassing scene with her gossip-hungry building manager.

"Isn't this carrying medical care a bit beyond the norm?" she asked.

"My apartment building is only a few blocks away," Michael explained. "And Beth Grant was worried about you, but there was no way she could leave the hospital to check on you, and when she tried calling she only got your answering machine. That was when she gave me your address." He placed one hand on either side of her head, gazing intently into her eyes. Not the look of a man fascinated but that of a doctor interested in her health. "How's the headache?"

"About as much fun as having your wisdom teeth extracted without the benefit of novocaine."

"Dizziness?"

"No."

"Nausea?"

"No, thank God." She stared back. "If it would make you feel better I'll recite the Gettysburg Address."

His slight smile warmed his features and deepened his blue eyes even more. Alex found herself utterly fascinated with the change just a smile could generate. "I think we can skip that." He drew back. "Why did you lie to me?"

She was instantly wary. "Lie?"

"You told me there was someone here to take care of you. By the way you spoke about your father somehow tripping you, I assumed you lived with your parents. Beth told me differently. Why?" It was apparent he wasn't going to leave until he received an answer.

Alex wasn't about to give him the truth, so she evaded as best she could. "I hate hospitals."

"No one is fond of them, but they aren't that bad, either," he said gently. "We have been known to help people."

"Look, my ex-husband is on staff there, and if he found out I was a patient there he'd either act the simpering concerned ex-husband, which would definitely send me into extreme nausea, or he'd try to poison my food. It was easier to just get out of there before he found out I was in the building."

"Who's your ex-husband?"

"Craig Sommers." She was secretly pleased to see the distaste briefly flicker in his eyes. "Ah, you've had dealings with the good doctor. Makes you seriously consider baking him cookies with Ex-Lax instead of chocolate chips, doesn't it?"

"Let's just say since we're both on staff we tend to run into each other." This time he was the one to evade.

She smiled. "Very tactful, Doctor. I never could understand why he became an OB when it's a well-known fact most babies are born at night. A big inconvenience for a man who likes to party until dawn. I realize I shouldn't let him bug me, but past dealings have left me none too eager to see him."

Michael smiled and shook his head. "At least you sound coherent. That's in your favor."

"Even if I'm not at my best," she muttered, turning away. She cast a quick glance around the living room, wondering where her parents might be. She could swear she heard her mother "gently" suggesting she offer the man something to drink. "Would you like some coffee?"

He shook his head. "No, thanks, I had to work two shifts because two doctors called in sick. I've probably had more caffeine in one day than I need for an entire year. I just wanted to come by and make sure you were all right."

"Well, as you can see, I'm just fine," she said brightly, then coughed to hide her gasp when she suddenly found her parents standing behind Michael.

He frowned. "Are you all right?"

"Fine," she croaked. "I just had something in my throat." She waved her hand in front of her face.

Michael shifted from one foot to the other, racking his brain for something brilliant to say. Being the kind of man who was more used to books and spending what precious little free time he had by himself, he wasn't used to male/female social interaction. Especially after his last attempt at male/female social interaction had failed miserably. Here stood before him one of the most fascinating women he'd met in a long time, and he had no idea what to say to her. He

doubted she'd be impressed if he told her how pretty he
thought she was. She probably heard that all the time. What
could he say that wouldn't sound like some pick-up line used
in a bar?

"It's nice you stopped by, Dr. Duffy, but I am tired."
Alex was the one to break the silence.

He smiled briefly and nodded. "Yeah, some kind of
physician I am. Just promise me something. If you have any
problems..."

She ignored the thumbs-up from her father and her
mother's nod of approval. "I'll go directly to Emergency
and not stop at Go or collect two hundred dollars. I promise."

He grinned. "Your promise didn't work before."

She couldn't help grinning back. "That's because I
crossed my fingers." She held up her hands and waggled the
guilty digits.

Michael opened the door and paused. "Good night,
Alex."

"Good night, Dr. Duffy."

"Dr. Duffy has a first name—Michael." He didn't want
to admit he'd told her, because he hoped to hear her say it.

She must have guessed his intention. "Michael. Good
night."

It wasn't until the door closed behind him that she turned
back to the pair standing nearby. "You two are terrible.
What if he'd sensed you? He might have psychic powers or
something."

"Michael Duffy. What a nice name," Marian mused.
"You're right, Alex. He has lovely eyes."

"I never said he had lovely eyes."

"You were a little out of it when you said it, but you did
tell us about his bedroom-blue eyes."

Alex threw her hands up in surrender. "Fine, he has bedroom eyes. And he's probably married with six kids."

"He wasn't wearing a wedding ring."

"Craig hasn't worn one for any of his four—or is it five?—wives."

"He mentioned his apartment. Six children and apartments don't mix."

Alex felt the need for a good, healthy screaming session. "So he has a wife and no children. It happens."

"He's an improvement over what's-his-name," Patrick declared.

She rolled her eyes. "You saw him for all of five minutes and you know that? He could be some kind of pervert!"

"It sounds as if you're trying to convince yourself, not us," Marian told her.

Determined to escape with as much of her dignity as she could, she breathed in deeply and held her head up high. "I think I'll go to bed now." She walked into her bedroom and carefully closed the door behind her.

Marian looked at Patrick. "Do you think we should have told her about the messages Jason left on her answering machine? He sounded very upset."

He shook his head. "She can hear them tomorrow."

BY THE TIME MICHAEL reached his apartment he knew what true fatigue meant. By his calculations he'd been awake almost thirty-six hours.

He skirted the boxes littering the entryway and headed for the kitchen, where he debated between a much-wanted beer and a glass of orange juice. He opted for the beer. Popping the tab, he threw his head back as he drank the cold brew, then walked into the living room and fell back on the couch.

"Alex Cassidy," he said out loud. "Obviously an extrovert, outspoken and very pretty." Still not bothering to turn on a light, he looked around a room that was littered with boxes he hadn't found time to unpack yet. And he had moved in six months ago. As long as he had clean clothes and food, he didn't worry about anything else. With the hospital keeping him busier than he expected, he had no idea when they'd get unpacked.

He lay back, resting the beer can on his flat belly as he thought over the night's events. Hands down, his most interesting patient had been Alex Cassidy. It had been a long time since he'd felt the least bit of interest in a woman, and when an unconscious woman was wheeled into the emergency room, it only took one look at her face to tell him she was different.

All during his drive from the hospital to her apartment he kept telling himself he was only doing it because, as a doctor, he needed to check on a patient. Sure. Right. Wrong. He just wanted to see if there was a chance that she might have dinner with him on one of his infrequent free nights. When she mentioned her ex-husband, he feared that she would reject any invitation to go out with him, so it remained unspoken. He wasn't sure Alex wasn't involved with someone. And he didn't feel comfortable enough to ask Beth Grant about her.

Michael hated to admit he was basically a shy man. The fact that he even showed the least bit of interest in Alex was a surprise to him. Now all he had to do was find a way to learn more about the lovely Miss Cassidy.

"SINCE I'VE REACHED your machine, it must mean that you're on your way to the restaurant," Jason's voice echoed throughout the room from the answering-machine speaker. "I had hoped you would have allowed time for traffic. Tardiness in a business situation isn't good, Alexis."

Beep!

"Alexis, where are you?" Jason now sounded impatient and angry. "Do you realize how late it is?"

By then Alex shut off the machine and merely rewound the tape. She dreaded finding out exactly how many calls he'd made. "No one mentioned Jason's calls," she said casually.

"We weren't here," Patrick smoothly lied.

She turned her head. "Where did you go? Wait, I know. Trade secret, right?"

"You weren't feeling well last night," Marian reminded her. "Why bother you with his calls? Besides, you were much too tired to speak to anyone."

And she thought the concussion was bad enough. "He obviously thinks I either forgot or deliberately stood him up!"

"He couldn't have thought that you might have met with an accident?" Patrick asked quietly. "If my lady didn't show up, I would be more prone to worry about her well-being than assume she was being callous."

"Jason worries about me," she defended him.

"I didn't hear concern in his voice, Alex. I heard impatience. It's not the same thing." He was adamant. "And this is the man you want to spend the rest of your life with?"

"If he asks me, yes! He'll be faithful and provide me with a wonderful home life," Alex argued. "He'll certainly give me more than Craig ever did!"

"Then, you start thinking about the most important part, love."

Alex opened her mouth for a rebuttal, but nothing came out. She was furious with herself for not being able to come up with a quick reply.

"I'm sure you didn't come back here for us to argue, so I think I'll call Jason and explain to him what happened." She picked up the receiver. Except she turned out not to be so lucky when Jason's secretary put her on hold, then returned to explain that Mr. Palmer would return her call later in the day. "He's punishing me," she muttered, not realizing how irrational she might sound. She glared at her parent. As far as she was concerned they were completely at fault. "Please, do me a favor. *Don't* do me any favors!" She stomped off to her studio, slamming the door behind her.

"I always hoped she would learn to control that temper of hers," Marian sighed.

Patrick shook his head. He sat down on the couch and picked up the television remote control, switching on ESPN. "She takes more after your side of the family every day."

"Mine? If I recall correctly, it was your mother who was known to throw the good china at your father. How many sets did they go through? And none of that now!" Marian snatched the remote control from him and punched the off button. "Patrick, we have to do something about Alex."

He didn't try to regain ownership of the remote. He knew his wife only too well. "Marian, you've said that for the last thirty years and Alex has always gone her own way. I don't think we'd have a chance of changing that routine now. We already inadvertently sabotaged her dinner plans. I think that's a pretty good start."

Marian shook her head as she paced back and forth, tapping her finger against her chin. "That Dr. Duffy seemed very nice. He looked about the right age for her and he's not married."

"How do you know?"

"I ran a check on him. In fact, Chloe, you remember her, is his aunt. She said he's always been a quiet, well-mannered boy. He needs a bit of a shake-up in his life and who better than a whirlwind like Alex? He can settle her down and she can give him a good kick in the pants."

Patrick didn't look convinced. "Something tells me you've come up with an idea."

She smiled. "Oh, yes, I have."

He considered it. "Is this an idea that could get us in a lot of trouble with Alex when she finds out?"

"Most definitely."

His rakish grin still melted his wife's knees. "Then I'm all for it."

"MY, MY, DR. DUFFY has an admirer."

"My husband didn't send me such an elaborate bouquet when I had our first baby."

"What do you think it takes to receive flowers like those?"

"Michael, my boy, you sure did something right!"

"That must have been one hot night!"

By now Michael Duffy sported a bright red face and fervently wished he was anywhere but walking toward the nurses' station where, he was told, something special was waiting for him. When he reached the station he discovered the reason for all the teasing remarks. A large crystal vase with an intricate display of colorful flowers dominated the counter.

"For you, Doctor." One of the nurses, with a sly grin, handed him a white envelope with his name scrawled across the front.

Cursing the flush heating his cheeks, he accepted the envelope between his fingertips.

"What does it say?" One of the doctors leaned over his shoulder.

"None of your business," he growled, twisting his body to one side. He slipped the envelope into his pocket and walked away.

"What about the flowers?" Cathy, one of the nurses, asked.

"I'll get them later." For now, he merely wanted a little privacy so he could read the card and discover who had sent them. And around here there was little chance of him finding any. Even his office was shared with another doctor because space was so precious in the small hospital. He ducked behind a swinging door and opened the envelope, pulling out a white card.

Many thanks for your medical expertise. Perhaps next time we can meet without a stethoscope swinging between us.

Alex Cassidy

"Hey, Duffy, what does it say?" A banging on the metal door startled him.

"Dammit, Dennis, can't a guy have any privacy? Even in the men's room?" Michael groused, hurriedly pushing the card into his shirt pocket.

"Not if it might have something to do with a sexy brunette in here a few nights ago sporting a concussion and the name of Alex Cassidy."

Aware his colleague wasn't about to leave, Michael walked out to find Dr. Dennis Conway leaning against one of the sinks, his arms crossed in front of his chest. Tall with black hair, green eyes and a smile that melted the hardest of hearts, he was well-known for cutting a wide swath through the nurses. His love life was legendary in the hospital, next to that of Dr. Craig Sommers.

"You treated a bona fide celebrity, old buddy. Alex Cassidy is the creator of the 'Chuck-it-All' comic strip, not to mention being Craig Sommers's ex-wife," Dennis offered, the glitter in his eyes indicating he hoped he'd dropped a bombshell. He always enjoyed stirring up trouble. And if he could ruffle the feathers of the unflappable Michael Duffy, so much the better.

Michael smiled. "Yes, I've heard." Although the disclosure about the comic strip was a surprise. So she was the creative force behind the first thing he read every Sunday morning. In fact, some of Fritzi's madcap adventures resembled a few of his own less happy trips. He could have laughed at the crestfallen expression on Dennis's face. "I've got patients to check on."

"Doesn't anything faze you, Michael?" Dennis followed him out into the hall. "You're cool as a cucumber, whether this place is a madhouse or so quiet it's spooky. Nothing gets to you."

Ice blue eyes get to me. A mouth that some might call lush gets to me. Exotic beauty gets to me. A brash, outspoken manner gets to me. But these weren't words he would dare speak out loud to anyone.

"No, I guess not," he said quietly, walking away. As he walked he was very much aware of the card seeming to burn a hole in his pocket.

"Well, then, old buddy, I can't wait to see the woman who finally topples the mighty Duffy," Dennis called after him.

"One topple off the mountain is more than enough, thank you," he muttered under his breath, already wondering how he was going to make it out of the hospital with those flowers without all the questions he knew would be forthcoming.

"ARE YOU STILL not talking to us, or are you willing to come out for some dinner?" Marian stuck her head around the door.

Still lost in another world, Alex looked up with a distracted expression. "Huh? Oh, dinner? What happened to lunch?" She looked around surprised to find it dark outside and with food mentioned, her stomach was now angrily rumbling. Where had the time gone?

"When I asked about lunch you told me a concussion was enough to recover from, without compounding it with food poisoning."

Alex couldn't help but see the hurt look on her mother's face. Marian knew only too well her culinary skills were nonexistent, but it never stopped her from trying.

"Jason didn't return your call, did he?"

"He probably will this evening. I only wish you and Dad could apologize for starting this fiasco." She climbed off her high stool and placed her hands against the small of her back, arching up to relieve the ache. "What's on the agenda?"

"Pizza."

Images of smoke curling out of her oven assaulted her imagination. Then sanity intruded. "I don't have the ingredients for pizza."

"No, but you do have the phone number for a pizza place that delivers."

Alex frowned. "I thought you told me no one could hear or see you. Wait a minute." She held up her hand. "Trade secret, right?" She began cleaning off her drafting table, capping her bottles of ink and laying her finished pages on a nearby table. She hadn't accomplished as much as she would have liked today, but she couldn't fault the work she finished. The frizzy-haired character with her oversized glasses, eternal grin and uniform of black skirt, white blouse and running shoes had turned out to be popular with her readers.

"You know something, Fritzi, I think your life is a great deal less complicated than mine," she muttered to the character. She looked up at the sound of the phone ringing. Nerves tightened as she picked up the receiver and heard the caller identify himself.

"Jason, I'm glad you called," she said warmly.

"Alexis, I'm very disappointed in you," he began without preamble. "If you weren't able to come, couldn't you have at least contacted me? You knew I considered that dinner very important. I had no idea what to say to the Bishops when you didn't appear or call."

"Yes, I know, Jason," she replied, effectively cutting into his tirade. "And believe me, I have an excellent reason for not making it. I ended up spending the evening in the hospital emergency room. I fell, hit my head and was knocked unconscious."

"Alexis, I counted on you to help me make this dinner special for the Bishops," he went on, not bothering to listen to her explanation. "Couldn't you at least have had someone from the hospital call me?"

She gritted her teeth. "Jason, listen to me. I fell, hit my head and was knocked out. I was unconscious for a while and by the time I came to I had a roaring headache and all I cared about was coming home and going to bed, although the doctor insisted I remain overnight." She didn't care if her agitation zinged across the telephone lines.

"I've been incredibly rude, haven't I, darling? Here you were lying ill in the hospital and I was angry because you didn't call. That was unfair of me. I can only hope you'll allow me to make it up to you by suggesting a dinner at Antoine's tomorrow evening." He lowered his voice to an intimate one.

She was slightly mollified. "I think it can be arranged."

"I'll pick you up at seven, then. Good night, darling."

"He didn't exactly apologize for his rude behavior, did he?" Patrick stood in the doorway. "He sounded more worried about his precious clients than your health."

She spun around. "Eavesdropping? Is that another trade secret, Dad?"

"I just wanted to tell you that the pizza delivery boy is at the door. I could open the door, but I don't think he would understand how it opened itself or why the money was floating in the air."

She nodded and quickly left the room, calling out she'd be right there. After paying the boy, she accepted the cardboard box and carried it into the kitchen.

"I forgot how good hot pizza smelled," Patrick sighed, standing over the box and inhaling the rich fragrance of tomatoes, spices and cheese.

"Sausage and extra cheese. Perfect," she murmured, her taste buds already salivating as she picked up a slice and bit into it. She closed her eyes, savoring the spicy flavor exploding inside her mouth. She had barely finished the first piece before she started in on the second. By the time she finished devouring half the pizza she felt more like her old self.

"Why don't we have an old-fashioned gabfest?" Alex suggested, as she searched for her pack of cigarettes and lighter. When she discovered the half-full carton missing she looked at her mother accusingly. "All right, what have you done with them?"

"I threw them away. They're not good for you, dear."

"Mom, when I'm ready to quit, I will. Just please don't force me into it." She rummaged through the trash bin until she found the carton and breathed a sigh of relief to find the packs intact. She looked up. "I'm not a chain-smoker. Just remember you only got on my case about smoking when you quit five years ago, and you never were able to persuade Dad to give up his cigars."

"I have no choice now," Patrick said ruefully. "Something else I miss, along with pizza and golf."

"Then, why would you come back to a place where you see all the things you miss?" Alex asked curiously.

"Because we had the chance to be with you again," Marian explained. "That was something we wouldn't give up for anything."

Alex reached out, almost afraid to touch her for fear she'd disappear before her very eyes. "I've missed you so much these months," she said softly. "There were days something would happen I'd want to talk to you about and you weren't there. You two were more than my parents. You were my best friends."

Her mother's eyes misted. "As we've missed you. That's why we had to come back, Alex. You're our only daughter and we love you dearly. We wanted to know you'd have a happy life and share the same kind of love your father and I've had all these years. We love you, Alex. We only want the best for you, and we'd do anything in our power to see you have that kind of love and happiness."

Alex blinked rapidly. "It's still hard to understand, but how can I argue with two parents who love their daughter so much they actually come back from the dead to see her again?" she sniffed. "The thing is, what you two have is so special I doubt it could be duplicated, even for me."

Marian smiled. "Of course it can. With the right man, that is. That's all we want for you, dear."

Alex looked at her parents, still unable to comprehend the kind of love that would enable them to do this wondrous thing for her. She opened her mouth to ask something else when the phone rang. She reached for the receiver.

"Hello?" A faint hint of something undefinable flashed across her face that her parents, knowing her so well, easily read. "Yes, Dr. Duffy. I remember you." She tucked the receiver under her chin and half turned away from the two avid eavesdroppers. "Oh, you did? Really?" She turned to face her parents with an accusing glare. Patrick whistled under his breath and studied the vase sitting on the lamp table.

"Well, yes, I can understand that is something that doesn't happen to a doctor too often. Well, I'm glad you enjoyed them." Her smile froze on her lips as she turned away from the offenders. "Dinner? I'm sorry, I have an engagement tomorrow evening." She ignored her mother tapping her shoulder a bit too hard. "No, I'm sorry, I'm busy then. Another time. Good night." She hung up the receiver with great care before turning to face the guilty pair. "Tell me how you did it. And don't use that nonsense about trade secrets, okay? Tell me exactly how you ordered flowers for Dr. Michael Duffy in my name."

"It was very easy." Marian was the one to reply with pride ringing in her voice at the idea their scheme worked so well. "We charged them on your Visa card."

Chapter Four

"Did he like them?" Marian asked brightly.

Alex threw her head back and uttered something between a soft scream and a curse. "Why did you do this?"

"Because he did something nice by coming by to check on you and the least you could do is thank him."

"A note would have been sufficient. Why flowers? I'm afraid to ask how much they cost," she muttered.

"Your father chose them. He wanted something that wouldn't appear too ostentatious or feminine."

Alex felt the horror wash over her. She remembered the flowers Patrick sent Marian for special occasions. He never considered the cost. "How much?" she uttered between cold lips.

"It was worth it. In fact, perhaps it's something you could write off your income tax," Patrick suggested.

"I sincerely doubt it. How much?" She stressed the last two words.

"Seventy-five dollars."

Alex felt the air leave her lungs in a hard whoosh. "Seventy-five dollars! What country did they come from?" She held up her hand. "Never mind. I don't think I could handle any more." She snatched up her pack of cigarettes and lighter and quickly lit up, giving her mother a telling look that warned of retribution if she dared say one word. She puffed several times before speaking.

"We need to discuss something," she began. "I know you think that this Dr. Duffy is the answer to your prayers, but you have to understand my feelings. You two share an incredible love, the kind of love that doesn't happen to just anyone. I thought I had it with Craig and I learned very quickly that I wasn't even close. Then I looked around at my friends who were married. Some were on their second, a few even on their third marriages. Most of them were happy if they were just compatible. No one has what you have. So I decided I would look for a man who could offer me a stable life, a nice home and wasn't threatened by my work."

"You mean you'll settle for second-best," Patrick said flatly.

"Jason is not even close to second-best," she argued.

"Oh, Alexis." Marian's dark eyes were full of what suspiciously looked like pity. "Just because what you thought was love turned out to be lust and betrayal doesn't mean the right man isn't out there for you. If you enter into a commitment with Jason feeling this way, you'll soon feel dissatisfied with what you have and you'll only grow bitter as time passes."

Alex sank down on the couch, reaching for the ashtray. She tapped the ashes into the ceramic center. "I'm trying to be honest with you and you're talking emotions again."

Patrick sat down next to her. "Baby, you have a very strong sense of emotion. You always have. I was always surprised you never became an actress, because you always knew what to do to keep us on your side."

She closed her eyes, wishing they would listen to her. "Then be on my side now when I need you the most. You keep saying you came back because you wanted to see me married to the right man. Please, accept my choice."

"Even if he's wrong for you?" Marian asked quietly.

"How do you know that? You've never given Jason a chance. He'll be here this evening to take me out to dinner. I'll suggest he have a drink first and we talk. You'll see how charming he really is," she told them. "Is that so much to ask?"

The two exchanged a silent communiqué.

"You're right. We aren't being fair to him," Patrick was the one to reply. "I just wish I could ask him some questions. In fact—" he looked too crafty for Alex's peace of mind "—I could ask you to ask him something."

"It would never work." She tamped out her cigarette and stood up. "I have to go over my final sketches before mailing them out."

"Where did Fritzi take her victims this time?" Marian asked.

Alex smiled. "Transylvania. We're starting with the werewolf's moonlight tour of the forest. Actually, this is a series for the month of October. There will also be an overnight stay in Dracula's castle and a fix-it seminar with Frankenstein, but I'm calling him Frank N. Stein." She drew out the name to indicate the middle initial used.

Patrick chuckled. "I don't know how you can come up with so many funny ideas."

"I'm just glad I've resisted drawing a daily, because there's times when coming up with an idea for a weekly is bad enough. Holidays are pretty easy, and sometimes ideas crop up. A couple of months ago I drew up a cruise on the refurbished *Titanic* with the assurance that just because it sank once didn't mean it would happen a second time." She headed for her office. "I'll see you two later."

Patrick frowned at the door Alex closed after her. "I can't believe she truly intends to talk that pompous ass into a marriage proposal."

"She might be right, you know," Marian said softly. "We never did give him a try after that first meeting."

"He sat there the entire evening trying to talk me into investing in some South American company that manufactured adult sex toys." Patrick rolled his eyes. "He kept yammering on how I'd see a large return on my investment within six months. And when I flat out told him no, he implied I didn't have the assets for such a wonderful investment or the brains to recognize it." His lips twisted with disgust. "He sat there in his Italian suit and Italian handmade shoes and looked down on me. I'm surprised he wasn't in on all those junk bonds."

"Perhaps he was and got out before it all blew apart," Marian considered.

Patrick looked up. "Maybe. I just wish I could talk to my stockbroker."

"He's Alex's now. She inherited him along with your portfolio."

He nodded absently. "Unless..." His eyes widened with horror. "She wouldn't have handed it all over to *him,* would she?"

"You forgot. She couldn't."

"Why not?"

"You stipulated in your will that if Alex dared to give her portfolio to anyone other than the four names on your list your broker would end up owning it instead."

He grinned at the recollection. "Oh, yes, now I remember. One of my smarter moves. Marian, I agreed we would give the jerk a chance, but that doesn't mean I'll like him. My money's still on Michael Duffy, as soon as we can get the two of them together again."

ALEX WAS IN THE MIDST of pinning her hair back in loose curls when the doorbell rang.

"Want us to answer that?" Patrick's voice was a shade too innocent.

"No!" She paused to take a deep breath. She'd forgotten her father's puckish sense of humor. She took another deep breath before walking out to the living room. "Very funny, Dad." She hesitated at the door as she glanced at her parents standing near the window. "Just give him a chance, okay?"

"I promised," Patrick replied, nothing in his face to indicate his emotions.

She pasted a smile on her lips and pulled open the door. "Jason, right on time, as usual," she greeted him.

"Alexis, you look lovely." He leaned over to brush a light kiss on her lips, careful not to smudge her lipstick.

"Come in and have a drink." She stepped back.

A frown marred his handsome features. "I told you I'd be here at seven-thirty, that we had reservations. I assumed you'd be ready to leave."

"I am," she assured him. "I just thought it wouldn't hurt for us to relax for a moment." She gestured to the couch as she sat down, adjusting the folds of her dark red silk dress around her legs.

Jason stood over her, a handsome man in his late forties with sleekly styled iron-gray hair, brown eyes that could never be described as puppy-dog brown and the lean figure of a man who indulged in daily visits from his personal trainer. He'd risen in his field due to his sharp business sense, cold, calculating mind and an unerring sense of what to do when. And once he'd gained that top rung, he'd done everything possible to remain there. Now he felt it was time to move on to another phase in his life, that of acquiring a suitable wife. In his eyes, the lovely Alexis Cassidy was the perfect choice. Especially once he had her in hand and weaned her away from drawing that deplorable comic strip. His smile revealed expensive dental work and nothing else, because it didn't reach anywhere near his eyes.

"I spoke to Leland McKinley today. He's flying out from New York next week, and if I have any say in the matter he'll be handing over all his investments to me before he leaves Los Angeles." His voice was heavily laced with satisfaction and confidence as he went on to tell her about another one of his pending deals.

"Doesn't he ever ask you about your day?" Patrick grumbled, glaring at the younger man.

"Of course," Alex hissed, then jumped as Jason looked at her strangely.

"I beg your pardon?"

She offered him a bleak smile. "Sorry. Something came to mind. Something that happened today." She waited for him to question her about it.

He merely nodded and continued with his own tale. This unsettled Alex. That and the glare her father was directing at Jason. A glare she remembered well. Patrick had glared at most of the men she dated. Craig headed the list. She looked down to hide her smile. She reached for one of the cigarettes she kept in an inlaid box on the coffee table when the lid suddenly dropped smartly across her knuckles.

"Ouch!" She looked up wide-eyed to find her mother standing over her. "Cute, real cute," she mumbled.

"Alexis." Jason's voice was sharp.

She looked at him. "I'm sorry."

"I said we should leave now if we're to make our reservations." He glanced at his watch with impatience.

She nodded as she stood up. "I'll get my purse and wrap."

As they walked out the door, Alex spared a quick backward glance that said it all. *We'll speak of this later.*

"I hope you don't mind if we wait up for you," Patrick called out cheerfully.

What might have been a gasp was quickly smothered by Alex's hand.

"Are you certain you're all right?" Jason asked as he ushered her into his dark blue Mercedes sedan. "You don't seem to be yourself this evening. Perhaps this wasn't a good idea. After all, you did say you took a nasty blow to the head only a few days ago."

"I'm fine," she assured him. "Actually, I'm glad we have this evening together." She reached out to caress his arm. "We seem to have so little time together."

"We would have more time if you had more evenings free. Perhaps you should arrange your work time more efficiently, so you wouldn't run into these little scheduling problems." His voice was tinged with just the right amount of censure meant to make her feel guilty.

It worked.

"Jason, you know how crazy things get when I'm up against a deadline," she explained, suddenly angry with herself for even bothering to explain. "Sometimes, my ideas don't come easily and I have to work harder at smoothing out my strip. It isn't as if there haven't been evenings when you needed to work. I never feel slighted when you have to cancel a date because of business."

"That's different."

She bristled. "Different? Why?"

When he stopped at the red light he reached out, taking her hand and offering her a warm smile. "Darling, we haven't seen each other in over a week. Let's not argue, shall we?"

Alex's first impulse was to disagree and insist they clear the air. Except Jason didn't believe in arguments. He once told her a disagreement was a waste of time because there could only be one person who was right. And naturally Jason was always right. She ignored the little voice inside her brain taunting her that she was acting like a wimp. This is *not* the normal Alex Cassidy; she was acting like *Alexis* Cassidy. Jason didn't like nicknames, along with fast-food restaurants, horror or science-fiction movies and most especially, heaven forbid, any kind of clothing off the rack. She bit down on her lower lip to forestall any words that might begin a disagreement she would surely lose. She tried to tell herself it didn't matter, but deep down she knew it did.

She mustered up her gracious Alexis smile, although it felt stiff on her lips. "You're right, darling. Now tell me what you've been doing."

From then until they reached the restaurant, Jason talked animatedly. They were greeted by the maître d' before he guided them to their table, a journey that was frequently interrupted as Jason was hailed by clients and co-workers. This wasn't unusual, since Jason frequently chose restaurants where he would run into people he knew and people he wanted to know better. He once explained to Alex that being seen in the right places and appearing to be easily accessible was good business. She learned early on that Jason didn't mind letting their dinners get cold while he chatted with people who stopped by their table. Not as long as he was able to follow up on a hot tip, nab a new client, or do anything else that would build up his investment business.

"It's always so lovely here," Alex murmured, accepting her menu. She opened it, scanning the offerings that changed every day according to the chef's whims. Naturally there were no prices listed on her menu. The first time she came here she had dreaded what the prices might be. She looked over the top of her menu, idly scanning the room for possible comic-strip subjects. Suddenly her attention stopped and shifted to a corner where two wisps of smoke floated upward and hovered in midair. She uttered a curse she only used under great duress.

"Alexis?" Jason frowned, looking up from his menu. "Is something wrong?"

She snapped to attention. "No, nothing. I just thought I saw someone I knew." She hid behind her menu and when she figured Jason's attention was diverted she sneaked a glance toward the same corner. The wisps were still there, and as the restaurant didn't allow smoking, the smoke had no reason to be there.

"They can't be here," she whispered to herself. "There's no way. Is there?" She racked her brain for any hints of what exactly her parents could and couldn't do. All she could recall were those two words she'd grown to hate—trade secret.

"Alexis, are you ready to order?" The impatience in Jason's voice indicated this wasn't the first time he'd asked her.

"Oh, I can't really decide. Why don't you choose for me?" Her gaze strayed involuntarily toward that corner. The wisps of smoke were gone. She breathed a sigh of relief. She must have just imagined them.

The wine steward poured wine for Jason, waiting for his approval before pouring some for Alex. She smiled at the man before picking up her glass.

"A belated happy birthday, darling." Jason tapped his glass against hers. "I'm only sorry I was unable to attend your party."

Alex thought of the male stripper her friends brought in as a joke. She knew Jason wouldn't have thought it amusing. "Oh, you probably wouldn't have enjoyed it very much."

"To be honest, I don't feel entirely comfortable with your friends. I've always felt you could do much better than many of the people you associate with," he went on in the tone of voice that meant what he said was for her own good.

"Jason, I don't care to have this discussion again," she said firmly but gently. "You are talking about people who have been my friends for years. Perhaps you don't feel they're appropriate for me, but they've been there for me during the good and bad times. I'm certainly not going to cut them off.''

His eyes cooled. He drew back in his chair. "I'm only thinking of you, Alex. For our future."

"I realize that...." Her attention was diverted by what appeared to be...no, it couldn't be. It was just her eyes playing tricks. Could that spoon be floating across the room?

"Alexis." Jason's voice sharpened.

She tore herself away from the intriguing sight. "Jason, did you see...?" She stopped when she saw the expression on his face. He was *not* amused. "Never mind."

His lips tightened with anger. "I'm beginning to think you still haven't fully recovered from that concussion. You don't appear to be listening to one word I've been saying."

Alex was never so grateful for an interruption as when the waiter appeared with their food. By now it was only too clear. Somehow, her parents had employed their "trade secrets" to sneak into the restaurant and sabotage her dinner with Jason.

"If they weren't already dead, I'd kill them with my bare hands!" she muttered, cutting into her meat with savage strokes of the knife. Then she looked down, horrified by the contents of the plate set in front of her. The meat facing her was white with a cream sauce. "Is this halibut?" she whispered.

He didn't look up from his meal. "Of course. You eat far too much red meat. You should keep an eye on your cholesterol."

Alex was never very picky about her food, except for one thing. She hated halibut with a passion. In fact, she hated most members of the fish family. She knew she once told Jason that, but he merely brushed it off, saying all she had to do was eat more fish to become accustomed to it.

Jason looked up, a frown marring his handsome features. It was clear he wasn't happy with her this evening. "Is there something wrong with your fish?"

She opened her mouth, then quickly closed it. "No, it's fine." She speared a piece and quickly put it into her mouth, chewing rapidly. "Just fine." She snagged her wineglass and downed the contents, swallowing the fish at the same time as if it was nothing more than nasty medicine.

Jason carefully set down his fork and half leaned across the table. "Alexis, that's wine you're drinking so enthusiastically, not water." His tone carried a warning. "I don't think you want people to assume you have too much of a fondness for alcohol."

She offered a stiff nod. "I'm sorry. It appears not to be my evening."

"Not when you act as if the wine is more important than your meal." He lowered his voice. "The Gladstones are just over there at the next table, and if I play my cards right, he'll be handing over three million dollars to me. But he won't be impressed if he sees my date drinking wine as if it was water."

His officious statement irritated Alex. Just as too much had irritated her this evening. She was already positive her parents were somewhere in the dining room. She looked around, surveying the area, fearing what might happen next. It wasn't difficult to miss. The drapes twitched, a waiter halting to rearrange them, they promptly returned to their earlier folds. The next time, a glowering maître d' moved forward to fix them. The moment he turned his back, the drapes twitched back. Alex stifled a moan.

I just bet they're now sitting with the Gladstones, she thought to herself. *Get a hold of yourself, Alex. They're just trying to ruin your dinner with Jason and if you keep acting like this they will have accomplished their objective. Don't let them win!* She took several deep breaths, forcing herself to calm down. "Gladstone. Is he the one who bought that plastics firm you spoke about?" She lowered her voice to the pleasant tone Jason always appreciated. The sudden warmth in his eyes told her he was pleased.

He immediately launched into the story of his machinations and meetings to persuade Isaac Gladstone to hand over a small fortune for investment purposes. It was clear to Alex that Jason was confident he wouldn't fail.

Except her attention couldn't remain on his talk. Not when she happened to look across the room and see those wisps of smoke again. And they looked as if they were moving toward her table! Luckily, before she could do anything further to embarrass herself they disappeared again. Fortunately Jason didn't notice her inattention.

She cut another tiny bite of halibut and raised it to her lips. This time she chose a sip of water to wash it down. It was the only way she could finish her meal.

By the time their plates were whisked away, Jason had relaxed. "I ordered something very special for dessert," he told her, expectation lighting his dark eyes.

Very special turned out to be Cherries Jubilee, which a beaming waiter presented to them with a theatrical flourish.

"Oh, Jason," Alex breathed, pleased he'd remembered her favorite dessert. She watched eagerly as the waiter lighted the brandy-soaked cherries, the flames whooshing upward. "This is wonderful, Jason." She viewed the treat before her with delight.

"I wanted this evening to be very special for us," he told her, picking up his spoon. "And not just because we're celebrating your birthday."

This is it. He's going to propose. His birthday gift to me is an engagement ring.

So why didn't she feel the excitement she had expected? It was almost anticlimactic, now that she'd led him down the garden path to exactly where she wanted him.

"We've known each other a long time, Alexis," Jason began. "And I feel during that time we've had an excellent chance to know how compatible we truly are."

"Yes," she breathed.

He reached into his jacket pocket. "Therefore—" Whatever he was to say was halted when his dish somehow slid right off the table and onto his lap. Choking back a curse he leapt to his feet, wiping at his slacks with his napkin. Within seconds several waiters swarmed over him and the maître d' clucked, murmuring assurances that all would be taken care of by the restaurant, of course.

"But it wasn't their fault," Alex mused, watching the scene unfolding before her like a horror movie. She fully expected to see a monster's hands rise up from the dishes and pull her down into the depths of a nasty creature's lair.

"Everything is fine!" Jason snapped, his usual cool composure strained to its limits. "Could we just have our check, please?"

The man held out his hands. "Please, Mr. Palmer, you have suffered enough this evening." He snapped his fingers. "Miss Cassidy's coat."

Jason's face was a bright red as they exited the restaurant.

"I can't believe this," he said between clenched teeth as they waited for the parking valet to bring up his car. "They were damn right they weren't going to charge me for that meal. This will be all over town by morning. It will take me weeks to live down." He glared at the valet who bounded around the driver's door as another valet opened the passenger door for Alex.

"Jason," she murmured. "It wasn't their fault."

He shot her a look that suggested she keep quiet about the entire episode.

The silence during the drive to Alex's apartment was so thick it could have been cut with a knife. For the first time she could remember, Jason raced through three yellow lights and cut off another car so sharply she was certain she'd end up in the emergency room again. For a man who rarely allowed his emotions to show, he was doing an admirable job of displaying them tonight.

"I was made to look like an idiot in front of the Gladstones," he muttered as he waited impatiently for a red light to turn green. "How can I hope for him to turn over those funds to a man covered with brandied cherries? That idiot waiter. I'll make sure he loses his job over this."

Alex was stunned. This was a side of Jason she'd never seen before and she didn't like it.

"Jason, it was an accident. It happened after the waiter left, so you can't blame him," she insisted.

"Yes, I can," he gritted, gripping the steering wheel with white-knuckled fingers. "He set the bowl too close to the edge of the table."

"No, he didn't! The bowl was just pushed onto your lap by some gremlin!"

Jason turned his head, looking at her as if she had lost her senses. "I can see I shouldn't have brought you out so soon after your accident. You've obviously not recovered yet. It would be better if we didn't speak of this again."

Alex slumped back in her seat. She knew when it was time to stop. Besides, she had to shore up all her energy for her confrontation with her parents. She had been prepared for them to pull a few tricks at her apartment. She hadn't expected them to go public.

Jason stopped the car in front of Alex's building and got out, opening her door for her. After they rode the elevator upstairs and halted in front of her door, he took her key from her and inserted it in the lock.

"Would you like to come in?" She asked more as a courtesy than because she wanted to prolong an evening that had gone from bad to worse.

"I don't think so."

Her smile froze on her lips. "I'm afraid you were interrupted at the restaurant when you were speaking about something important."

"The mood is gone." He brushed a cool kiss across her lips. "Good night, Alexis. I'll phone you later."

The moment she had the door closed between them, she leaned against it. Her parents were sitting on the couch, watching television, looking like something out of a Norman Rockwell painting. Marian looked up with an expectant smile.

"Have a nice evening, dear?"

"You know very well I didn't. Why did you do it?" She pushed herself away from the door. "Floating spoons, moving drapes, wisps of smoke in a dining room that has no smokers, and then the fiasco with the Cherries Jubilee. Why?"

Patrick looked confused. "What are you talking about, Alex?"

"You know very well what I'm talking about!" Her voice rose with her agitation. She held up her hands and took several calming breaths before recounting the evening.

"Alex, we told you before. We can't leave the apartment," Marian explained. "We can't go any farther than your doorway. It was one of the conditions of our coming back."

"I could only get your newspaper that morning because your paperboy left it against your door," Patrick spoke up. "We can't cross the threshold."

They looked so sincere Alex felt her anger ebbing, although suspicion still lingered. "Really?"

"Really." Patrick got up and walked over to her. He reached around and twisted the doorknob. He waited for Alex to move aside as he opened the door and walked outside. Or tried to. He seemed to come up against an invisible wall. He turned around. "See?"

Now she didn't know what to believe. "But the things that happened at the restaurant. They couldn't have been some kind of crazy coincidence."

"Since we weren't there, I can't tell you how or why they happened. Perhaps it's a sign." He patted her shoulder.

Alex groaned. "He was getting ready to propose. I know he was. Then the Cherries Jubilee hit his lap. I have never seen him so angry. He blamed the waiter for the accident when he had nothing to do with it." She sighed. "I'm going to bed. This has been an evening I'd really prefer to forget."

"Would you like me to run you a hot bath, dear?" Marian asked, motherly concern etched on her face.

She shook her head. "No, thank you. Sleep is all I want right now." She entered her bedroom and turned, holding onto the doorknob. "I was so angry that you were behind this. I'm glad to know you weren't. I'm sorry I blamed you without listening to your side." She smiled wanly and closed her door.

Marian turned to Patrick. "We might have been able to swear we weren't in that restaurant, but we're very lucky she didn't ask if we were behind that episode. I would have told her the truth if she'd asked, Patrick. I can't lie to her."

He nodded. "I know. It's just a good thing I could prove we can't leave the apartment. At least she'll never learn that doesn't stop us from finding someone who can enter the restaurant." He grinned. "Cherries Jubilee. I imagine that left quite a stain on that fancy tailored suit of his. I bet it won't even come out." His chuckle turned into a full-fledged laugh. "I wish I had been there to see it. With luck, this pushes that stuffy what's-his-name out of the picture. Now if we could just get that doctor into it."

"We'll find a way. We did before."

Chapter Five

"Hey, Mr. Party Animal, you going to join us for softball this weekend?" one of the doctors called out to Michael as he walked down the hallway to the cafeteria for a long-overdue dinner break.

He smiled and shook his head. "Sorry, I'm still trying to unpack my things, and this is the first weekend I've had off since I arrived." He paused when he noticed the blond nurse standing with the doctor. She smiled and nodded, indicating she remembered him.

It took a moment for the memory to click in his weary mind...Alex Cassidy's friend. The one who asked about her and was kind enough to give him her address. "How's your friend doing?" he asked.

She shrugged. "Fine, I guess. With my crazy schedule I haven't had much chance to talk to her except for a quick phone call the other night to make sure she wasn't suffering from any headaches," Beth replied. She added with a sly smile, "If you want to find out for yourself, you should come to our game. Alex plans to be there."

A tiny flicker of something that had been dead for a long time briefly came to life deep within his senses. "Perhaps I will." His tone was all too casual. He smiled and nodded before heading back down the hall.

"Why did you bother, Beth?" He could hear the man ask. "He's not going to come."

"You asked him."

"Yeah, but I knew he'd say no. He never bothers with any of our activities. The guy is a real hermit. Or did you think those luscious charms of yours will succeed where others haven't?"

She looked over her shoulder to make sure Michael was out of earshot. "No, but I have a friend whose charms just might."

While Michael lingered over his dinner he thought about a pair of exotically slanted ice-blue eyes, a thick mane of sun-streaked brown hair and a lush mouth. Amazing that the memory of a woman he'd only spoken to a short time would linger so long in his thoughts. Especially a woman who clearly didn't share the attraction he felt.

"Custard soup isn't a pretty sight."

He looked up and found Beth standing beside him, a tray in her hands.

"Mind if I sit down?" she smiled.

He gestured toward the other empty chair. "Be my guest."

She arranged her dishes on the table and set her tray on an empty one nearby. "You've become the hospital mystery, you know. The nurses complain because you haven't made a pass at them. Others complain because you don't react when *they* make a pass at you. You don't party, you don't play golf, you work incredible hours, if someone wants a weekend off you work their shift and as far as anyone knows you have nothing resembling a private life." She shook her head. "Doctor, you really need to loosen up."

Michael shrugged. "I'm happy with my life, dull as it is."

She reached across the table, snatching the spoon out of his hand. "Stirring that custard will only make it worse. The hospital grapevine will tell you that I'm very outspoken and that I tend to make assumptions where they aren't invited. Probably because I'm usually right." She eyed him over her linked hands resting against her chin. "So tell me, what did you think of Alex?"

"She seemed to be completely coherent that night. No aftereffects."

"That isn't what I meant and you know it. What do you think about *her?*"

"I don't know her well enough to give a proper answer," he evaded, fervently wishing he had something to occupy his hands which now fidgeted with the sugar packets on the table, aligning each one neatly with the print right-side-up.

Beth watched his nervous gestures. "Ex-smoker?"

He grinned sheepishly. "Shows, huh?"

"Only to another three-pack-a-day inhaler. I quit two years ago and drove my friends up the walls with my more than compulsive behavior. My kitchen cabinets were rearranged every other day." She reached for her coffee cup. "Alex and I have been friends since kindergarten. Our standing joke is we've remained friends so long because we have so much dirt on each other we don't dare split up. I think the two of you would get along very well together."

"Is that why the invitation to the softball game?"

She didn't flush or show any signs of embarrassment at being found out. Michael had to admire her composure.

He looked wary. "Is she really attending this game?"

Beth's smile was broad and warm. "She will be."

"YES, SIMON, I'm listening," Alex sang out, rolling her eyes. That was what she loved about the phone. She could make all the faces she wanted and the person on the other end never knew her true reaction. Her agent, Simon, was a prime example. The man was a classic worrier and his main bone of contention was Alex's breezy way of conducting business. His excited chatter rang in her ear. She bared her teeth in a mock growl as she stared in the mirror. "Simon, there's nothing for you to worry about. Put down the bottle of Maalox and just relax. I've got it all taken care of." While her face looked like something out of a horror film, her voice was a soothing croon.

"How do I know that?" he fretted, not the least bit reassured by her words.

"Because I said so. I'll meet with those lovely executives from that newspaper syndicate, charm the socks off them and show them that Fritzi would be a welcome addition to their Sunday papers." She leaned forward, looking closely into the mirror, fingering what appeared to be a tiny pimple on her chin, then crossed her eyes.

"You keep doing that, your eyes will remain like that," Marian warned, walking past her.

"Alex, are you listening to me?" Simon demanded in a querulous voice.

"Yes, Simon, you're coming through loud and clear. Look, sweetie, I've got to go. Call me when they get to town and we'll set something up," she told him. "Don't worry, I promise to behave."

"Alex, we need to discuss this!"

"There's no need when we don't even know when—or if—they're coming. Bye." She hung up quickly. "The man needs to slow down."

"Then why do you stay with him?" Patrick asked.

"Because he's the best in the business." Alex ran her fingers through her hair, pushing the heavy waves away from her face. "And I'm sure I make him just as crazy as he makes me."

"Alex, do you realize you haven't done anything with all these tapes I bought you?" Marian looked up from her crouched position in front of Alex's videotape cabinet. "They're all still wrapped in plastic." She held one up as an example.

Alex silently wished she had hidden the collection of exercise tapes her mother had given her over the years.

"I don't have time."

"You could make the time. Some of these workouts for specific parts of the body are only fifteen or twenty minutes. You know, all the experts say it's harder for a woman to remain in shape after she reaches thirty," Marian reminded her. "That's why I went to that exercise studio four days a week. You should think seriously about using them now. You're not getting any younger, you know."

Alex dropped onto the couch and buried her face in the pillow, agitated sounds rising from her smothered lips.

"No wonder I have so much trouble working," she mumbled. She uttered a stifled scream when the doorbell rang. "With my luck it's Ed McMahon telling me I've won a million dollars and you'll show up on the television camera." She pushed herself off the couch. She peeked through the peephole and opened the door, grateful to see a friendly face. "Hi, Beth."

"I'm not disturbing you in the middle of your work, am I?"

Alex shook her head. "No, come on in."

Beth entered, halting to see Suzi Q seated on top of the couch tapping at something and yowling away. "If I were you, I'd take that cat to a feline psychologist. She's definitely gone over the edge. Who knows, maybe her mother didn't nurse her enough as a kitten or something."

"She's not the only one going over the edge," Alex muttered. "How about some coffee?"

"Sounds good." Beth seated herself at the counter overlooking the kitchen. "You have any plans for Saturday?" She traced the design in the tile with her fingernail.

"Not really."

"So, Jason hasn't called you since your exciting evening out?" Beth had heard the story the night before when she called Alex.

Alex handed her a filled mug. "Not yet."

Beth sipped her coffee. "Do us both a favor, Alex, admit he acted like a first-class jerk. You said it wasn't any of the restaurant staff's fault, yet he blames them. He even wanted the poor waiter fired, for God's sake! He got a free meal out of it and he's probably even found a way to gain sympathy from the whole deal."

"So he overreacted. He expected to enjoy a lovely romantic evening when it went up in flames." Alex looked over Beth's shoulder at Marian and Patrick. She still couldn't believe they had nothing to do with it. She even wondered if there wasn't a gang of ghostly parents roaming the earth helping each other so their poor, misguided children would get married to the people they deemed proper.

"A bunch of us are getting together Saturday afternoon to play softball and go out for pizza afterward. Thought you might like to come along. I know you've enjoyed the other times you've joined us."

Alex looked impressed. "How did you ever get a Saturday off? You once said you couldn't get a Saturday off if you were dying, that they'd just hook you up with an IV and portable oxygen that you could drag along behind you as you finished your duties."

"Somebody must have done something crazy with the budget, because they actually allowed us to add two nurses to our floor and one of them will be taking my Saturdays. She isn't too happy about it, but I told her after she's worked there for a hundred years or so she'll get a Saturday off, too." Beth chuckled. "Come on, Alex. You know you'll have fun. You always do. Besides, you're the only decent shortstop we've got."

She considered the offer. "I don't know. What if Jason calls?" Inwardly she was appalled at her dithering. Alex, who never dithered. Who never believed in sticking around the house to wait for a phone call from the opposite sex. Who always went merrily her own way.

Beth slammed down her mug on the counter. "So what? Alex, you're losing your old edge. You've never allowed a man to walk all over you the way you allow Jason. The old Alex would have told him to get lost a long time ago." Her voice softened. "Sweetie, I know how much Craig hurt you, and the death of your parents was another hard blow, but this crazy idea of yours that marrying Jason will make everything right is only going to end up hurting you more, because you're doing it for all the wrong reasons. Be honest with yourself. You only latched on to him because he was the exact opposite of Craig. Fine, he's served his purpose. He got you over the rough spots. Now it's time for you to move on."

Her smile softened her words. "Believe me, Beth, I know what I'm doing."

She sighed, recognizing it was time to back off. "So will you come to the game Saturday?"

Alex wrinkled her nose. "I don't know."

"You know Dennis will beg you to play shortstop and we just love to hear him beg."

She took that under consideration. "Who all is going?"

Beth knew she had her hooked. Now all she had to do was reel her in slow and easy. "The usual. Although I did ask Dr. Duffy in Emergency if he'd like to join us. He's new there and doesn't know many people."

Alex couldn't miss her friend's all-too-casual tone. "The last time you tried that tactic with me was the homecoming dance our junior year, and you wanted to go with Neil Harris and needed a date for his cousin."

Laughter danced in her eyes at the memory. "Neil told me Derek looked like a movie star!" Beth defended herself between laughs.

"Oh, sure, Pee-Wee Herman!" Alex broke down in laughter. "I wasn't at all surprised when he told me he was on the debating team!" she giggled.

Beth shook her head, still laughing. "I wonder what happened to him."

Alex choked. "I saw him once." She paused for effect. "On Saturday-morning cartoons!" she literally howled.

"This is what I truly miss," Marian told Patrick, settling herself on the edge of the couch listening to the two friends reminisce. "Those two always had the most enjoyable times together. I only wish we could join in."

"Don't worry about Beth, too, Marian," he told her in a low voice so Alex wouldn't hear him. "Her parents are still alive and kicking. Let them worry about her. We have enough problems with Alex."

"At least we have Beth unwittingly helping us. Didn't you hear her say that that Dr. Duffy will be at the softball game? And even if Alex doesn't want to admit it, her eyes did light up when Beth mentioned his name. I have a good feeling she'll go to that softball game."

Patrick grinned. "Only if she can play shortstop."

"Come on, Alex, you know you want to go," Beth coaxed. "Besides, if Jason calls and you aren't home, he'll realize you aren't at his beck and call. It will do him good to worry a little about where you are and who you might be with. You always did a great job of making your men suffer."

Alex laughed and held her hands up in surrender. "All right, all right, I'll go."

Beth looked sly. "And just maybe you wanted to be persuaded to go because Dr. Michael Duffy is going to be there?'' She picked up her mug and walked into the kitchen to rinse it out. "I'm off."

Alex followed her to the door. "Is Dr. Duffy going just to meet the others on a social basis?'' she asked too casually.

Beth's smile had brought many a man to his knees. "I told him you would be there." The words followed her out the door.

Alex stared wide-eyed after her friend. "Age has made you even sneakier! Just for that, I won't go!" She slammed the door.

"Yes, you will," her smug tone floated through the door. "Because you want to see him again just as badly as he wants to see you. Plus, you know our team needs a good shortstop."

Alex spun around to see just what she feared most. A pair of smiles too smug for their own good.

"I always had a soft spot for that girl," Patrick announced, turning on the television to watch the ski championships on ESPN.

MICHAEL WAS INDECISIVE all week about whether he would go to the softball game. When Beth tracked him down Friday afternoon to remind him about it, he opened his mouth ready to use whatever excuse sounded most plausible, but none came to mind. Instead he merely nodded and accepted the sheet of paper she gave him listing the time and location of the game.

Boxes filled with who-knows-what remained filled while he enjoyed the pleasure of sleeping late, lingered over brunch and showered and dressed in jeans and a soft green T-shirt. One last look at his littered apartment was enough to make him exit quickly rather than stay home and unpack the rest of his boxes. In no time he arrived at the edge of the baseball diamond, where he found the large group picking sides.

"No, no way I'm taking Cathy," Dennis objected loudly, waving his arms around.

"And what's wrong with me?" the nurse screeched, her hands braced on her slim hips.

"You haven't hit the ball once in three years, that's what's wrong. And you refuse to stay in the outfield, for fear you'll catch a ball and break a nail," he snarled.

She narrowed her eyes. "When you get sick, Doctor, I'm going to make sure you're placed on my floor."

"Okay, I'll take Cathy," Jay, the captain of the other team, interceded. "But I get to choose Alex as a consolation prize."

"No way! She's our best shortstop! Take Beth or Sheryl instead."

"I want Alex."

Nose met nose, as the two men glowered.

"Why not flip a coin to decide?" Alex suggested before war could erupt. "After all, this is only a game, guys, not a major debate."

The men stepped back, looking sheepish.

"I left all my change at home," Jay muttered.

"So did I," Dennis admitted, staring down at the ground.

Mumbling something about little boys who never grow up, Alex dug into the pocket of her khaki shorts and pulled out a quarter. She tossed it high into the air. "Call it."

"Heads," Dennis said swiftly.

"That's what I was going to call," Jay argued.

The coin was snatched by a hand before it reached the ground. "It seems you need a different system here." Michael walked over to stand beside Alex. "Why don't you try odds or evens? Jay, you call it."

Jay narrowed his eyes. "Evens."

The two men closed a fist and pumped them up twice before each throwing out a certain number of fingers. The to-
tal was six. Dennis swore under his breath.

"Two out of three," he pleaded.

"No way."

Alex looked up at Michael. "This is the first time one of
their arguments has been settled so easily."

He tried to look everywhere but at the woman wearing a
pair of shorts displaying a great pair of legs. A bright orange
sweatshirt with a picture of the frizzy-haired Fritzi silk-
screened on the front and a brightly colored CHUCK-IT-
ALL TOURS, WE SEND YOU WHERE YOU DON'T
WANT TO GO emblazoned underneath. With her hair
tucked up under a baseball cap and scuffed running shoes
on her feet she looked adorable. He'd never have the nerve
to admit it out loud, though. Instead, he discreetly looked
his fill.

Alex leaned over, talking out of the corner of her mouth.
"I heard you were practically dragged here."

There was something about her vivacious manner that
brought a smile to his lips. "Kicking and screaming."

She shook her head in mock sympathy. "Let me give you
fair warning. One shortstop position is already spoken for."

"Is that why they were arguing?"

"I'm the best in the business. They wanted me to go to
medical or nursing school, so I could be an official member
when they play other hospital teams," she explained. "But
I told them I can't even remove a splinter without passing
out."

"No wonder you didn't want to stay in the hospital overnight," he murmured, looking into eyes that looked back at
him so directly that he felt as if he was drowning in a blue
haze.

"Michael, you playing?" Dennis called out.

He absently nodded, his attention still centered on Alex.

Dennis grinned broadly, stared up at the heavens and muttered a heartfelt "thank you."

"It appears we'll be competitors," Alex murmured. "Why is Dennis so happy?"

"Probably because I went to college on a baseball scholarship."

She looked ready to burst out grinning. "Don't tell me. Shortstop?"

Canary feathers could have been plastered to his chin as he nodded. "I was also a pretty good hitter."

There was nothing Alex loved more than a challenge. "We'll cream you."

"Private bet?"

"Loser has to eat anchovies on *his* pizza."

"Suppose I like anchovies on my pizza?"

"No one in his right mind likes anchovies on pizza."

"Alex, come on!" Jay called.

Alex ran backward, blowing a saucy kiss in Michael's direction. "I'll ask them to give you double anchovies."

"Something tells me you've got a thing for my friend," Beth murmured in Michael's ear.

"A thing?"

"Yeah, fascinated, interested, all that good stuff."

"She is different," he admitted.

"And you've already made it over the first hurdle."

Michael turned his head. "Hurdle?"

"Usually she won't give a doctor the time of day. She's not only given you the time of day, she's made a bet." She patted his shoulder. "Don't deliberately lose the game. She loves nothing more than playing the role of the gloating winner." Beth giggled. "I love being the brains behind this." She sauntered off to the outfield.

Dennis's team was up first, so Michael took his place on the bench, where he could watch Alex take her assigned spot behind and near the pitcher.

Michael continued watching Alex during the first inning. He noticed how relaxed she was, her body slowly swaying from side to side. Not a lot, just enough to keep him from looking away. He was so involved in watching her he didn't hear any of the teasing catcalls coming from both teams.

"Hey, batter, batter, batter, batter, su-wingg, batter!"

"Yo, Hank took off his shirt!" Feminine wolf whistles shrilled overhead. "Be still my heart! Take it off, baby. Take it *all* off!"

Michael laughed and shook his head in wonderment. "Is it always like this?"

"Nah, usually we're a lot wilder," Dennis replied. "One night a bunch of us guys came out here about midnight for a quick game after treating about fifty victims from a multi-car pileup. We had a couple six-packs of beer and pretty soon felt the effects of the alcohol." His eyes misted over. "Hell, that was a game."

Michael remembered those kind of feelings. "How many did you lose?" he asked quietly.

"Five small kids and seven adults." He shook his head to dispel the memories. "That's why I can't understand how you can work in Emergency full-time. It seems that's all you would see. The hurt and dying."

Michael shrugged. "There's pluses, too. I delivered a baby girl yesterday. The mother never made it up to Maternity."

"Yeah, I guess you do have to look at it that way."

Michael could easily guess his colleague's state of mind. Burnout, especially in emergency medicine, was very high. There were times he felt close to it. In fact, he'd been so tired lately he had seriously considered not coming today, so he could stay home and unwind. Now all he had to do was look at Alex Cassidy's animated features and feel remarkably energized.

He wished he knew what there was about her to attract him so strongly. Several times she looked in his direction and gave him a hundred-watt smile that left him smiling back. Too bad they weren't on the same team. He would have liked the chance to talk to her. Still, sitting here and looking his fill at her wasn't all that bad, either.

"You didn't have to catch that ball, you know," Michael later told Alex as they traded places when the third out was announced.

"But, darling, I thought that was what I was supposed to do." She batted her eyelashes at him. "You hit it right at me so nicely I had no choice but to catch it in my li'l ol' glove."

"I guess then I'll have to return the favor," he bantered.

Alex looked over her shoulder as she walked toward home plate. "Maybe."

"My, my, what a change in you today," Beth commented as they sat down on the bench.

Alex looked puzzled by her friend's teasing remark. "What do you mean?"

"You keep up that flirting much more and the guy's tongue will be hanging on the ground." Beth pulled off her sweatshirt and tied the sleeves around her waist. "What's with you? Usually you don't flirt so openly with any man, much less a doctor."

She opened her mouth, then closed it when she realized she didn't have an answer. "I don't know," she seemed to say as much to herself as to her friend.

Beth knew right away that Alex was being honest with her. "Then back off a little, if you're just teasing. He's a nice guy and you're my best friend. I don't want to see any unnecessary casualties here."

Alex was startled by her words. "If anyone's been hurt in the past, it's been me."

"Yes, but you've hardened yourself where men are concerned. You did it when you decided marrying Jason would be a good idea." Beth looked up when her name was called. "Looks like I'm up next." She stood up and walked toward the plate.

Alex was troubled by Beth's blunt words. She knew her friend wasn't trying to hurt her, but to help. Still, that Beth thought she was deliberately stringing Michael along for the fun of it did hurt. Between her parents' candid observations and Beth's comments, this week was turning out to be a revelation.

She looked across the field where Michael stood, utterly relaxed. As if feeling her gaze on him, he half turned his head and sent her the warmest smile she'd seen in a long time. This wasn't like Jason's smile, which never seemed to reach his dark eyes. No, Michael's smile began in his eyes and radiated outward until it lit the world around him.

With that smile, Alex knew she was well and truly hooked.

Chapter Six

This can't be happening! Alex forced herself back to earth with a bone-jarring thud. *He's a doctor. Doctors only mean trouble.* She looked around with narrowed eyes. *Therefore, there has to be a logical reason why I'm suddenly noticing a nice-looking man who could easily inspire lust if I'm not careful.*

"It was just a smile, nothing more," she whispered fiercely. "It's going to take more than a smile to turn my knees to jelly. So get your hormones back on track."

"What'd you say?" one of the men said, turning to her.

She forced a weak smile. "Just psyching myself up for the game." Except she knew she'd need more than a good pep talk to do that. She began to wonder if her parents didn't have something to do with what was going on. But they swore to her they couldn't leave her apartment! No, this was just some kind of overload on her part, that was all. She slowly released the breath she was holding. She looked up when a pair of legs appeared before her.

Jay crouched down, his narrow features intense. "Alex, this is our first chance to win a game against Dennis's team. When you're up at bat you've got to hit that sucker clear out of the park. I know you're a strong hitter and you can do it." He silently pleaded with her.

"It's not going to be easy with Dennis as the pitcher. He knows all my weaknesses and you can be sure he's going to use that knowledge against me when I'm up at bat."

He threw his head back and groaned. "Can't you outwit him?"

She felt so bad for him that she could only promise, "You know I'll do my best."

Jay's face lit up. "Thanks, babe." He patted her knee and moved on to the next player to deliver a pep talk.

"I can do it. Just don't look at him," Alex muttered when she took her place at bat.

She hefted the bat and took several practice swings before approaching home plate. The first thing she saw wasn't the pitcher but the shortstop watching her with those enigmatic deep blue eyes that she sensed saw more than she was comfortable with.

"Not him, you fool," she mumbled. "Just concentrate on the pitcher."

Alex swung the bat back to rest lightly against her shoulder. "Let's go for it." She looked grim enough to chew nails.

Easier said than done, Alex soon learned as she refused to look at Michael. Instead, she concentrated on Dennis. She'd played with him enough to know most of his moves, and hopefully could predict his pitch. Even softball had a few surprises in it.

Dennis stared at her a long time, probably in hopes of unnerving her. Alex narrowed her eyes and stared right back.

"Come on, Dennis, let's see that wimpball of yours!" she shouted, flexing her back muscles.

With a growl he let loose with the ball. Alex waited until the right moment and let the bat fly forward. The wood hit the ball with a satisfying *whack!* With a grin of pure pleasure she took a split second to watch the ball sail toward center field.

"Run, Alex!" The scream was deafening.

Without hesitation she was off. Her feet flew over first base, tapped second base and she was on her way to third. She knew she had more than enough time to make it to home plate.

"Pump it, Alex!" Jay yelled as she passed third base.

She put on a burst of speed as she saw home plate looming ahead and knew if she didn't hurry she would have to slide—a painful prospect. Gritting her teeth, she forced herself to pump her legs as hard as possible.

"There's no stopping me now." She sailed over home base.

"You're out!" the umpire shouted.

Alex skidded to a stop, almost losing her balance in the process. "I'm *what?*"

The umpire shrugged. "You're out, baby."

She planted her hands on her hips, fully prepared to do battle. "Out? That ball is still out in center field."

"Oh yeah? Then what's this?" He pointed to the ball the grinning catcher held.

Alex's eyes almost bugged out. "Where did that come from?"

"Looks like you weren't so lucky, after all." The catcher, a technician from Radiology, gloated.

"This is ridiculous." She stomped back to the bench. "There was no way that ball could get back here so fast. I practically hit it out of the park. And I hit it toward Janis, who ducks when a ball comes within ten feet of her."

Hal, who played second base, shook his head. "Not this time. That ball dropped right at Janis's feet. She scooped it up and threw it further than I ever thought she could."

Alex saw red. "Why did she have to pick now to improve her game!" She stalked down to the end of the bench.

Feeling someone's eyes on her, she slowly lifted her head and found Michael watching her from his position as shortstop.

Good hit, he mouthed.

"Don't worry about it, Alex," Jay consoled, patting her on the shoulder. "Your hit helped get two of our guys in."

She couldn't contain her anger. "I should have slid in."

"I don't think it would have made any difference." He looked up at the sound of collective groans. "Looks like Stan just got tagged out."

"We can still cream them," she vowed darkly, brushing past Jay.

"You were right," Michael commented as they traded places. "You're very good."

Right about now, she wasn't in the mood for any compliments. "Obviously not good enough."

He smiled. "It was a fluke. The wind probably hit the ball."

Her eyes gleamed with the light of battle. "Just don't expect me to be so kind when you're taken out."

"I knew you were a no-mercy woman. Don't worry, I can handle it."

She should have known he was the kind of man she couldn't stay angry at long. Her eyes lighted with laughter. "Yes, I'm sure you can."

"WITH THE WAY Alex is playing today, I'm sure glad she's with the opposition." Dennis settled on the bench beside Michael. He gave the other man a sly glance. "I wonder if it doesn't have something to do with our newest player?"

Michael never believed in deliberately misunderstanding a coy remark. "She's probably faking you out and waiting to clobber us when it really counts."

"Naw, it's not her style. She prefers taunting you to your face, just as she's pushing said face in the dirt. She loves nothing more than a challenge and meets it head-on."

"Sounds like a man speaking from experience." He hoped his tone sounded casual enough. He hated to admit he was more than a little curious about the real Alex Cassidy, not just the facts he'd seen written on her medical chart and what little he'd learned that evening in her apartment.

Dennis laughed as he shook his head. "Don't I wish? The lady isn't interested in doctors. Not after what happened with her ex. As far as she's concerned, we're good enough for softball buddies, treating an occasional ache and pain, but as for romance, well, we members of the medical profession are just not stable enough. Craig Sommers, with his eye for pretty nurses and anything else in skirts, left an indelible black mark against all of us. I guess we should feel honored that she'll still play softball with us. Well, I'm up."

Michael rested his back against the fence with his legs stretched out in front of him, ankles crossed. With his arms crossed in front of his chest, he appeared the picture of a relaxed man while he studied the woman manning the shortstop position. Strands of hair now escaped her ponytail, hanging down her cheeks and along her nape, but she appeared oblivious to them, and whatever makeup she might have put on that morning had already worn off from her exertion. She pulled the bill of her cap down over her eyes to shade them from the sun as she joined in raucously taunting the other team. She shifted her weight from one foot to the other, clearly unable to stand still for more than a minute.

How does she manage to stay at a drawing board for hours at a time, when she can't even stand still for more than thirty seconds out here? he wondered. Or is this how she takes care of energy she can't expend while she's working?

His intense gaze remained on Alex, who appeared more than a little distracted. From what the others said about her playing ability she was usually so alert during a game it was downright scary. No ball got past her and her energy level never lagged. So what had happened to change her so dramatically? Today she seemed to concentrate more on him than the game. His eyes narrowed as his ever-sharp brain tried to put all the pieces together. Unfortunately, he was used to diagnosing a human being's suffering, not the emotional makeup of an intriguing woman. He might not indulge in gossip, but that didn't mean he didn't hear it from time to time. And Alex's stuffy banker friend was a good topic among the people present today. If Alex was seeing someone else, why was she watching him so intently? And why did she send him the flowers? He found himself with a lot of questions he wished he had answers for.

"What's your game, Alex?" he murmured. "What are you trying to prove?"

ALEX SIGHED. This would be her last game with this group unless she could find a way to redeem herself. She couldn't believe how badly she was playing!

She flubbed a fly ball that a small child could have caught. Then when she finally scooped it into her glove and turned to throw it to third base, something happened to her that had never happened before. She somehow got confused and threw it to first base instead. Her teammates' groans were not a pretty sound.

"What the hell is your problem?" Jay screamed, finally at the end of his rope. The cheerful captain who had expected an easy win became a raving maniac with each point the other team scored.

"You're the doctor, you tell me," she screamed back. "Maybe it's PMS!"

After that, Alex threw all her concentration into the game. With the same grim purpose she used when facing a deadline, she made sure a ball didn't get past her. When her team was up, she used the time before she was up at bat to focus on how to hit that ball as hard and far as she could.

"What is wrong with you today?" Beth sat down beside her.

"Beth, if I told you what was going on, you'd have the men in white coats haul me away. And straitjackets don't do anything for me."

"At the rate you're going, sweetie, you won't have to tell me a thing."

"It's all because of my birthday," Alex muttered, tracing idle circles in the dust with the toe of her shoe. "Things happen to you when you turn thirty. Strange things you can't even imagine."

"Something tells me forty is going to be hell for you." She plopped down beside her. "You're already not making much sense."

"I know," she sighed.

"Then tell me what's wrong," Beth persisted.

She took the plunge. "My parents."

"Come again?"

Alex drew in a deep breath. "My parents. I bet even this is all their doing. The way I suddenly can't catch a ball or hit. Even my falling and hitting my head on the coffee table. I'm sure they knew I'd meet what they consider an eligible man in the emergency room. You'd think they'd leave well enough alone. I mean, I am thirty and I've been married and divorced, lived on my own since I was twenty, so I should have some common sense, shouldn't I?" She looked at her friend with pleading eyes.

By now Beth was past confusion to full-scale alarm. Alex was known for flights of fancy but never anything like this. "Alex, we need to talk."

Feeling a little better, she patted her friend's hand and stood up. "You're right, we need to sit down and have an old-fashioned gabfest, but I'm next up at bat."

Beth cast her gaze around, hoping no one else had heard Alex's irrational conversation. Especially the psychiatric resident who was convinced everyone was a potential patient. Wouldn't he have a field day with Alex right about now!

"And here I thought she suffered only a mild concussion."

"I CAN'T BELIEVE we're not further ahead," Jay groaned, tunneling his hands through his hair, sending the cropped dark brown strands standing high. He looked accusingly at Alex.

"This is not my fault," she argued.

"Then how come Dennis always wins when you're on his team, and now that you're with us you can't play worth a damn?"

"Everyone has an off day!"

"Why did yours have to be today!" he practically screamed.

"Think you two could settle this battle after we've won?" Dennis called out.

Jay's reply was profane and to the point. "Let's get on with it," he growled, stomping off. He spun around, pointing a finger at Alex. "You better hit the ball clear into hell."

"Jay, if I were a physician I would recommend a lobotomy, stat."

Growling something uncomplimentary about her under his breath, he returned to the bench and plopped himself down.

"Okay, let's show him how it's done," Alex muttered, hefting the bat in her hands and giving it several experimental swings. She spread her legs slightly in a comfortable stance and forced all her attention away from Michael.

"Are you going to stand there talking to yourself all day or are you going to play ball?" the portly umpire asked, looking up at the heavens as he uttered a long-suffering sigh.

Alex flashed him one of her deadly smiles. "Stan, my dear, I'm going to play ball like you've never seen it played before. I'm going to hit the kind of ball you guys in Urology will be talking about for years. I'm going to hit it clear into the heavens."

Stan groaned. "Don't talk about it, sweetheart, just do it, okay?"

Alex's first swing would have been perfect, if she had waited just a split second longer before she leveled the bat at the ball. The second was a ball. Third time was the charm. She swung into the ball as if she, the bat and the ball were one.

"Yes!" she squealed, taking off the moment she knew the ball was heading out in a graceful arc. She was halfway to first base when she realized the roars of excitement had changed to groans of disappointment. Just before she tapped the sandbag, she noticed the ball she thought she'd hit out of the park now resided in Michael's mitt and was being swiftly thrown to first base. She did the only thing she could to save time... she flattened out and slid in on her stomach. Quite painfully, too.

"Oomph!"

"You're out!"

Alex slowly straightened up. "I should have stayed home." She pulled her shirt up to inspect the damage. She wasn't surprised to find angry-looking abrasions across her stomach. She tentatively touched them with her fingernail and winced. She didn't have to look at her knees to see the damage. They stung just as badly.

"You did a good job of scraping yourself up." Michael stood next to her, studying her wounds.

She wrinkled her nose. "How many years of medical school did it take for you to figure that out?"

He chuckled. "Too many. Come on, I've got my bag in my car." He draped an arm around her shoulders and guided her off the field.

"Jay must be hopping mad."

"He did say something about taking up chess."

Alex looked around for Beth. "Look, thanks for your offer, but I came with Beth."

"I told her I'd drive you over to the pizza place. She said you could give me directions." He led her over to a sixties-model black Mustang whose body shone with a loving wax job.

She expelled a low whistle. "Very nice. Where's the Mercedes or equally ostentatious car every doctor believes he should own?"

He unlocked and opened his trunk, pulling out a dark leather doctor's bag. He slammed the lid closed and indicated that Alex should hitch herself up on the trunk.

She looked warily at the shining surface. "I'm afraid of scratching it."

"Not much can scratch this baby. If you're so worried, I'll give you a boost." He carefully placed one hand on each side of her waist. Both froze as his hands made contact with her bare skin when her sweatshirt rode up. Startled sky-blue eyes looked into deeper blue ones.

It's a foregone conclusion our children would have blue eyes. The thought came unbidden to Alex's mind.

Quickly recovering, Michael easily lifted her onto the trunk and turned away to open his bag.

Alex could only sit there stunned. Not even when she thought she was madly in love with Craig had she felt the instant magnetic connection she felt with Michael. And all he'd done was touch her in what many might call an impersonal way! What would have happened if...? She shook her head almost violently. She dared not think about it.

Michael noticed her action. "Are you all right?"

"A piece of dust or something settled against my nose." She'd been evading the truth all day.

He smiled. Alex already figured out that Michael Duffy's smile was a rare event.

"You found that funny?"

He shook his head. "To be honest, I was fascinated by the way the late afternoon light caught in your hair." His hand lifted slightly in that direction but he quickly brought it under control and reached back inside his bag instead. "I've got some damp cloths here that will clean the abrasions." He tore open a foil packet.

"The last time a man opened a packet like that around me it wasn't for a wet cloth," Alex muttered, then swiftly clapped her hands over her mouth as she realized how it sounded. "Pardon me while I stuff my foot farther into my mouth."

He smiled again. He was learning that he liked smiling around her. "What's so wrong with being outspoken?"

"There's many a time when speaking before running said thoughts through one's brain can get one into a great deal of trouble," she intoned.

Michael carefully ran the cloth across Alex's exposed abdomen, forcing himself not to think about how soft her skin was or how the angry-looking scrapes only enhanced the pale gold color of her skin. He inwardly winced as he thought how much the raw skin must burn.

"You should have slid in on your side," he said quietly, going about with his usual efficiency as he finished cleaning the wounds and disposed of the cloths in a nearby trash can. He hoped she didn't notice how badly his hands were shaking.

Alex wrinkled her nose in distaste at the idea. "No thanks. Not when I'm wearing shorts. I tried it once and I walked funny for a month." She cocked her head to one side, enjoying the chance to study him without being too obvious. "You're not the boisterous type, are you, Dr. Duffy?"

"Not really," he said without a trace of apology. "I'm usually bogged down with my work and have stacks of medical journals to read during what little free time I have. I guess you could say I'm a pretty boring guy." He looked away for a moment to hide the pain he felt at admitting something once told him in sharp, concise terms.

"Ever been married?"

His features closed up tighter than a drum. "Close. It wasn't meant to be."

As an artist, Alex read expressions easier than many people. And right now she could see that Michael had suffered a great deal of hurt. She found herself wanting to reach out and soothe his pain.

"And you don't care to get caught up in that mess again," she guessed.

"Correct."

She smiled and held out her hand. "Then, my friend, I'm the perfect woman for you, because I don't care to get caught up with a doctor again." Even if he does have a smile that could melt a woman's knees and looks good enough in those jeans to eat. She tried to remind herself that she was only doing a good deed. She was offering a lonely, wounded man her friendship. There was nothing wrong with that. Of course the idea that something other than friendship might happen occurred to her also. There was something about him that did strange things to her hormones.

Michael wasn't as impulsive in his moods. "Why?"

"Why not?" She pulled down her shirt and carefully eased off the trunk so as not to scratch its surface.

"I ask you out and you're basically tied up. And I've heard that you're practically engaged to an investment banker. So why all this flirting and saucy byplay today?" he demanded, planting one hand on each side of her thighs so she was trapped. The scent of male flesh warmed by the sun and the afternoon's exertion and an expression that threatened to bore into her innermost thoughts sent immediate signals to her brain. This was one man who refused to be put off with careless words. He'd want the truth and nothing less.

"There's no game," she said softly.

He had to believe her. He hoped to believe her. She looked too sincere to lie. "Then, why?"

"I don't know." The admission came out as a whisper that barely reached his ears.

Working purely on instinct, he slid his hands slowly up and down her arms. It would only have taken a little pressure from him to bring her closer, closer until their lips could meet.

Alex wasn't aware of her face lifting just enough and tilting at just that right angle. Her lips were parted slightly, moist and most definitely inviting. Even her body leaned into his just enough for an embrace they both so obviously wanted.

They were so unaware of the parking lot around them they could have been anywhere. All they needed was a blazing sunset and violin music to make the romantic scene complete.

Michael was the one to abruptly break the spell. His arms dropped and he stepped back before he could change his mind and take what she was so sweetly offering.

"We better catch up with the others before they send out a search party." He unlocked the passenger door and quickly walked around to the driver's side.

Alex was still recovering from the force of what *hadn't* happened. She could feel all her nerve endings quivering.

"If my parents knew what almost happened," she muttered, "they would have found a way to lock us inside the park."

Chapter Seven

"What happened to you two?" Beth cornered Alex as soon as she and Michael reached the Italian restaurant known for its spicy food and friendly atmosphere. Dennis and several others had already swept Michael back to one of the rear tables the two teams commandeered upon arriving. "We were about ready to send out a search party. Or..." she drew out the word, her eyes sparkling with mischievous delight, "were the two of you planning on a private celebration?"

Alex sent her an eloquent look. "He cleaned my scrapes. Wanna see?" She started to lift her shirt.

She rolled her eyes. "Very funny, Alex. You were gone long enough for those scrapes to heal completely. Tell all."

Alex took a deep breath. "He took out his black bag and played doctor, *literally,* while he cleaned my scrapes, probably because he didn't want to risk an infection. That was all. Sorry I don't have any titillating news for you."

Beth studied her face closely. "He didn't kiss you?" She sounded disappointed more than anything.

Alex was prepared for the question so she could reply without hesitation. "No." *But he tried to. At least, I think he did. And I hoped he would have.* "Beth, I can't...I don't..." She expelled a sigh of frustration. "He's a doctor." As far as she was concerned, that was more than enough of a reason why she wouldn't allow anything to go further. Not to mention, she was *afraid* of allowing it to go any further.

Beth understood only too well. "I swear, you need a psychiatrist to work out this aversion you have to dating doctors."

"My love life is full enough, thank you." She held up her forefinger, requesting silence. "Please, Beth, you're my best friend and I love you dearly, but I've been given so much unwanted advice lately regarding men that I honestly can't take any more." She turned away to walk back to the tables.

Beth grasped her wrist to halt her escape. "Do me one favor. Think long and hard about what marriage to Jason would be like. How are you going to feel about living with him for the next forty or so years? And more importantly, what if he insists you give up your strip after you're married? Would you honestly be willing to do that?"

She turned her head. That was something she hadn't considered. Or, a tiny voice in her brain prompted, was it that she hadn't *dared* consider it because she feared Jason would do just that? Funny, she never had doubts about him before. What had happened to cause them now? "He would never ask that of me. He knows how important it is to me," she declared with false bravado.

"Really? You don't sound all that convinced. You forget I've been around when others have brought up Fritzi in front of him. He may have smiled, but it never reached his eyes, and he was always uncomfortable when the subject came up. He considers cartoons to be beneath him, Alex. And that means he'll feel they're beneath his wife. I can see it happening. He'll start out with little biting remarks, but soon enough you'll decide it would just be easier if you give up the strip, and if you do that you've given up the last part of yourself, Alex. Don't let that cold-blooded vampire suck away every drop of your life." This time her vibrant eyes glittered with purpose. The purpose of protecting her closest friend from hurt.

Alex looked around furtively, ensuring no one could overhear their conversation. "Everything you're saying is hypothetical, Beth," she hissed. "Not to mention I don't care to discuss this now."

"It's the first time I've been able to. Whenever I've tried to bring it up, you've put me off. I wasn't about to let you do it again. Michael Duffy might be a doctor, but he's nothing like Craig. Whether you like it or not, he does something to your hormones. I'm not going to apologize if you don't like what I'm saying. I'm your friend and I care about you. I don't want to see you hurt again, and if it takes some plain speaking to help you, then that's just what I'll do." She lowered her voice. "Admit it, Alex. The man has given you something to think about." Having said her bit, Beth released Alex's wrist and walked away.

Alex stood frozen for a moment, stunned by Beth's verbal attack. Beth had always been fairly laid-back and not the type to butt into another's business unless she felt she had a good reason. Alex didn't want to dwell on that reason. She squared her shoulders, pasted a broad smile on her face and headed in the same direction as Beth.

Michael looked up at Alex's approach. He hadn't missed the tension in Beth's face when she drew Alex to one side for a low-voiced conversation. He didn't have to guess that the main object of that conversation was himself. Several others slyly asked what took them so long. Sounds of disbelief met his explanation that he wanted to take the time to clean her scrapes to prevent any chance of infection.

"Maybe this doctor knows the way to soften our hardhearted Alex toward the medical profession." Dennis grinned. "Why didn't I think about patching up her skinned knees and other parts of her anatomy when she scraped herself up?"

"If my first introduction to the male side of the medical field had been Craig Sommers, I wouldn't even walk on the same side of the street as any of you," said Jennifer, Dennis's latest girlfriend.

"Hey, there's nothing wrong with a man liking his ladies," one of the other doctors spoke up, leering at the woman seated beside him. He yelped when she pinched his waist.

"There's a lot wrong with it, if there's a wife involved," Jennifer argued. "I worked with that sleaze for six months before I could transfer to another floor. He thinks he's God's gift to women and we were all eager to jump into bed with him. There may be stupid bimbos around who fall for his line, but I'm proud to say I wasn't one of them." As tense silence descended, she looked up, her face turning a bright red as she realized Alex stood nearby. "Oh, Alex, I'm sorry," she whispered, stricken.

She offered a reassuring smile. "Don't be, Jen. I'm just glad to know you weren't one of those stupid bimbos. Personally, I always felt Craig would have been happier if he could work as a stud in Las Vegas. At least then he would be paid for doing what he *thinks* he does best."

"That sounds a little bitchy, Alex," Lisa, a sloe-eyed brunette, purred. It was a well-known fact that she had been one of Craig's many late-night diversions during his marriage to Alex. "Perhaps you're not over him as much as you think."

"Trust me, I'm over the man. As for what you thought was a bitchy remark, it wasn't. I was merely stating the facts." She seated herself at the other table next to Michael.

"Friendly enemy?" he murmured, handing her a glass of wine.

"Far from it. I think she wouldn't mind having my heart on a silver platter. She's still convinced I forced her breakup with Craig instead of the new nurse in Orthopedics. None of them ever lasted more than a few months.'' Ignoring her first inclination to down the wine like a glass of water, she merely sipped the rich burgundy and set the glass down in front of her. ''So where's the menu?''

Michael shook his head. ''Don't worry, I already ordered your dinner. A large pizza with plenty of anchovies. Just the way you like it.''

Alex's dazzling smile gave no indication that she hated anchovies with a passion.

''Didn't I hear once that anchovies give you hives?'' Jay asked with devilish glee.

''No, Jay, *you* give me hives,'' she bantered back.

Michael settled back in his chair, one arm draped over the lattice back. He was fully prepared to sit there and enjoy the show Alex was putting on. This was clearly her element—the center of things. Not that she deliberately sought the spotlight, just that people naturally gravitated to her outgoing personality. He remembered once reading an article about the right-brained creative personality and how most of them were introverts, happiest with their own company. Alex's work clearly defined her as a creative personality, but there was nothing introverted about her. He also noticed she answered questions about her cartoon strip but didn't elaborate, preferring to switch the conversation around to the others. Talk among the group wasn't so much about medicine as it was about anything that struck their fancy, from the new puppy one of the doctors had just bought to the number of new restaurants that had sprung up in the past six months.

Even after their energetic afternoon he could swear he smelled a faint whiff of cologne coming from Alex's skin. Just as he thought he noticed it during that charged moment at the field when he almost kissed her. Now he wished he'd given in to his first inclination. And was it his imagination, or was that her bare leg resting so close to his own that he could feel her body heat? He cradled his glass of wine with his hands.

"Lighten up, Doc, this is our victory celebration," one of his fellow players teased. "We won hands down." He ducked his head when several losers pelted him with wadded napkins. "Hey, don't be sore losers!"

His smile was fleeting. "Sorry. I guess I sort of drifted off." Thinking about what it would be like to have Alex Cassidy all to himself.

"Look, old buddy, it's time for us to party. Waiter, could we have another couple bottles of wine over here?" Dennis called out. When they arrived, he filled everyone's glasses except Michael's, whose hand covered the top.

"I'll wait until I have some food in me."

"They'll keep it up until they have a good buzz on," Alex said in a low voice, picking up the basket of soft, warmed bread sticks drenched in garlic butter. She offered the basket to Michael and took one out, sinking her teeth into it. "Mm, I can live on these alone. Well, not really, but they hit the spot as an appetizer."

For one brief second, he envisioned those teeth sinking into his skin. He blinked several times, dispelling the image before it started taking over. As he watched her, he couldn't help grinning at her restless energy. "Don't worry, your anchovy-drenched pizza should be arriving soon."

Alex studied him carefully. "You should do it more often."

"What?"

"Smile."

"I do smile," he pointed out, a bit put out she might see him as unfriendly. Especially considering the thoughts he'd been having about her.

She shifted in her chair so that her back was to the others as she faced him. "Not as much as you could." With her cap off, her ponytail dragging and makeup worn off by her exertions she looked more like a cheeky sixteen-year-old than a woman just hitting thirty. "My mother's favorite phrase was 'don't frown, dear, they only cause wrinkles,'" she chuckled. "But then she also used to tell me not to lie because my nose would grow, so I was never sure what to believe."

"I won't tell you the old wives' tales my parents used to tell me."

She lifted her eyebrows comically. "If you were a precocious boy, I can well imagine what they warned you against," she teased.

"There was one thing they didn't warn me against."

"What was that?"

"You."

Not by a blink of the eye did Alex show any reaction to Michael's blunt statement, but it did throw her off. She felt it in the pit of her stomach as she stared at his face, looking for a sign, any sign that this was light flirtation. The trouble was, it wasn't there. He was very serious and she found it thrilling along with a bit scary.

This one is different, her brain insisted. *He isn't more concerned with himself than others. Just remember, all his attention has been directed toward you. And you have to admit you love it. Hey, who wouldn't? The man is good-looking, has excellent manners and there's something about him that appeals to all your hormones.*

Of course it does, the doubting side argued. *He's trying to impress you. Just as Craig did. Remember how he acted as if you were the only woman alive? How he'd look deep into your eyes, telling you you were the only woman for him? Then he'd leave you to meet some nurse at her apartment for a few hours of anatomy lessons.* She felt saddened that there could be even the slimmest of chances Michael was like Craig.

Michael recognized Alex's retreat immediately, by the way her eyes showed a faint touch of pain in their pale blue depths. The warm, teasing woman with the sly come-hither smiles of just a few moments ago was gone. The only reason for her withdrawal had to be what he said, an impulsive statement he'd never made to any other woman. He cursed himself for speaking without thinking. He turned his head when he heard his name called.

Alex was pleasantly surprised when a plate of Tortellini Alfredo, one of her favorites, was set in front of her. She looked up at Michael.

"Something told me anchovies aren't your favorite any more than they're mine," he admitted. "And I won't even bring up that hated cholesterol word, either."

"Cholesterol never looked so palatable," she replied, picking up her fork and digging into the pasta with the ferocity of a hungry woman who clearly didn't bother to watch her calorie intake.

"Alex, I'm sorry if I embarrassed you a few minutes ago," he said in a low voice, concentrating on his own meal. "I usually have a stricter rein on my tongue. Maybe it was the wine I had."

Her fork paused in midair. It was clear from the expression on her face that an apology from him was unexpected. Deep down, she knew it wasn't the wine that caused him to say what he did. He hadn't drunk enough. No, what he spoke was the truth, and all she did was retreat when a part of her wouldn't have minded advancing. She slowly turned her head. "You aren't the impetuous type, are you?"

He shook his head. "It took me five months to settle on which couch to buy. Does that tell you how impulsive I am?"

She grinned. "How about deciding on a color scheme for your home?"

His lips twitched. "There's supposed to be a color scheme?"

Alex leaned over, confiding under her breath, "It helps you tell the difference between the kitchen and the bathroom."

"You'd find apartments in the east that have the bathtub in the kitchen. Think that confuses people?"

"It would sure confuse me."

"You two having a private discussion or can anyone horn in?" Dennis asked, leering at them.

"Not if you're going to talk about autopsies, lab serums or something equally gruesome," she retorted. "I almost lost my dinner the last time, listening to three of you talk about your cadavers in medical school." She wrinkled her nose in distaste.

"Herbert was very special to me," he said, affronted.

"Herbert? Mine was named Ralph," Michael chimed in. "I especially remember my excitement to learn he had webs between his toes. I thought I'd made a great medical discovery until my instructor caustically pointed out that this wasn't the first time he'd seen it. I was crushed for days."

"Please." Alex held up her hand in surrender. "I have a strong stomach for gory horror films, but not for listening to you people talk about the real thing. I'll stick to special effects, thank you very much."

"Maybe you should put Fritzi in the hospital for a while," Jennifer suggested.

Alex's eyes became unfocused as she thought about it. She gradually returned to the present. "I don't think it would work. There are no viable tours in hospitals. I once thought of a tour of Watergate, but I figured it was more Garry Trudeau's style than mine."

"I would think after all this time you'd run out of tour ideas," Michael commented, fascinated at the way she so easily slipped into her creative mode. As a logical, left-brain individual, he envied the right-brain part of the human race because they always seemed to enjoy the world more.

"There's times when I wonder if I might have run dry, but then something seems to come up. And if I ever do feel it's time to move on, I'll just go through my folder of ideas and see if there's anything I want to work with." She forked up the last of her tortellini.

"What you do fascinates me," Jay admitted. "I mean, you take a vague idea and breathe life into it. Not just words but pictures, too."

"Yes, but I couldn't find a person's lungs without a road map."

Dennis snapped his fingers. "A map! That's our problem, guys. We just get in there and root around when we should be consulting a map!"

The others hooted with good-natured laughter.

"You are all so very sick." Alex stood up. "Now I know it's time for me to leave."

Beth looked dismayed. "Actually, Alex, I've got to work tonight."

She looked at her friend suspiciously. "I thought you had the weekend off."

"The hospital called just before I left to ask me to come in tonight."

Alex didn't believe one word. Not when Beth hadn't breathed a word about working earlier.

"No problem, I'll run you home," Michael offered.

She didn't take her accusing eyes off Beth. "No, that isn't fair to you."

He stood up. "As I said, no problem. I'm ready to leave, too." As far as he was concerned, there was nothing more to say on the subject.

If Alex hadn't turned her head just that moment she would have missed the tiny smile of triumph on Beth's face. She and Michael had walked right into her trap.

I'll get you for this, she mouthed to her friend.

Beth merely smiled back. "I'll see you later, Alex."

"Oh, yes, you will." It was more a threat than a promise.

Alex held her tongue until she and Michael were in the parking lot.

"I hate to tell you this, but Beth isn't working tonight," she sighed, waiting for him to unlock the passenger door.

"I know. She agreed to go out with Greg for a drink after everyone split up." He looked up. "Does it bother you that I'm driving you home?"

"It bothers me that you were tricked into it," she said quietly.

Michael turned to rest his hip against the cool metal of the door. "Let me set you straight, Alex. If I felt used or tricked into this, I wouldn't have offered to drive you home. If it makes you feel any better, you don't live out of my way—and I'm not the party type, so you're not taking me away from anything I don't want to be taken from. All right?" His eyes bored into hers.

Those all-seeing eyes were the first thing she'd seen when she came to in the hospital. She wondered what he saw now. She knew what she saw. And what she saw she very much liked.

Skin used to sterile hospital lighting now in the beginning stages of a fairly nasty sunburn. Creases along the eyes and mouth indicating he wasn't always as serious as he looked now. She wouldn't mind seeing that mind-blowing smile of his again. Hair still tousled from the afternoon breeze on the playing field. When they arrived at the restaurant he'd pulled a sweatshirt on and pushed the sleeves up to his elbows.

"Very all right," she said huskily. Whether she was talking about what he just said or what she was looking at, even she wasn't sure. At that moment, Jason Palmer was very much out of her mind.

His face creased in a smile. "Good." He moved away and opened her door, closing it after her as she settled herself in the seat.

The ride to Alex's apartment building was made in comfortable silence.

"Does Dr. Duffy know enough to take a cool shower tonight to ease that sunburn?" Alex asked as Michael parked the car in the guest parking lot. She dared to reach out and run her fingers across his cheek, finding it pleasantly rough and warm to the touch. Jason's face was always baby-butt smooth from his constant shaving. She found this faint hint of stubble very sexy and couldn't find the strength to order her fingers to stop touching him. "And use some lotion?"

"That will be my first task when I get home. I haven't had too much time outside lately and I should have remembered to use some sunblock." He ignored the tight, itchy feeling to his skin as he grasped her wandering hand around the wrist.

"I hope you enjoyed your day," she whispered.

"Very much. Perhaps next time we can play on the same team."

She felt as if there was something unspoken going on here. "It's kind of difficult to have two shortstops on one team."

"I'm sure we could work it out." His fingers rubbed in a circular motion against the tender spot on the underside of her wrist.

"Yes, I guess so." She felt mesmerized by his gaze and caress that sent signals up to her brain. How easy, just move forward a few inches, he'd move forward a few inches, and *voilà!* Close enough to kiss. She discovered more and more she wanted to find out what kind of kisser he was. The car was in shadows, the streetlights spaced far enough to give them a bit of privacy. At the same time, this waiting, the anticipation only heightened her senses more. And judging by his rough breathing and tension, he felt the same way. If anyone dared ask her about Jason Palmer that moment, she would have looked at them blankly and asked, "Jason who?"

"I guess I should go in," she whispered, all the while feeling the exact opposite.

Little did she know he would take her literally. He slowly released her arm and sat back. He climbed out of the car and walked around to the passenger door, assisting her out.

"Thank you for driving me home," she said, her voice trailing off. There was so much more she wanted to say, and she toyed with the idea of asking him inside.

"Alexis?"

She spun around at the sound of the familiar voice. "Jason?" Her mind went into overdrive. Had she forgotten a date they planned? Had her parents mixed up her schedule again? She didn't stop to question her displeasure at seeing him so unexpectedly.

Jason, immaculate as always, looked at her rumpled clothing, untidy ponytail and baseball cap with distaste. Her companion, just as disheveled, earned another curl of the lip.

"I didn't realize you had plans this evening," he said stiffly.

"Jason, this is Dr. Michael Duffy." She decided it was best to ignore his remark.

Jason barely nodded at him. "I thought you didn't care to have anything to do with doctors."

She was stunned by his rudeness. Jason didn't believe in being rude. At least, she had thought so until now. "Jason, what is wrong? This isn't like you."

He continued looking at her as if Michael didn't exist. "I'd like to talk to you privately."

Alex was torn. This was a Jason she wasn't used to, and she wasn't sure she wanted to spend any time alone with him. Besides, she had been about to invite Michael in for coffee when Jason appeared.

"Well, it is late," she murmured, shifting from one leg to the other. To be honest, she had no idea what time it was. Even if it wasn't late, she knew she didn't want Jason, in his present mood, in her apartment.

Jason stuck his balled fists in his topcoat pocket. He easily read her mind. "I see."

"I'll get going, Alex." Michael touched her shoulder.

She looked up. "Thanks for the ride."

"Any time." He nodded at Jason and moved toward his car.

"Could we go upstairs?" Jason requested.

Deciding she wasn't going to be able to get rid of him easily, Alex nodded and walked toward the front door. She wryly noticed that he made no move to get too close to her when they stepped into the elevator. She wondered what her parents would think when they saw him.

"I can't believe this!" Patrick was more than a little surprised when Alex walked in with Jason behind her. "What's *he* doing here?"

"You can't tell me this man attended the softball game." Marian looked at Alex. Her daughter's stormy gaze eloquently informed her she'd explain later. "Obviously not."

"I can't believe you could be so rude, Jason," Alex said without preamble. "You acted as if I stood you up. I don't believe we had an engagement this evening."

"Was he the doctor who treated you in the emergency room?" he demanded.

"Yes, what about it?" Then it all became clear. "I see. Because I fell for one doctor, there's a chance I would be stupid enough to fall for another. The man drove me home after a softball game, that was all." She perched on the couch arm near him, wishing she had a few trade secrets of her own to banish the two blatant eavesdroppers standing by. She ignored the little voice inside that reminded her she would have done a great deal with the *doctor* if he'd cooperated!

"Oh, don't worry about us, dear," Marian cooed, perching herself on the couch arm. "Just pretend we're not here."

"I only wish I could," Alex muttered.

Jason looked up. "I beg your pardon?"

"Nothing."

He drew back, looking at her dusty figure and cap perched on top of her head. "Wouldn't you like to freshen up after your day of exercise?"

Alex had had enough. After playing the worst game in her life, finding herself growing more attracted to Michael by the minute, not to mention running into Jason who was acting even more like a boor than he had that night at dinner, his inference that she didn't smell fresh as a daisy was the absolute last straw.

"Are you trying to say that I stink?"

He wrinkled his nose. "I wouldn't put it that way."

"But that's what you mean," she pressed, deliberately leaning closer. "Honestly, Jason, are you saying that you can play racquetball without working up a good sweat? I've been on a softball field all afternoon, and that kind of workout leaves one smelling less than desirable." *Except Michael's after-shave still lingered along with the undertones of soap and pure male,* her treacherous mind prompted. She quickly quashed that thought.

It wasn't until then that Alex truly realized how inflexible Jason was. She was beginning to see the man in a new, unflattering light.

"I guess I should have telephoned first."

She closed her eyes and silently counted to ten. "I'm sorry, Jason. Our game didn't go well and I appear to be taking it out on you." *Wait a minute,* that same brain cell spoke up, *he's the one who was rude to Michael. He was the one who showed up here without warning, so why are you apologizing?* "Would you care for a drink?" *Don't offer him a drink! Show him the door instead!*

Jason shook his head. "Basically I'm here because I have something to discuss with you." The red tones in his face told her this subject wasn't pleasant.

"Yes?"

Alex couldn't remember ever seeing Jason look as uneasy as he did now. "I spoke to a colleague of mine today, Steve Taylor of Charles Daily and Associates." He looked up.

She had no idea where this was going. "Am I supposed to know the name?"

He coldly pointed out, "Since he handles a fairly extensive portfolio for you, I would assume you'd be very familiar with his name. In fact, I was very impressed with the investments you've made the past couple years. Not to mention the ones left to you by your father."

"Oh, oh," Patrick muttered, earning a freezing look from his daughter.

"Jason, my business manager, Doug, handles all that. Although I happen to use the same broker my father did. What are you trying to get at? Is this Taylor unscrupulous or what?" She now wished she'd poured a drink for herself. A good stiff one.

An atom bomb couldn't have broken Jason's outer shell. "Naturally, we rarely speak of the specifics regarding a client's portfolios, but when he learned that you and I are involved, he was quick to point out he has been handling your investments for the past few years, and it didn't take much to figure out the amount he handles for you."

She wished he would just spit it out. "Jason, I told you, my business manager is in charge of all that. Why don't you cut to the chase? What is the problem here?"

"I want you to transfer the portfolio over to me. Naturally I had no idea that your silly drawings brought in that kind of money, and Taylor has done quite well for you, but I know I can do much better."

Alex's features tightened. "I do not appreciate you disparaging my work that way," she coldly stated. "As for handing my portfolio over to you, my answer is very simple. No."

He was stunned as if he couldn't believe she would reject his suggestion. "Why not?"

"Because I go by Doug's recommendations, and he hasn't been wrong yet. As long as he's happy with Raymond Taylor, so am I." She saw no reason to tell him that her father's investments left to her were specified to a certain broker or she lost them. She felt that was none of his business.

His face flushed a deep color. "You sound as if you don't trust me."

Alex had no desire to have this conversation now. She was still smarting from his remark about her "silly drawings." "Jason, I don't tell Doug what to do. He's the expert in these matters."

He stood up, the movements jerky. "Once we're married it would only be natural for me to handle your investments, but it appears you aren't sure yet. Perhaps you should think on it and give me your decision on Monday when you've had time to calm down." He stormed out of the apartment.

"That man has something to hide," Patrick announced, flopping down on the couch.

Alex threw up her hands. "I've had it! What's going to happen next?" She narrowed her eyes. "Great-aunt Sophie isn't going to show up, is she? Because if she does, I'm definitely calling an exorcist.''

"No, of course not," Marian replied, running her fingers over Suzi Q's sleek fur as the cat purred contentedly under the attention.

"I can't believe today! I'm suddenly seeing Michael Duffy as if he was the greatest thing since hot-fudge sundaes. And now this problem with Jason. If this is some kind of spell, I want it taken off right now." She sliced the air with her hand.

"Spell?" Patrick shook his head. "Alex, we can't do any of that. You've been watching too many B movies."

"Then whatever you're doing, stop! I just want my life back!" she wailed, heading for the bedroom and slamming the door shut behind her.

Marian turned to Patrick. "Do you think we'll ever find out what happened at the baseball field?"

He shrugged. "I don't know, but whatever it was seems to have given her some food for thought, pardon the pun. She compared the man to a hot-fudge sundae. That was a good sign, if I ever saw one."

Chapter Eight

"Nice legs."

Michael couldn't conjure up one logical sentence, much less a word. Not when he was too busy grabbing the rapidly slipping towel around his middle and gaping at the woman standing in the doorway whose eyes were busy inspecting the hair-dusted bare legs.

"I didn't expect you."

Alex's lips twitched. Her eyes floated from his eyes down to the towel barely covering a wet male body, to the feet shifting one to the other in an uneasy stance. Her gaze wandered just as leisurely upward. "Yes, I figured that out already. May I come in?"

The good manners drummed into him from birth prompted him to step back. "Sure." Why was she here? At the same time, he wasn't going to look the proverbial gift horse in the mouth. She was here; wasn't that enough good fortune for him?

Alex moved to one side, out of sight for a moment before reappearing holding a large green leafy plant in a basket. "A housewarming gift," she announced, walking inside. "Since you appear to have your hands full, I'll take care of this." She looked around at the boxes littering the living room and stacked on the breakfast bar, save for a small area Michael used for his meals. "You weren't kidding about a lack of color scheme, were you?"

Michael, still confused by Alex's unexpected presence, stood there stupidly holding the towel in a knot at his waist. "How did you find out where I live?" He pushed the door closed before any more surprises appeared.

She cocked an eyebrow. "I had my methods. Don't doctors usually advise damp bodies to stay out of drafts? Why don't you go dry off while I find the right place for this." She held up the basket.

He quickly retreated to his bedroom, where he didn't waste any time in pulling on a T-shirt and shorts. A hand dragged across his jaw told him a quick shave wouldn't hurt, either.

Alex wandered through the maze of boxes, breathing deeply to quell the rapid thudding of her heart. It might not have been the first time she'd seen a nearly naked man, but it was the first time she'd seen Michael, and Michael just wearing a damp towel was more than impressive!

"Who'd've thought surgeons' greens could hide such a great body," she muttered.

"There's coffee in the kitchen," the subject of her thoughts called out from the rear of the apartment. "Ten to one you'll find clean cups in the dishwasher."

Alex set the plant on top of a box and headed for the kitchen. Judging from the spots on the plates and glasses, she easily assumed the dishes in the dishwasher were dirty. She quickly washed two cups before filling one of them with coffee. Taking matters into her own hands she poured soap into the dispenser and switched the dishwasher on.

"I—ah—I guess I forgot to run it last night." Michael walked in, looking dryer, a bit more composed and no less appealing.

"I tend to do the same thing. I even got in the habit of filling the soap dispenser first because that was the only way

I knew if they were clean or dirty." She refilled the cup by the coffee maker and handed it to him. "I thought you moved here a few months ago."

"I did." He lifted the mug to his lips.

Alex found she couldn't keep her eyes off his bare midriff where the shirt rode up. She quickly concentrated on her coffee. "Oh, I see. The boxes are your furniture. I admit, it's a novel idea."

"My schedule has been so crazy since I arrived that I haven't had time to unpack, so I tend to empty a box whenever I need something." His eyes fell on the colorful plant sitting on a box. "That's really nice of you to bring me a plant, but I'm afraid with the kind of schedule I keep it might not get the care it should."

Alex's laughter spilled outward. "Don't worry, Doctor, I already thought of that. It's silk. There's no way you can kill it."

"Silk?" Now why did that word make him think of sexy lingerie and dresses that slide across the skin like a whisper? Funny thoughts for a man who'd always been accused of not having a romantic bone in his body.

"I may work out of my home, but I tend to forget about watering and feeding, so all my plants are silk. Guaranteed unkillable. Before that, yellow and brown leaves littered my carpet like crazy. I either overwatered and underfed or the other way around." She waved her free hand in a wagging motion.

Now that Michael's senses were returning to normal, he was able to feast his eyes on the woman standing in his kitchen talking so blithely about killing poor defenseless plants. Her rich brown hair with intriguing paler streaks swirled around her shoulders in loose waves that begged to be touched, and her pale blue shirt, which stopped just above the waistband of her full calf-length skirt, hinted of a romantic nature. He liked the way the skirt hem was hitched up every few inches to reveal a lace-trimmed petticoat. While it might have been the design of the skirt, he liked to think he was seeing something he wasn't supposed to.

"I didn't come by just to bring the plant." Alex's voice broke in his wandering thoughts.

He looked up from his perusal of her slender ankles defined by pale blue ballet slippers. "That wasn't your only reason for interrupting my shower?" he teased.

She shook her head. All signs of humor were now gone, something Michael didn't want to happen. "I also wanted to apologize for Jason's behavior last night. He was very rude to you and there was no reason for it."

"It isn't your responsibility to apologize for him, Alex," he said quietly.

She traced the rim of her cup with her fingertip. "He's not normally like that."

Michael frowned. "He didn't hurt you or anything, did he?"

"No, that isn't Jason's way. He's very aware of his professional standing and wouldn't allow anything like emotions to interfere with that." She made a face. "I guess you could say he received a sharp blow to the ego and he couldn't handle it very well."

Michael leaned against the counter, still drinking his coffee, just waiting.

Alex paced back and forth, unable to keep still for more than a few seconds.

"He learned that I have an investment portfolio with someone else," she blurted out.

"Is that a major crime?"

She looked at him as if he should have figured out the answer to that by himself. "In his eyes it is, since we've been seeing each other for quite a while. He's upset that I don't have it with him."

"Do you have your portfolio with someone else for a special reason?"

"Some of my investments I inherited from my father, with the stipulation I use the same broker he had for years, so I just transferred everything else over to him. My business manager oversees it from there. Oh, I know I have investments, and I know enough not to be taken to the cleaner's, but my manager is a very reliable man and I trust him."

"And Jason doesn't agree," he stated.

She wrinkled her nose. "That's an understatement. He wants me to transfer everything to him. I guess he feels it's his right."

"And you don't want to."

Michael put into stark, clear words what Alex had been pretending wasn't running through her mind.

"It's not that I don't trust his judgment," she began, faltered and went on. "It's just that sometimes he comes across a little too eager for the almighty dollar. For the ultimate coup. He collects prestigious clients the way someone else would collect stamps. He likes the names he can drop to make him sound even more important." Her expression changed, twisted like that of a small child told something she didn't want to hear. "He called what I did silly drawings! I didn't like him saying that and I told him so."

Now it was out. That was what really bothered her. Jason Palmer was obviously condescending when it came to Alex's work, and she didn't appreciate it one bit. Neither did Michael.

"I work damn hard on my strips," she ranted, continuing to pace back and forth. "People seem to think they just flow out of my fingertips—well, they don't. There's days I practically work myself into a migraine to get my ideas on paper. Days when I throw away more paper than what I keep."

Michael's hand snaked out, grabbing the coffee mug Alex was waving around wildly. He set it out of harm's way on the counter behind him.

"Do you think it's easy to just come up with new tours?" Alex demanded, stopping long enough to poke a finger in his chest. "Well, it's not. My Christmas strip dealing with the North Pole took me months to get right! Then there was the hike down a volcano! Wh—!"

Michael could think of only one way to shut up Alex. He grasped her arms, pulled her close to him and covered her mouth with his in one fell swoop. And with her mouth already open on a surprised gasp, he took immediate advantage of the situation. The first sensation was a mouth that softened and felt like silk. The taste of coffee mingling with the mint from his toothpaste. His tongue circled the tiny O her lips made, dipping leisurely for a more thorough taste. He next realized she wasn't pushing him away but had slipped her arms around his waist and she was moving closer to him until her body was neatly nestled in the cradle of his spread-legged stance.

"Alex," he murmured, giving in to his earlier temptation and combing his fingers through the thick waves. The faint citrus scent of her shampoo teased his nostrils.

She had no response to give him other than a physical one. Not when she was swimming in a sensory maelstrom caused by Michael's mouth doing incredible things that brought to mind silk sheets and candlelight. Even his hands stroked her nape in a way that she wouldn't associate with a doctor. Doctor. Craig. Her fingers tensed.

"I'm not Sommers," Michael muttered, easily reading her thoughts. Another surprise for her. No man ever mentally connected with her so easily.

He shifted his weight, easing one leg between hers and settling her more comfortably against him. More comfortably? He was so aroused he wondered if just kissing her could kill him!

"I—" she sighed, moving her face to one side. That didn't deter him. He concentrated on her ear, then, bypassing the large gold hoop earring brushing the side of her neck to nibble on the lobe. "I—oh God, what are you doing to me?" she wailed, running her open mouth over his collarbone barely visible above the T-shirt neckline.

"Making you as crazy as I am." His fingers at her bare waist tightened a fraction before relaxing and smoothing their way down over her buttocks, pulling her even tighter against him.

It would have been so easy to give in. To just drift along, with Michael making her feel like the most sensual woman alive. Wouldn't her parents have a laugh if they saw her now!

"No," she moaned, planting her hands against his chest, lingering for a moment against the heat, then quickly pushing away before she lost her sanity again. "This is not a good idea."

He took a deep breath that rasped through his chest. "You seemed to think so before."

Alex's respiration wasn't any calmer. She wasn't surprised to find her hands trembling as she raised them to push her hair away from her face. She flushed and quickly hid her hands behind her back. Too late, because Michael couldn't miss her loss of composure.

"Why did you kiss me?" Her voice was low and husky, a hint of tension underlying her usual calm self.

"You were ranting and raving, and it seemed like a good way to shut you up before you worked yourself into a hysterical mess."

"Thank you for your practical solution," she said wryly, looking away.

Michael winced. If only she knew how much he hated that word! "Practicality had nothing to do with it."

Most people would have missed the rueful tone, but Alex was nothing if not observant.

"You don't like to be accused of being practical, do you?"

"Just as you don't like people to call what you do little drawings, I hate to think of myself as a dull, practical man. Even if that is what I am."

Dull would have been the last word Alex would use to describe Michael Duffy. Not after the soul-shattering kiss he just delivered. Even thinking about it was enough to weaken her knees. And here she thought there wasn't a man alive to send her thoughts skittering the way marbles rolled across a bare floor. In her eyes, there could only be one reason behind his statement.

"I can't believe a woman would have the nerve to call you dull and practical. Not with the way you kiss." Along with being observant, she was also thoroughly blunt.

He smiled wanly. "It doesn't take a genius to figure that one out."

She touched his arm. "Michael, I may not know you very well, but I wouldn't think of you as dull. And being practical isn't a sin. There's times when I wish I was more practical. Then perhaps my parents—" She clapped her hands over her mouth.

"Your parents?" he prompted, puzzled by the shock in her eyes.

"Nothing," she said too quickly. "Just old thoughts that really don't have anything to do with this."

"Beth said they were killed about a year ago and that you were all very close. I'm sure it's rough for you."

Alex turned away so he wouldn't see the expression on her face. "More than you know." She spun back around. "Do you have anything planned for today? Do you have to report to the hospital?"

He shook his head. "I was lucky enough to get the entire weekend off. It probably won't happen again for the next five years, and to be honest, I was afraid if I made specific plans something would happen to cancel them."

She smiled. "Then let's make the most of it. How about we get these boxes unpacked? I wouldn't be surprised if we found more of your plates and coffee mugs somewhere."

"My silverware."

Alex rummaged through the drawers, finding most of them empty except for the basic utensils, obviously new, and a box of plastic knives, forks and spoons. "This is really sad, Duffy." She looked up in time to catch the smile in his eyes. "What?"

"Michael sounds dull and practical. Duffy sounds more human."

"Well then, Duffy, let's get cracking!" She walked out of the kitchen and picked up her leather tote bag. She muttered under her breath as she rummaged through the contents. "I know it's in here somewhere."

"What?" He peered over her shoulder. "Good Lord, woman, you could run away from home with all you have in there."

Alex pulled out two candy bars and a pack of gum which she set aside. Her wallet, checkbook, business-card case, mirror, makeup case and a pack of Kleenex quickly followed. "I knew it was in here somewhere." She held up a small pocketknife. "I didn't see any scissors to cut open the tape," she explained. "And I didn't think you'd appreciate my borrowing one of your scalpels."

He couldn't remember the last time he'd smiled so much in such a short period of time. "What makes you think I have one?"

"You're a doctor. Naturally, you'd have one. And just as naturally you'd protect your scalpels from me."

"You could be right."

"That's why I'm glad I found my knife." She flipped it open. "Where do you want to start?"

He held his hands up. "I'm just the manual labor here. You choose."

Alex looked around. "Definitely the living room. At least all the boxes are marked. The last time I moved, I packed everything without marking the boxes. The stuff for my bathroom was in the kitchen and my drawing materials were in the bedroom!" She fingered several boxes before selecting one. A flick of the wrist and the top was gaping open. Within seconds, she pulled out a couple of vases and a modern sculpture with no recognizable shape.

"This gets pitched." Michael took the sculpture out of her hands and dropped it in a wastebasket.

"What are you doing? That looks expensive. Even if it was ugly as sin."

He stared downward. "Expensive in more ways than you know."

Alex looked at him for several long moments before returning to the open box. "When Craig and I split up, I broke an entire set of dinnerware," she said casually. "I started out with the cups, then moved on to the saucers and dessert plates. I felt fine by the time I reached the bowls, but it was the dinner plates that left me feeling great. Breaking plates is better than any tranquilizer in my book."

Now she had his attention. "Why?"

"Why not? They were ostentatious, just his style, expensive, and he wanted custody of them and I, feeling bitchy at the time, refused to give them up." A glimmer of amusement lit up her pale eyes. "It was horribly childish of me, but it helped me come to terms with myself." Laughter spilled out, along with a beige tablecloth pulled from the box. "Craig screamed when he heard about it. All he could think about was the cost. Seeing his red face and the veins sticking out from his neck was more than worth it. I can just imagine how much I raised his blood pressure that day."

Michael couldn't help but join in her laughter. "You are something else, Alex Cassidy. I sure wouldn't want to get on your wrong side."

"I don't get mad, I get even." Alex held up the tablecloth and matching napkins. "Very boring, Duffy. Don't you believe in anything but beige?"

He shrugged. "Beige goes with everything."

She shook her head as she tackled another box. "It appears, Dr. Duffy, that I was brought into your life to liven things up."

"I'd say you've already done an excellent job of that," he said quietly.

Her fingers stilled. "I usually don't react that way with men I barely know." Her voice was barely above a whisper.

He pushed aside her hair and curled his fingers around her nape. "I didn't think you did. I'm just glad you did with me."

She spun around, but his hand didn't leave its wrapped position around her nape. It was a comforting pressure she didn't want to lose. She wryly wondered what her parents would think of this turn of events. Knowing her mother, she'd be planning a ghostly wedding reception!

"You don't understand." She felt helpless under his touch and she wasn't sure if that was a safe thing to be. "You're a doctor."

He bit his lower lip to keep his smile from appearing, since she was so serious with her statement. "Yes, that's what my diplomas say."

"Doctors are unstable!" she cried out. "They look upon medicine as a way to meet women and party all the time. Look at your colleagues last night! You know very well they closed down that restaurant. Jeff was coming on to the new waitress with his stock line, "'Trust me, I'm a doctor.'" She ran out of steam.

Michael folded his arms around her more in a comforting embrace than a passionate one. "Remember what I told you in the kitchen?" he rumbled softly in her ear. "I'm not Craig Sommers. I'm me, Michael Duffy, a hardworking trauma surgeon who meets all members of the human race in emergency rooms. I can't remember the last time I attended a party. Last night was the first time I've been out socially in the past year. My idea of dining out is the hospital cafeteria. My world is made up of automobile accidents, gunshot wounds and stabbings and an occasional pregnant woman who can't wait to get to Maternity. It's not always a pretty sight in there, Alex. More reality than most people even want to think of."

Alex remained quiet in his arms, digesting his speech. She wondered if the other woman in his life knew just how special a man she'd given up. "Then we definitely need to do some shopping," she said finally.

He pulled back his head and looked down quizzically. "Shopping?" He couldn't imagine where that idea had come from.

She nodded. "If that's the only world you know, you need to come home to some color." With that decision in her mind, she stepped back and reached for her knife. She quickly opened several more boxes and found something she should have expected. "How many of these boxes hold books?"

"Just about all of them," he had to admit.

She shook her finger at him. "You're as bad as I am." She grabbed her purse. "Let's go."

He reached out and grabbed her hand. "Can I change first?"

"I'll give you ten minutes."

As Michael walked down the hallway, he could hear Alex muttering to herself about primary colors versus desert pastels as she rummaged in her bag for a piece of paper.

"Sommers, the best thing you ever did was screw around on this lady," he murmured, as he pulled a pair of jeans off a hanger. "Because now I've got a chance with her and I don't intend to blow it."

MICHAEL SOON LEARNED that Alex didn't believe in doing anything halfway. Once they were in his car, she directed him not to the nearby mall but another larger one a distance away.

"They've got the kind of shops we'll need," she explained, once they reached the freeway. "Judging from what I found in those boxes, you're going to need everything."

He winced at the gleam in her eyes. Like most women, she appeared to take her shopping duties very seriously. "Just remember, I'm a poor, humble doctor."

"I don't intend to blow your credit limit, just add color," she said softly, thinking of the bland walls in his living room. She'd hazard a guess his bedroom wasn't any different. "Everyone needs color in their lives."

"Is that why your cartoon strip seems to explode off the paper in all those bright colors?" he asked.

"Color makes the world seem more palatable," she explained. "I can handle anything as long as there's color around."

Michael flipped the turn signal when they came to the off ramp Alex directed him to. "Then why are you wearing a blue so pale that it's almost white?"

She grinned. "Because it matches my eyes. One reporter described them as exotic blue ice. I have to admit I liked the exotic part because I never thought of myself in those terms. All I see is a mouth that's a bit too large.''

Lush.

''Eyes too pale.''

Compelling.

''A nose that's also a bit too large.''

Elegant.

''And a face that shows off too many heritages.''

Ah, there's the exotic part, Alex. A face that I wanted to keep on kissing if you hadn't pulled away when you had.

Oblivious to Michael's wandering thoughts, Alex directed him to an empty parking space and hopped out of the car before he barely stopped it.

''Be prepared to shop till you drop,'' she announced, walking around to the driver's side.

''Something tells me you're a dedicated shopper,'' he groaned theatrically.

''Only when I have a purpose, and you're about the best excuse I've come across in a long time.'' Alex grabbed his hand and dragged him across the parking lot to the mall entrance. ''Don't worry, one of these stores should pretty much have everything you need.'' She turned to the left, heading for the escalator. ''It's on the third level.''

Michael caught quick glimpses of storefronts as Alex led the way to a store advertising everything for the home.

''Many of the items here are from Europe,'' she explained as they entered.

He stared at a deep purple rectangular cushion with a horrendously expensive price tag attached. ''Not that.''

She followed his gaze and the laughter bubbled out again. ''No, not that. Let's work with the kitchen first.''

Michael looked at the metal racks of tablecloths, then shifted to kitchen appliances fit only for gourmet cooks. ''I don't know what size my table is.''

"I measured it while you changed your clothes." She picked up a stark white cloth splashed with brilliant red, yellow and blue tulips. "Pretty, but not you. No flowers."

"I'd need sunglasses to eat on that." He examined a cream-colored cloth with a pale green-and-lilac design.

She took it out of his hand. "Nothing even close to beige."

Alex dug through the stacks of patterned tablecloths. She knew what she wanted. Something bright and cheerful to greet Michael when he came home from one of those nights of fighting death. Splashes of color to make getting up in the morning worth it. When he spoke of his world she wanted to cry, but she knew it wasn't tears of sympathy he needed. No, he needed laughter.

Without even thinking of what the words truly meant she whispered under her breath, "He needs me."

Chapter Nine

"I have to admit, Ms. Cassidy, you've got a magic touch with dull, practical apartments." Michael looked around a room he wouldn't have recognized if it wasn't for the furniture he knew to be his. "You've created a miracle."

Color blazed everywhere he looked, from several prints hanging on the walls to the bright print pillows arranged on the couch and a shallow bowl brightening the coffee table. The kitchen boasted new towels and a saucy print hanging on the wall of jungle animals gorging on a huge banana split. The bathroom had bright teal towels on the racks and a coordinating rug on the floor. Alex might not have seen Michael's bedroom, but she knew enough to find a new bedspread and sheets in the rich colors of a desert sunset. And Alex hadn't stopped there. When they returned from the mall, she set him to unpacking boxes while she hung pictures, covered the table with the bright cloth and found a place for the plant she'd brought over that morning.

Alex's pride in her handiwork shone on her face as she surveyed the changes. "This is what I wanted to see," she murmured.

"What did you want to see, Alex?"

She slowly turned, looking up at him. "Color. Bright, living color. This will be the first thing you'll see when you come in. It will either soothe or energize you, depending on what you require."

He couldn't help but smile. "You really believe in this, don't you?"

"Of course. It's been proven that color is important to a person's well-being. No wonder I felt so terrible in the emergency room." She shuddered dramatically. "All that white. Uch!"

"That's because you were in the section that hasn't been repainted yet. They're working on a soft blue. Almost the color of your eyes," he murmured.

Alex, normally not one to back down, decided this might be a good time to retreat. Michael's earlier kiss still lingered in her mind in stunning detail. She was convinced all she had to do was lick her lips and she would taste him there.

"I guess I've done enough damage for one day." She turned away, intending to grab her purse and run.

"Wait a minute, please." His fingers curled around her arm. "The least I can do is take you out to dinner to thank you for all the work you've done."

"That isn't necessary." She refused to look at him. She, who was never uncomfortable around a man, found this one very disconcerting to be with.

"Yes, it is," Michael said quietly, firmly. "Besides, it's a good excuse not to lose you for another couple of hours. Unless," he hesitated as something else came to mind, "you have other plans."

Alex had to put him out of his misery fast. "No, no other plans. But I would like to change my clothes first."

"How about I pick you up in an hour?" he suggested.

"Perfect. I'll see you then." This time she left, fully aware she was going home to two parents who were just going to love the news she was going out with someone other than Jason.

"That nice doctor from the emergency room is taking you to dinner? How nice!" Marian followed Alex into the bedroom. "When did you see him? What are you going to wear?"

"Today when I took a plant over there as a housewarming gift." Needing some sort of calming agent, she quickly lit up a cigarette under her mother's censorious eyes.

"It took you all day just to deliver a plant?" Patrick stood in the open doorway, looking the part of the suspicious father. Except there was also that betraying twinkle in his eye.

Alex pulled open her closet doors and rummaged through the contents. "No, I also helped him with some decorating. The only colors that man knows are hospital white and boring beige. Where are my red slacks?" she muttered, pushing hangers to one side. She was so intent on her search she missed the knowing look Marian and Patrick shared. "I know they've got to be here. I picked them up from the cleaner's last week."

"To your right," Marian pointed out.

Alex grabbed the appropriate hanger and pulled it out. The blouse she chose was white with a low vee neckline. Splashes of green, red, blue and black dotted the white silk. She pulled out a pair of red shoes and matching clutch purse.

"I've been dressing to go out for more than twenty years," she reminded her parents.

"I'm gone." Patrick disappeared, in more ways than one.

"I guess I should be grateful that you don't go up in a puff of smoke or flames or something." Alex stared at the empty spot where her father had stood. "My smoke alarm would never recover from the shock."

Marian remained seated on the bed. "I suppose you want me gone also." She looked so wistful that Alex relented.

She sat down next to Marian. "No, Mom, it's just that you two are acting as if this man is going to make all your dreams come true. He's only taking me out to thank me for helping him decorate his apartment."

"You certainly can't still want to be with Jason after last night?"

She slowly shook her head. "No, I think last night told me something about him I used to pretend wasn't true. Now I almost wonder if he wasn't after my portfolio all the time." She sighed. "I'm beginning to wonder if there's a man alive who will ever want me for myself," she whispered, betraying a vulnerability she rarely showed to anyone.

Marian put her arms around her the way she had when Alex was a little girl. "I know that kind of man is out there," she assured her. "Just don't be so picky!" she scolded playfully. "Sometimes the most unlikely ones are the best catches."

Alex mustered up a smile and laid her head on Marian's shoulder. "I've missed you so much," she told her. "There were days when I'd pick up the phone to call you because I'd heard or read something I knew would interest you and then I'd remember that it wasn't your phone number anymore." Her laughter held a strong hint of tears. "Do you know I even resented the people who bought your house? I didn't like the idea that they could live there because you couldn't. I hated fate for taking you away from me before I was ready to lose you."

Marian patted her shoulder in typical motherly fashion. "Are the new owners nice? I hope they left the tree in the front yard," she mused. "It gave such lovely shade during the summer. Even if your father did complain about all the leaves he had to rake up every fall."

"Uh-hmm, they have two small children and a dog. They're your typical all-American family." She enjoyed the idea of her mother hugging her again. "When I first heard

you and Dad were dead, all I could think of were the things
I wanted to tell you. I felt there were so many things I didn't
have a chance to say," she said in a small voice.

Marian smoothed her hair from her forehead. "Such as
what, dear?"

"Oh, that I finally understood why you grounded me
when I came home four hours after my curfew that time I
dated Ron Thomas, and I wanted to relive that time we
drove through Arizona and got lost and had so much fun
wandering through the small towns. I know I acted like a
little brat then because I was fourteen and felt I was too old
to be on vacation with my parents and every time I later
thought about it I was afraid I had ruined it for you."

"No, Alex, you didn't. We knew you were trying so hard
to let us believe you weren't having fun when you were."
Marian smiled. "When I realized I was taken away from
you, all I could think of was that I would never have the
chance to tell my daughter again how much I love her.
That's what hurt for me the most."

Alex sniffed. "I never even had a chance to see you one
last time. We only talked on the phone before you left on
that trip, because I felt I was too busy to go over and see
you."

Marian kissed her cheek. "Then let's consider ourselves
lucky to have this second chance and perhaps say a few
things we weren't able to before."

"I'd like that." Alex spied the clock. "Oh no, I didn't
realize how late it was getting." She hesitated, not anxious
to break the special mood.

"And you must look your best for Michael," Marian told
her. "Don't worry, darling, we still have plenty of time," she
said easily reading her daughter's thoughts.

"Mom," she hesitated, clearly uncertain how to phrase
her request. "You and Dad won't try anything strange with
Michael, will you? He's a nice man and if you tried the

tricks you pulled on Jason, well..." She lifted her shoulders in a small shrug.

She was very careful to keep her smile of triumph to herself. "We wouldn't dream of doing anything, darling. His Aunt Chloe would never forgive us. After all, she's hoping he'll find the right woman, too."

Alex literally ran into the bathroom to escape any further assurances that didn't sound the least bit reassuring! "I don't want to know. I don't want to know."

Alex was ready with several minutes to spare. She used the extra time to remind her parents not to try any ghostly tricks they might have up their sleeves. And she refused to hear any more about Michael's dear Aunt Chloe.

"And you stop that," she admonished Suzi Q, who sat by Marian yowling her own part of the conversation. "Or you'll end up in a kitty straitjacket."

"And he's the doctor who treated your concussion?" Patrick beamed. "He seemed a good sort when he stopped by that night. Not many doctors would bother to check on a patient who's no longer under their care. Especially one who walked out against his advice. Shows he truly cares about human beings and not what kind of fees they can contribute to his practice."

"He's strictly staff at the hospital. He prefers dealing in trauma medicine." Alex set a bowl of gourmet cat food on the kitchen floor. She stood there, her arms crossed in front of her chest, toe tapping a merry tune while Suzi Q circled the bowl her usual seven times and sniffed the food twice before crouching down to feast on her meal.

"It's about time," Alex muttered to the cat. "Everything with you is a ritual! If you met a gentleman cat to your liking, you'd probably set up another crazy ritual before settling down to business."

Suzi Q looked up and yowled, her delicate features twisted with disdain at her human's idea of sarcasm. With a

Siamese, ritual was a way of life—didn't anyone else understand that? After informing Alex of those very important facts, she returned to her dinner.

"It's probably a good thing I had that nice veterinarian operate on you," Alex let out her parting shot and exited the kitchen to a screech from Suzi Q.

"Sometimes that cat seems more human than feline," Patrick remarked.

"Sometimes? I think that she changes into an oriental beauty during the night and goes out nightclubbing," Alex grumbled, snatching a sly look at the clock, not without her parents noticing her impatience with the passing moments.

At the first chime of the doorbell she spun on her heel to confront her parents.

"I mean it, not one ghostly trick," she warned. "Or I'll call the Ghostbusters."

"Just what we need, Bill Murray making jokes," Patrick mumbled as Alex's hand covered the doorknob. He held up his hands in surrender when he caught her threatening expression. "No problem, we'll behave."

Michael, dressed in gray slacks and a blue-and-gray striped shirt, smiled at Alex who gestured him to enter.

"Quite a change from the softball field," he told her, stepping inside.

"I try to keep people guessing," she quipped.

"Offer him something to drink, dear," Marian prompted.

A flash of impatience entered Alex's eyes and left swiftly. "Would you like a drink?" she asked pleasantly, one hand hidden behind her back as she waved "get lost!" to her parents.

"No, thank you. I guess you could say I'm a wet blanket when it comes to drinking. I've seen too many victims of drunk drivers," he said without apology.

"A big difference from Jason, who seems to enjoy his wine a little too much," Patrick commented.

"He had three glasses with dinner that one time we had him over, along with a brandy afterward," Marian recalled. "And he didn't appear to hold alcohol very well."

Alex bit back a scream. "Let me get my purse." She turned around and her eyes flashed a warning message before she hurried into her bedroom.

"You have a very nice place here," Michael told her when she returned. He held an ecstatic Suzi Q purring in his arms, not caring that cat hairs might end up on his shirt.

Alex couldn't remember the last time that cat had been so comfortable with someone she wasn't familiar with. Come to think of it, there were a few people she was familiar with she didn't act that friendly with. Including Alex.

"Thank you. I moved in just after my divorce. I felt very lucky to find it. It's so difficult to find apartments that accept pets, although Suzi Q doesn't consider herself anything close to a pet."

Michael's hand rested against the small of her back as they left. "I hope you like Mexican food," he was heard to say as they walked out the door.

"Mexican food gives her heartburn," Marian commented. "That's one thing she's always known—to tell a date that she can't abide Mexican food."

"It's one of my favorites." Alex's reply floated back as the door closed.

Patrick chuckled. "After that dinner, she's going to be in for a long night—and not the way she might enjoy it, either."

Marian stood up and headed for the bathroom. "I'll put out the Maalox."

Within moments they were downstairs and walking toward Michael's car.

"I'm surprised you haven't bought a house by now." He assisted her into the car.

"That's what my business manager says, but I haven't seen anything that strikes my fancy, and I won't buy a house just for the sake of owning one. He thinks I'm crazy."

"Let him. You're the one who has to live in it."

She was pleased by his comment. "You're right."

"How do you look for a house? The newspaper ads? Real-estate agencies?"

Alex shook her head. "I'm someone who isn't sure what exactly I want. I just watch the real-estate ads on cable, where they show houses in the area. What I'm afraid of is that Suzi Q is so used to apartment living that she'd have trouble adjusting to a house with a real yard. And Mom and Dad definitely wouldn't like to move now that they've settled in so well," she muttered under her breath.

"I beg your pardon?" Michael glanced at her briefly as he drove.

She smiled and shook her head. "Nothing important. Just my brain going off in different directions."

"Did it do that before your concussion?"

"Unfortunately, yes. I've been told it's an occupational hazard with creative people."

"From what you've said, creating a comic strip is hard work, so I guess your mind is going whenever it's necessary," Michael replied.

"Yes, it is. Not to mention, I've been approached to do a book of cartoons and they want new material, not what's been printed already," she sighed. "I've been putting them off for almost a year now, but I'm going to have to come to a decision soon."

"It sounds as if you don't want to do one."

Alex shrugged. "I have plenty of work to keep me busy, so I guess I'm not as worried about it as some people think I should be."

The restaurant Michael chose was large, colorful and somewhat noisy with cheerful diners.

Alex ordered a margarita first thing, in hopes it would numb her stomach to what she knew was coming. Why hadn't she told him that she had a cast-iron stomach for every kind of food except Mexican? She could eat the hottest of oriental and Indian cuisine and not suffer a twinge, but one lowly taco could send her stomach into absolute agony. She made a mental note to check the contents of her purse for antacid tablets. She perused the menu and decided she would be safe with chicken with rice. That couldn't be too spicy. She winced as she listened to Michael order *carnitas* with plenty of hot salsa and flour tortillas on the side.

"Are you settling in all right?" she asked after their drinks arrived. She sipped the tart liquid with pleasure.

"As well as someone who works an eighty-hour week can. I found a grocery store and dry cleaner between home and the hospital and a few fast-food restaurants." A wry smile lit up his face.

"If it's such a hectic life, why do you work in trauma medicine?"

"For the satisfaction," he said simply. "Trauma medicine is still a relatively new field, and most hospitals don't have anything even close to a trauma center or doctors equipped to handle large-scale emergencies. There's nothing more grievous than for a hospital to be the recipient of victims of a multi-car accident and not know enough about triage and the handling of trauma cases."

Suddenly he appeared uneasy. "Sorry. I can go on about this ad nauseam. Usually people's eyes start to glaze over before five minutes are up."

"Do my eyes look glazed?" She batted her eyelashes at him.

"No, they look lovely."

Alex blinked. It wasn't the first time she'd received a compliment, but it was the first time she felt she heard one that was truly sincere without any hidden meaning.

"You were talking about trauma medicine," she prompted softly.

"Basically it's the idea of dealing with several cases at once, knowing which ones are the most critical, which ones can wait and who handles what. It's very high-pressure and burnout isn't uncommon."

"You're so calm, so laid-back that it's difficult to imagine you in something that intense." Alex sipped her margarita and chose a warm, salty taco chip. Michael, likewise, took a chip, but dipped it in salsa before eating it.

"It's better that way," he explained. "Maybe it's this laid-back attitude of mine that helps me cope with it all. While others run around like chickens with their heads cut off, I'm plodding on." He ducked his head. "I generally don't go on like this. Which accounts for the once bland and boring apartment that now looks as if someone stole in with buckets of bright colors."

"Hey, Duffy, there's nothing wrong with being committed to your work." Alex reached across the table to cover his hand with hers. "And as I said before, I never thought of you as bland and boring, so cut it out, okay?" She closed her hand around his in a mock-fierce grip. "We've got to work on that male ego of yours, buddy. It's much too big!"

He couldn't help but join in with her laughter.

"Doesn't anything ever get you down?"

"Only seeing my ex. He gets me downright depressed."

He found himself hating the idea of vibrant Alex married to a jerk such as Craig. "Because the marriage was so bad?"

"Because he has enough arrogance for ten men. Have you ever seen his office nurse?"

Michael rolled his eyes. "Matilda the Hun?"

She laughed at his more-than-accurate description. "Personally I always felt she looked more like Margaret Hamilton. Do you know why he has a nurse who looks like her? Because he's afraid a young, pretty nurse would only fall in love with him and complicate matters. With Irene he doesn't have to worry about constantly interviewing new office nurses. Now, *that's* a big ego."

"He is a good-looking guy," he admitted.

Alex chuckled. "And he knows it. I think what I hate more is that he's the male equivalent of a slut and he doesn't look one bit debauched!" she exclaimed. "The least he could do is have gray skin and a paunch. Instead, he always looks as if he just stepped out of a health club."

"It will all catch up with him someday."

Alex looked down as the waitress slid a plate in front of her with the murmured warning that it was hot. "I don't love him anymore, if I ever truly did, but it wouldn't hurt to see his sins show up in his face."

Michael leaned across the table. "Maybe he has a painting of himself hidden in the attic," he whispered.

Her eyes lit up. "I can see it now. Deep crevices along the cheekbones." She fumbled in her purse and pulled out a pen. She grabbed a napkin from an empty place setting and made quick strokes with the pen on the paper. "Maybe a few scars, real ugly ones—the kind Frankenstein had."

Michael watched her, amazed at what so easily appeared under her pen. "Warts?"

She chewed on her lower lip as she drew. "Of course. *Voilà!*" She handed him the napkin which was now covered with a face that was only barely recognizable as Craig Sommers. The features were there, with the addition of scars, several warts, a drooping eye, a mouth that turned up hideously on one end and a throat covered with ugly growths.

"You'd be a natural drawing for horror comics. This is even better than Dorian Gray." He handed her back the napkin. "You most definitely have a talent for sketching the ugly and unusual."

She wrinkled her nose, warming under his praise. "If Beth saw this, she'd put it on the hospital bulletin board for all to see."

Michael loaded a flour tortilla with cooked pork and vegetables and salsa, and wrapped the tortilla around the spicy meat. He bit into it and uttered a low groan of pleasure that ran along Alex's nerve endings. Without thinking of where her thoughts might be taking her, she wondered if that was the way he sounded when he made love. To mask her wandering thoughts, she took a quick bite of her meat and almost choked as the spices exploded in her mouth. It took all of her willpower to leisurely reach for her water glass instead of grabbing it with feverish haste and inhaling the icy liquid.

"Too hot?" Michael inquired.

"No," her voice came out as a high-pitched squeak. "No, it's fine. A piece was caught in my throat and I figured I could wash it down with water." To prove her words, she took another bite, adding some rice with the chicken in hopes of tempering it. The rice was just as spicy. She was surprised her eyes weren't watering and her face wasn't a bright red.

Michael looked concerned. "Are you sure the food isn't too spicy?"

"I eat Thai food all the time, and my stomach hasn't complained once," she said brightly. No, it's only burritos, tacos and all sorts of Latin cooking that sends you running for the Maalox, her brain reminded her. She picked up her fork, determined to eat every damned bite!

By the time they left the restaurant, Alex's stomach was already sending out warnings.

Michael made no move to turn the ignition key once they were settled in the car.

"I want to see you again," he said quietly, staring out through the windshield, afraid he might see rejection in her eyes. "I understand that doctors aren't at the top of your list. And I have no idea what Jason Palmer is to you, but if there's a chance..." He felt her touch before he heard her words.

"I'd like for us to go out again where it's not one of us feeling we owe the other something, but just because we enjoy each other's company." Alex's tone matched his. "As long as you remember that you aren't bland and boring."

"Someone used to tell me that until I believed it."

"A woman?"

"We lived together, and I thought we might even have a future together, but she was going out in the evening and making new business contacts while I enjoyed spending my few free evenings at home. I'm not one for parties or small talk. She felt I could set up a private practice and make more money. Therefore, I was boring." He still hadn't found the nerve to look at her.

Alex's hackles rose at the unknown woman's callousness. "Perhaps we should introduce her to Jason. They could go out together and make all the business contacts they want. Maybe they could even have a contest to see who gets the most at the end of the evening," she said lightly.

"Rumor has it Jason was going to be husband number two." Michael wanted it all out in the open.

Alex knew she had to be honest with him. "I thought he was going to be, yes. But my doubts have been surfacing more and more lately. And after last night's episode, well, I don't feel I can trust him any longer. My parents will love to hear this," she muttered to herself.

He frowned. "Your parents?"

"I just like to talk out loud. I guess it's as if I'm still talking to them." Alex exhaled a silent breath. What if she told Michael the truth? Would he believe her, or would he merely send her to the nearest padded cell? She decided not to take a chance just yet.

Michael started to turn the key, then stopped. "My schedule isn't necessarily my own," he warned. "If there's a major emergency, I'm called in, and I carry a beeper at all times. To be honest, I'm surprised it was so quiet this weekend."

"And there's times when I'm against a deadline with blank sheets of paper in front of me and I'll work twenty-four hours a day until I get my work finished," she pointed out. "I guess that makes us even. There may be times I'll be disappointed. I wouldn't be human if I wasn't, but I will understand—just as I hope you'll understand when the position is reversed." She didn't stop to think she was well on her way to making a commitment here.

Michael released a shuddering breath. "Lady, you're too good to be true." He leaned over and brushed his lips across hers. But he wasn't willing to stop at something light, after all the anticipation that had built up between them. He wrapped his arms around her and pulled her into his embrace, deepening his kiss as his tongue slipped between her lips and stroked the interior, tasting the tart spices from their dinner. She moaned low in her throat and edged herself closer to him as her hands braced themselves against his shirt front. It was so easy, one light touch deepened into a stronger caress. Mouths nibbling and trailing across bare skin. Except it left them hungrier for more.

"Hey, Duffy," Alex murmured, placing love nips along his throat. "We're under a streetlight here, for anyone who leaves the restaurant to see. Why don't we make this a private show?"

"Good idea." He quickly switched on the engine and left the parking lot with a squeal of tires.

"One piece, Duffy, let's get there in one piece," she laughed, enjoying his usual lack of decorum. "And one more thing, we need lights." She leaned over and bit his earlobe.

"Then I suggest you leave the driver alone until we're locked inside your apartment," he growled.

They reached Alex's apartment house in record time and, snaking her fingers between his shirt buttons, she backed her way through the doorway and led him into the apartment.

"Time for us to leave," Patrick announced, standing up from the couch where he had been lounging, but Alex was beyond hearing. Or was she?

"Good thinking," she replied. Whether she was saying that to her parents or to Michael, who was rubbing his hands across the back of her neck, was anyone's guess. She closed her eyes and literally purred under his attention. "Why, Doctor, what nice hands you have."

"Surgeon's hands." Said hands were now working on her blouse buttons, easily releasing them from the buttonholes until they had room to slide between the folds of fabric and encounter silk-covered skin.

Their mouths rarely left each other as clothing was loosened and his hands discovered silky skin soft from applications of a scented cream and she found hair-roughened skin that she kissed and explored with her lips as they lay entwined on the couch.

"Oh, Michael," Alex sighed, as his mouth trailed across her bare collarbone. Her closed eyes opened to slits as she lay in his arms. They widened with horror as she found her parents standing just beyond him. And they were smiling broadly! She gasped, feeling the air leave her lungs. What were they trying to do?

"No talking," he muttered, returning to kiss her deeply.

Once his mouth covered hers again she could have cared less if the Vienna Boys' Choir watched them. She twined her arms around him, pulling him over her fully, shifting her body as she felt his hand cover her breast under her camisole, two fingers circling her nipple until it hardened to a tight bud.

"I hear bells," she gasped, as he grabbed her earlobe between his teeth.

"Hmm?" He paused a moment, then leaned back, swearing profusely as he recognized the metallic sound exploding through the charged silence. "It's my beeper," he groaned.

Alex didn't know whether to laugh or cry. She chose the former. "The phone's over there." She stepped back and gestured to the breakfast bar.

Michael swore under his breath and grabbed the cordless unit, quickly punching out the number. His mumbled words could be barely heard and their meaning was lost on layman Alex.

"Ten-car pileup on the freeway," he told her once he was off the phone. "They need every pair of hands they can get."

"And yours equals two pairs. All I ask is that you get some rest as soon as you can." She could see that his mind was already racing ahead to the hospital. "And if you get a chance, call me to let me know you're okay."

He pressed a hard kiss on her lips. "It could be late."

"I don't care."

Michael looked pensive, as if afraid to believe what was happening. "This is the beginning of our tests."

"Then let's pass them with flying colors." She linked her arms around his neck and gave him a kiss that sizzled right down to his toes. "Drive safely, Doctor."

"After that, I'll be lucky to make it there in one piece." With one last look at her flushed features, he reluctantly left.

"It appears you've changed your mind about doctors."

Alex shrieked and jumped at the unexpected voice behind her. "Don't do that," she panted, spinning around, holding her hand against her chest to still her rapidly thumping heart.

Marian held up her hands. "All right, next time I'll reappear in front of you. I'm just glad that you've found someone presentable. Chloe said he's a regular darling," she added.

"What's-'is-name called and didn't sound too happy you weren't home," Patrick announced, appearing next to Marian.

"How was your dinner?" Marian asked. "Did you have a nice time? Were you able to find something that wouldn't bother your stomach? Or did you finally confess to him that you can't handle Mexican food."

Alex clenched her teeth. "I don't need this." The earlier light warnings in her stomach had already begun escalating to a major explosion. She made a beeline for the bathroom, grateful to find the bottle of Maalox strategically placed on the counter. She popped four tablets into her mouth and chewed energetically.

"You're going to drop that idiot banker, aren't you?" Patrick called out. "He didn't sound very calm and collected on the phone tonight."

Alex didn't like the idea of Jason pushing her the way he was. In fact, the more she thought about events in the past, the more she wondered how she could go so long without seeing his true nature. She couldn't believe she had been so blind and she began to doubt her own judgment. She knew she would have to begin some serious thinking where he was concerned. With Michael coming into her life she had a pretty good idea where Jason stood, and she doubted the banker would appreciate his position.

"I'll listen to his message tomorrow." She read the instructions, wondering if she could take four more tablets within the next five minutes. Between her firestorm of a stomach and her parents eager to find out about her dinner with Michael, she knew she was in for a very long night.

Chapter Ten

"You ate Mexican food? You actually ate something filled with chili peppers?" Beth hooted, drawing one leg up onto her chair, the foot resting flat on the cushioned seat with her elbow resting on her raised knee. "Alex, Mexican food gives you third-degree heartburn. While you can eat Thai and enough curry to melt steel, you can't handle Mexican food at all."

"Thank you for that public-service announcement." Alex was bent over as she rummaged through the contents of her refrigerator. "For that you can just crawl off to your own apartment and make your own coffee."

Beth had appeared on Alex's doorstep fifteen minutes before, begging a cup of coffee. She had come off the late shift and arrived home only to discover there was none in her house, and contrary to most caffeine drinkers, Beth always drank hers before bed to relax and sleep. After spending most of the night with her mother hovering over her moaning figure, Alex was grateful for company that wouldn't disappear in a puff of smoke.

Beth looked up from the morning paper. "What are you doing?"

"Getting this out." Alex held up a milk carton. "I intend to coat my stomach with this stuff."

"You hate drinking milk. Besides, it won't work." Her words stopped Alex from pouring it into a glass.

"What do you mean, it won't work? That's what they tell ulcer patients to do. Well, actually they tell them to drink cream, don't they? But I don't have any, so I'll have to make do with this until I can get some."

"Not anymore. Not for quite a few years, in fact. You said you've been taking Maalox—that should have worked."

"I ran out of the liquid hours ago and the tablets don't seem to help as much." Alex picked up the pot and poured the steaming coffee into a mug. After handing it to Beth, she popped two slices of bread into the toaster.

"There's one thing that puzzles me. Who fascinated you so much you were willing to eat Mexican food?"

Alex buried her head in the depths of the refrigerator again, pretending to hunt for her favorite jam. "What makes you think I was with anyone?"

"Easy. You wouldn't be stupid enough to do it on your own, so it had to be some guy you wanted to make a good impression on." Beth's cup halted just as it touched her lips. "Michael Duffy."

"Ow! Damn!" Alex's head hit the top of the refrigerator when her body jerked in reaction.

"I was right!" Beth crowed, setting her cup down, her need for caffeine forgotten as something more important caught her attention. "It was Michael Duffy you went to dinner with. I thought there was the beginning of something hot between you two." She bounced in her seat like a three-year-old at the circus. "And you two make such a cute couple, too. You, so vibrant, and him, so serious." She braced her chin on her palm, dramatically batting her eyelashes.

"He's not boring," Alex pointed out with a sharp edge to her words.

Beth didn't even blink at the attack. "I never said he was, although obviously someone did, and I just bet it wasn't you." Her brilliant eyes softened. "Is that why he's so standoffish? Because he thinks he's boring?"

She needed to talk to someone, and Beth was the best person to air out her crazy feelings. "Last night he proved to me that men can be just as vulnerable as women when it comes to personal issues. Some woman really did a number on him, Beth. And for her to inflict that kind of mental damage, he must have cared for her a great deal. I went over to his apartment yesterday to take him a plant as sort of a housewarming gift. After all, he is new to the city." She defended her action.

"A plant? You with the black thumb that can kill a healthy leaf in ten seconds?"

Alex leveled her with a telling look which, to her chagrin, did absolutely nothing. "A silk plant, but that's beside the point. Beth, his apartment had no color. None whatsoever. No one should go without color in their lives. I couldn't let him live that way, so I dragged him to the mall and found him a few extras that would give him that color. Doing the kind of job he does, he can't go home to a place that's so dead-looking. He needed me to help him find that color, Beth." She was perfectly serious, without an ounce of conceit.

Beth knew Alex had nothing but color in her life, from the bright lavenders, turquoises and pinks adorning every corner of her apartment to the lively colors she wore. This was a new side of her friend, and Beth gloried in seeing it. For a woman who vowed never to have anything to do with a doctor, she was going to an awful lot of trouble to make one doctor's life more comfortable. Beth refrained from saying so out loud, because she knew her friend would only deny it. She bit down hard on her lower lip to keep her smile of triumph from blossoming forth. Now if Jason Palmer could just get out of the picture!

"What about Jason? Does this new turn of events mean he's gone for good?" This she did feel safe in asking out loud.

Alex hesitated. How could she truthfully answer a question she had been wrestling with lately? Jason had changed so much that she wasn't sure he was the same man she had considered marrying. And the more she saw of him, the more she knew she didn't want to be with him any more than she had to be. She opened her mouth to give the best answer she could when she was interrupted.

Beep! "Alexis, I thought you would have called me with your answer by now. It's urgent that I speak with you as soon as possible." Jason's agitated voice sounded tinny over the answering-machine speaker. "I hope you've given a lot of thought to my suggestion of the other night. I'm sure you'll do the right thing. Please return my call, so the paperwork can be put into motion. We can't afford to waste any more time."

Beth spun around and stared at the machine, which had seemingly come on by itself. "How did it do that?" she demanded, turning back to Alex. "I didn't hear your phone ring."

She too was shocked. She knew how it had come on, but she doubted her friend would believe her and she couldn't think of an explanation that would sound the least bit plausible. "Perhaps the machine picked up the call before the ring was completed," she said weakly. "Or perhaps there's an electrical short."

Beth rolled her eyes. "An electrical short? Alex, it was as if someone turned the playback on."

Someone did and if they weren't already dead, she would cheerfully remedy that.

"It's been acting up a lot." Alex knew her explanation was pitiful before she even finished it.

"That doesn't explain Jason's manner on the phone. The man sounded as if he was losing his cool. And here I thought he was made of ice. To be perfectly honest, Alex, he sounded desperate. It's a good thing you're not going to have anything to do with him. Or does his call have something to do with that?"

She grimaced. "You wouldn't think he was made of ice if you'd seen his tantrum two nights ago."

"I should have flattened the creep," Patrick grumbled, earning a warning pat on the shoulder from Marian.

Beth's green eyes widened. "Tantrum? Mr. Cool and Calm had a tantrum? Damn!" She slapped the counter with the flat of her hand. "And I had to miss it! This is something the eleven o'clock news should have been present for."

Alex retrieved the toast and spread strawberry preserves on top, slicing each piece in half and handing two halves to Beth on a napkin.

"Use a plate, dear," Marian scolded.

"All the plates are dirty," Alex mumbled, without even realizing she was doing it again.

"So what?" Beth asked, munching on the toast. "We've used napkins for plates lots of times. I've never complained, have I? At least our mothers can't see what bad habits we've gained over the years," she said mischievously.

"Oh, you'd be surprised what they find out about us," Alex said wryly, catching the smile on Marian's face.

"Back to Jason." Beth waved her piece of toast around. "What's his problem?"

Alex took the bar stool next to Beth. "He somehow found out that I deal with an investment firm, and he wants me to hand my portfolio over to him. I'd sure like to know who told him that,'' she muttered. "And here I thought these things were kept private.''

Beth considered this piece of information. "Maybe he isn't as pure in his business practices as you thought he was.''

Alex hated to admit that she was beginning to think the same thing. Here she thought she'd met the perfect man, and she was finding out just the opposite. She was starting to doubt her judgment regarding the opposite sex. "It's just that Doug and the broker who handle my dad's investments take care of that. They're both well respected in the field, and with so many con men in this business I'm glad I have people I can trust, so I know they don't have anything to do with it. Actually, Jason implied it was the broker who has my portfolio, which doesn't make any sense, since Dad used him for years and never had any complaints. I'm going to call Doug today and discuss this with him.''

"Why is Jason so eager to get his hands on your portfolio?'' Beth inquired. "I mean, he's always been so high-and-mighty about the many prestigious clients he has, and from the way he's put down your cartoon strip I'd think he wouldn't want anything to do with your business. Some of the clients he's mentioned have millions of dollars invested with him. And you once said yours doesn't come anywhere close to that amount.''

"I've wondered that, too,'' she admitted, idly munching on her toast. "I've been wondering a lot of things.''

Both women silently finished their quick breakfast.

"Alex, do you think Jason is in some kind of trouble?'' Beth spoke suddenly.

That was the last idea Alex would have come up with. "Trouble? Jason? The two don't go together.''

"Yes, but look at what's happening in the financial world. Drexel closed down, the erratic ups and downs in stocks, and you have to admit he's been eager lately to take on the kind of clients who have more money than they know what to do with.''

Alex hated to admit how logical it sounded. "And in his profession he can't afford the least hint of failure," she murmured.

Beth nodded. "Exactly."

Alex glanced at the kitchen wall clock. "I'm going to try Doug now. I need to get this settled." She grabbed her phone and quickly punched out a number. Within minutes she was talking to the man who handled her finances so ably. As she anticipated, Doug was not happy that someone might have been discussing her portfolio, even if it was with a man many thought she would be marrying in the near future. He promised to look into the matter and get back to her as soon as he had some answers. Judging from his grim tone, it boded ill for the hapless investment counselor.

"Tough lady," Beth teased, quickly rinsing out her coffee cup and setting it in the dishwasher. "I better get to bed. It's really lousy working a double shift. I lose all sense of time."

"And here I thought Pediatrics was a cushy job."

Beth laughed. "We have cycles like anything else, and this is our turn to have every bed loaded. And there's such a shortage at the hospital that a lot of us work double shifts. That's why I was so glad to see us receive some new nurses, even if most of them are floaters." When the phone rang she walked toward the door. "I'm off." She opened the door and halted for a moment. "Look, Alex, Jason didn't sound like his old stuffy self. If he shows up acting like Attila the Hun, call me, okay? Two can stand him off better than one."

"I can handle him."

"The old Jason, maybe. But this new one sounds as if he doesn't have anything to lose. See you later."

Alex nodded as she picked up the phone. She wasn't surprised to find it was Doug.

"Okay, kiddo, it's all taken care of," his cigar-roughened voice boomed in her ears. "It appears Roger has been out on sick leave and some big-mouthed kid was working on your portfolio without calling to clear it with me first. I chewed his butt out but good. He figured there was no harm, since Palmer said the two of you were engaged when they were talking about clients. I told the kid that even if you two were married he had no reason to mention your investments to Palmer, that it was up to you and you only. It appears the kid thought he would make a name for himself by working on something he had no business even looking at. He'll be looking for another job. Maybe next time he'll keep his mouth shut."

Alex chuckled. "You don't waste any time, do you?"

"Damn straight. I promise my people results and I'll do whatever it takes to get it. After his superior kicks his butt, that kid's going to think I let him off easy."

She chewed her lower lip while considering her next question, then plunged right in. "Tell me honestly, Doug. What have you heard about Jason Palmer's business dealings at Trainor and Associates?" A shiver traveled along her spine at his silence. "Please, I want to know."

"Okay, all I ask is that you don't shoot the messenger. Word has it he's overextended. He's lost quite a bit of money for his clients, and they're not happy. Most of them have pulled out. He's putting on a big front that he's not going to be able to keep up for long. Word has it if he doesn't bring in some well-heeled clients in the very near future he'll be losing his custom-tailored shirt right off his back."

Alex suddenly felt a chill, even though the room was warm. "And this has all been very recent," she said quietly, all too quietly.

"Yeah, it has."

The rapid surge in dinners and cocktail parties, the name-dropping, exchanging of business cards and setting up lunches with her. She merely assumed he was looking for her to get involved in his work. Oh, yes, he wanted involvement, all right. He wanted the income from her portfolio! Her rational side reminded her she was conjuring up irrational thoughts, but it sounded too logical as far as she was concerned.

"Thank you for your honesty, Doug," she went on in a soft voice.

"I—ah—I gather you're not seeing him anymore." He was hesitant in asking.

She gripped the receiver tightly. She had been the recipient of so many surprises lately that this one shouldn't be a shock. But it was. The man she once thought she loved had turned out not to be that man after all. Wasn't she ever going to get it right? Was she always going to choose the wrong man? She even began to doubt herself, doubt Michael. What if he turned out to have feet of clay, too? What if there was something in his past, or even present, that proved he wasn't the man she thought he was? She wasn't certain she could bear any more blows. "No, I won't be seeing him anymore," she murmured.

"It's about time you came to your senses!" Patrick hooted.

As she finished the call she waved a warning hand at her father, although she knew there wasn't a chance of Doug hearing him.

"All right, you've achieved your goal," she said wearily, sinking down in a chair. "I hope you're happy now."

Marian put her arms around Alex's shoulders. "We can't be happy when you're so unhappy, dear," she said quietly, frowning at her husband for acting so jubilant when their daughter was clearly in emotional pain. "But isn't it better to find out now rather than later?"

"Is it?" Alex rested her cheek against her mother's breast. Funny, she could swear she could inhale the Shalimar her mother always wore. She felt so solid beneath her cheek. So *real*. She wanted nothing more than to wrap her arms around Marian and bawl like a baby, in hopes she'd feel better afterward. "What is it about me, that I attract the wrong men? The first one couldn't stop chasing women and the other decided my portfolio was more fascinating than me! From now on, it's sane relationships that don't require anything on my part." She sighed. "It's much safer."

Marian shot a look of alarm at Patrick. "What about Dr. Duffy?"

Tears pricked her eyelids. "There's probably something wrong with him that I just haven't learned yet. There has to be. He's too good to be true."

Patrick laid his hand on top of her head, combing his fingers through the thick strands the way he used to when she was a little girl. "Third time's the charm, sweetheart," he reminded her.

"Or three strikes, you're out."

"Michael is a wonderful man. His Aunt Chloe has assured us he's not at all like Craig or Jason," Marian went on. "None of this is your fault, Alex. Those two men tried to use you because they saw something wonderful and beautiful in you. I'm just so glad that they didn't pull you down to their level. You're a survivor. You'll do fine. I know you will."

Alex managed a weak smile. "With the two of you in my corner, I guess I don't have any choice, do I?" She threw up her hands in defeat when the doorbell rang. "Now what?" Right about now all she wanted was an extra-large bottle of aspirin.

"Maybe you should just ignore it," Marian advised, sensing trouble on the other side.

"And miss out on Ed McMahon presenting me with my million dollars?" She headed for the door.

"You never enter those contests," Patrick added.

"So someone else submitted my name." She pulled the door open and cursed under her breath at the sight of her unwanted visitor. "Jason, you should have called first." Her clipped voice and stiff posture were perfect indications that she didn't care to see him. Although she had to admit this was a perfect time to tell him to erase her number from his phone book.

He rudely brushed past her. "I did and you didn't bother to return my call, so I thought I would come to see you." He looked around. "But then, perhaps you couldn't return my call because you were entertaining. Are you alone?"

"It isn't any of your business whether I'm alone or not." She injected pure frost into her voice to cope with the shock of his appearance. She had never seen him so disheveled. It was as if he hadn't shaved or changed clothes all weekend. "Jason, things just aren't going to work out for us. I feel it would be better if we didn't see each other anymore." There, she had said it. And felt so much better at saying it, too!

"I can arrange to have your portfolio transferred as soon as you sign these papers." He acted as if he hadn't heard her, as he pulled several wrinkled sheets of paper out of his coat pocket. "Just sign where the red X's are and we can get things rolling."

"Didn't you hear me? I don't want to see you anymore! And why should I sign anything?" She had a sneaking suspicion about exactly what he meant, but she wanted him to admit it.

He looked at her as if she had asked a stupid question. "Why, for me to take over your investments, of course."

Her eyes turned to ice. "I never said you could handle my portfolio."

Jason's dark features turned even darker with rage. His eyes flashed pure fury at being thwarted. "This is no joking matter, Alex. Just sign the papers."

Her eyes glittered with a temper her friends knew well enough to avoid. "Believe me, Jason, I am not joking. In fact, I would prefer that you leave right now. As I already told you, I don't care to hear from you again." She threw open the door and gestured outside.

"What are you saying?" he demanded, waving his hands around. "Do you realize what I did for you by presenting you to the right people, giving you some credibility even if you only drew those silly pictures?"

"No one asked you to!" she yelled. "Just get out, Jason, before I say something we'll both regret. And believe me, I'm well on my way to saying a great deal."

He advanced on her. "Not until we get this settled. You owe me!"

Her temper fired up at that. "I owe you diddly!"

"Why, you son of a bitch!" Wrapped in his own rage, Patrick took a swing at the unsuspecting Jason, but fell down as his arm swept right through the stockbroker without impact.

"I want you out of here now!" Alex shrieked at glass-breaking level.

"You're not going to cheat me out of what I'm owed!" he shouted back, grabbing her arm.

Her reply was loud and strident as she began calling him every name she could think of and a few Patrick gleefully threw in. She jerked her arm back and hit Jason square in the chest with her fist so hard the man fell back a few steps. With rage marring his face he advanced on her, but she was too angry to feel any fear as they waged a loud verbal war.

"You leave her alone, you cad!" Marian had her own ideas of punishment. She urged Suzi Q, who was already upset by all the yelling, toward Jason until the cat jumped onto him, leaving claw marks everywhere.

Jason yelped and batted at the irate cat with his hands.

"Don't you hurt my cat!" Alex jumped into the fray. A hard elbow in her ribs did nothing to stop her.

With the front door open and the war escalating, it was no wonder a concerned neighbor called in a complaint to the police. When two uniformed officers appeared on the scene and parted the warriors, Alex could only stand back, tossing her hair behind her shoulder as she tried to catch her breath.

"She assaulted me for no reason!" Jason shouted at the first officer who entered the apartment. "I want that madwoman locked up." He pulled out a handkerchief and dabbed at several bloody scratches on his face and freely bleeding gouges on his arms. "And I want that cat destroyed. It's crazy! I wouldn't be surprised if it has rabies. I demand to see a doctor right away!"

"You son of a bitch!" Only an officer's quick intervention saved Jason from further attack as Alex launched at him. "You were the one to come in here uninvited!"

"Ma'am, don't make matters any worse," the officer advised. "First of all, let's get you two fixed up." He eyed the bruise on Alex's cheek and said to his partner, "And here we thought it would be a quiet day."

"Don't say anything without a lawyer present," Patrick advised as the battling twosome were escorted out.

"You would have to throw the cat into this," she muttered to her mother on the way out.

At the hospital emergency room the officers were patient in their attempt to get the facts straight while Jason waited to see a doctor for treatment.

Alex sat in a chair, arms crossed in front of her chest, scowling at Jason with a look fit to kill as she listened to him pompously inform the officers she had attacked him without provocation.

"You should write fiction, Jason," she said with a curl of the lip. "That's the best tall tale I've heard in a long time."

He glared at her. "She hasn't been right since her parents died."

"Keep my parents out of this, Jason, or next time I'll knock your block off," she softly warned, her eyes narrowing to dangerous slits.

He pointed at her. "Doesn't that prove my point?"

"As far as I know the lady is more than stable. You're the one who looks like the rear end of a donkey."

Alex looked up at the sound of a familiar voice, then moaned with mortification and slid further down in her seat, her hands covering her face. "Just cart me off to jail now and make everyone happy."

"Hi, doc," one of the officers greeted Michael. "You know these two?"

He nodded, the smile on his lips slipping when he noticed the bruise blooming on Alex's cheek. "The *gentleman*—" his tone indicated the word was being used loosely "—accosted Ms. Cassidy a couple days ago. I gather this was a repeat episode."

Jason glared at him. "Her cat almost blinded me." He gestured to the bloody scratches on his face and neck.

Michael's lips tightened. "Bring him on back," he told one of the nurses.

"I want her in jail," Jason went on, oblivious to the storm clouds gathering in Michael's eyes. "That cat could have seriously injured me."

The officer raised an eyebrow of disbelief as he traded silent words with Michael.

Jason looked at Michael closely, recognition slow to surface. "You were with her Saturday night," he announced. "The woman is certifiable. I'm certainly glad I didn't propose to her. I can see I would have had too much trouble on my hands even after I persuaded her to stop drawing those silly pictures and get rid of that cat from hell." He bared his teeth. "I would have gladly driven that monster to the pound." He flinched when Alex growled at him.

"Aren't we all glad this didn't happen? I have an idea if you had tried it, you'd consider today just a picnic in the park compared to what the lady would do to you," the officer muttered, clearly wishing he was anywhere else.

"I don't want this doctor working on me," Jason told the officer. "He's involved with her. I won't receive proper treatment."

"Palmer, be happy you have someone at all treating you this soon," Michael informed him, pulling out antiseptics and bandages. "Unfortunately, cat scratches can get infected if left untreated. Have you had a tetanus shot lately?"

He stiffened. "I don't like shots."

"Well, you're going to love this one." Michael leaned over Jason who now sat on a gurney. "Palmer, I didn't like you the first time I saw you and I like you even less the second time. You are a hypocrite of the first order, and if you suffered at Alex's hands she must have been acting in self-defense. Now don't make me angry. Or I might accidentally stick this needle in a muscle, and believe me, that can really hurt."

Jason's face blanched at the implied threat. He sat back and shut up.

ALEX SLOUCHED DOWN in the chair with her long legs straight out in front of her, ankles crossed. It was bad enough to sit next to a police officer, worse when said officer was there to keep an eye on her in front of too many people who knew her. Especially when certain people walked by with broad grins on their faces, making cracks about San Quentin and what a shame Alcatraz was closed.

"I just want you to know that if I murder anyone here it's justifiable homicide," she told the officer between clenched teeth.

A pair of legs garbed in surgical greens planted themselves in front of her. "I wouldn't try that now, after all the trouble I went to on your behalf." Michael's amused voice floated down.

She looked up. "Damn. There's more than a few doctors in this place that deserve to die by my hand after their oh-so-cute comments, and now you've ruined all my fun. So tell me, what have you done on my behalf?"

"Well, Killer, I was able to persuade the nice officer to release you into my custody, as long as you promise to behave yourself."

Chapter Eleven

"This has been one of the most embarrassing days of my life." Alex picked at a cinnamon roll of indeterminate age as she drank black coffee that looked strong enough to float the entire U.S. Navy and tasted just as bad. She had never dreamed anyone could make worse coffee than her mother's. "I can't believe Jason would pull such an extreme turnaround."

"Desperation does that to some people," Michael replied, playing it safe with a large ice-filled cup of diet Coke. His fingers slowly ran up and down the plastic-coated cup in a dance that Alex wouldn't mind seeing them perform on her skin.

"Those officers weren't really going to arrest me, were they? Or take Suzi Q away? She was only protecting me."

"No, but they needed to get you two settled down. Jason could make a lot of noise about Suzi Q, but there's no proof she deliberately attacked him. Not to mention, cats don't get rabies as he tried to claim she had. Still, Palmer had some nasty scratches that needed treatment. I know Suzi Q is a clean cat, but a cat's claws do carry a lot of harmful bacteria, which is why the scratches needed to be cleaned." He suddenly grinned. "And he needed a tetanus shot."

Alex's eyes widened. "He hates shots."

His grin grew larger. "Yeah, I know."

A giggle escaped her lips. "I wish I had been there to see it."

"Nah, you already had your fun. This one was all mine." He looked very satisfied with himself.

She watched him under the cover of lowered lashes, while she pretended to study the oily swirls in her coffee cup.

"I learned that he's lost a lot of money and a lot a disgruntled clients have pulled their accounts," she said quietly. "His credibility is sinking fast and he's doing whatever is necessary to pick up new clients. I still don't understand why he felt taking over my investments would make such a difference. My portfolio is insignificant, compared to the accounts he's handled." She idly chewed on a fingernail. "I wonder..."

Michael looked up. "What?"

Alex pushed her plate to one side. "I just wonder if perhaps Jason hasn't been tampering with his clients' investments. You know, moving money from one account to pay another, and now he's caught short and needs new money to take care of the old ones."

"That's a serious accusation."

"And Jason was a serious player. Now that I think about it, I wouldn't be surprised if he was doing such a thing. I mean, he used to brag about some of the deals he pulled off. And while they didn't sound illegal, they didn't sound all that conservative either, considering his public image. Maybe it was all a facade." She shook her head, unable to believe the events of the past few hours. "And to think I was seriously considering saying yes if that jerk proposed to me!" She slapped her forehead with the palm of her hand. "I am such an idiot. You'd think I would have learned the first time around."

Michael's stomach seemed to drip acid at the idea of Alex marrying Jason. "Well, a lot of people aren't what they appear to the public eye."

"You are." Conscious of curious eyes directed at them every so often, she purposely kept her hands to herself. She kept them occupied rearranging the silverware, resisting the temptation to reach across the table for his hand.

Seemingly just as conscious, his eyes touched hers. "Are you sure?"

"There were no copies of *Playboy* hidden under the bed or in the boxes you haven't unpacked, so I feel pretty safe in making that statement." An impish smile curved her full lips, colored a deep rose. "Besides, I have to keep on your good side since the nice policeman left me in your custody." Her forefinger slowly stroked the fork from the tips of the tines to the flat edge of the handle. "Tell me something, Doctor, did the police insist you take full-time custody of the prisoner?"

His eyes followed the movements. "That's negotiable."

"That would mean twenty-four hours a day," she said huskily, keeping eye contact.

"Just about."

"So-o-o," she drawled. "You would have to watch over me during the night as well as the day, am I correct?"

His gaze lingered on her slightly parted lips, then dropped down to sweep over her body before moving back up to her mouth again. "I'd say so, yes."

Alex could feel the heat of his gaze. Except right about now she'd prefer feeling a lot more than just his gaze on her! She injected a sultry note in her voice. There was no reason for her to be the only one affected by this two-edged conversation. "Well, then, doctor, I put myself in your hands."

His lips barely moved. "Excellent." He suddenly glanced toward the clock on the wall. "I guess I better get back to work."

Alex quickly masked the frown she could feel furrowing her brow. After her not-so-subtle comment, he was thinking about work! What did she have to do to get this man's

full attention? "I can catch a cab back to my apartment."
She hid her disappointment as she rose to her feet the same
time he did. She walked quickly by his side as they headed
for the elevator. She looked furtively down the long, wind-
ing hall.

Michael noticed her quick glances. "What's wrong?"

She lowered her voice. "I just want to know if the morgue
is in the near vicinity. I mean, we're not going to run into
anyone, are we?"

He draped an arm around her shoulders as they rounded
a corner. "No, you're safe." He looked around. "For the
moment."

Before Alex could question his cryptic comment, she
found herself hustled around another corner and into a
closet that turned out to be filled with shelves containing
linens.

Her lips curved in a wicked smile he could barely see in the
light filtering under the closed door. Maybe their conversation had some effect on him, after all! "Why, Duffy, you
devil, you. We're not in here to count the linens, are we?"

"Far from it." His eyes were filled with equally wicked
promises. "I'm sure we can find something else to do," he
said, reaching out for her.

Smiling broadly, she edged away from his grasp. "I don't
think I should make it easy for you."

"You agreed to my having custody of you."

"Yes, but that has nothing to do with this." She swept her
arm around the tiny room. Truth was, she couldn't move
two steps without running into Michael. Which wouldn't be
all that bad, to her way of thinking, as long as it was *her*
idea.

When he moved to the left, she moved to her left. The
next time, he was able to outwit her and caught hold of her
upper arms. "Gotcha."

She twined her arms around his neck. "Maybe I've got you."

"Then we'll call it a tie." His mouth hovered a fraction above hers.

She could smell the coffee on his breath, mingled with the starchy odor of clean linens around them. Not one of the sexier combinations she'd ever encountered, but where Michael was concerned, a lot of things had changed for her. She flicked his upper lip with the tip of her tongue. "I made the first kill. I win."

"Maybe the battle, but you still have the war to conquer," he told her just before his mouth captured hers in a spine-tingling kiss.

Alex wasn't about to argue. Not when she was caught up in returning Michael's caresses. She needed the feel of his warm skin beneath her hands to assure her this was real. She moved her hands over the front of his shirt, taking in his body warmth, stroking what skin she could find in the vee-neck of his cotton shirt. A faint odor of disinfectant on his hands, coupled with a musky after-shave, teased her nostrils. Funny, for someone who usually looked upon the world with colors in mind, her sense of smell was receiving quite a work over today. She opened her mouth wider as his tongue thrust inside. She was as close to him as she could get, but it wasn't enough. Not when a part of her reminded that someone could walk in at any moment and it wouldn't look good for Michael.

"Michael," she moaned, when he lifted her sweater, "do you really think this is a good place?"

"Do you know of a better one?" By now his lips were coursing a scorching path down her neck.

"Yes, my apartment."

He stopped abruptly.

"Where I can take the phone off the hook, lock all the doors and we wouldn't have to worry about anyone walking in on us," she said breathlessly.

He angled back to get a better look at her flushed features and mussed hair. "You have an excellent idea, Ms. Cassidy."

"Then you agree? After all, you'd be able to keep a better eye on me there."

He tucked his shirt back into his waistband. "Just as soon as I get off duty."

She smoothed her sweater down over her hips. "I'll be waiting."

They were so caught up in each other they were unaware of a shadowed figure standing along one of the side hallways watching their exit with malicious amusement etched on his handsome face.

Alex grasped Michael's hand, threading her fingers through his as they walked toward the ER. "Come on, Duffy, we've got to get you back where you belong. I'll fix you something healthy to eat tonight. I can't believe all the junk food in that cafeteria! I'm surprised more nurses and doctors aren't patients here."

Within two minutes, Alex and Michael parted company in the Emergency Room where he handed her some money for taxi fare. She used a telephone to call a cab and luckily didn't have long to wait. She didn't look back when she walked outside to her cab. There was no reason, since Michael was already hard at work.

When she returned to her apartment she sought out the building supervisor to let her in since she didn't have her purse with her and dreaded being overheard asking her dead parents to open the door. When she entered she found her parents pacing the length of the living room.

"Are you all right?" Marian demanded to know. "They didn't throw you in jail, did they? Oh, my poor darling, would you like some tea?"

"Mom, I have never liked tea," she replied, collapsing on the couch. "To me, it's nothing more than dirty water. All I want is a cigarette."

"But tea is very soothing, and a cigarette will do the opposite," she protested.

"If I want soothing I'll take a hefty shot of brandy." She stretched her arms over her head.

"That's more like it," Patrick agreed. "So what happened to that idiot?"

Alex wrinkled her nose. "He tried to have me arrested for assault. I understand he also called Suzi Q a psychotic and wanted her taken to the pound." Her hand rested on the sleek back of the purring Siamese. "Needless to say, Jason isn't welcome here anymore. As if he'd even want to come around after what happened today."

"He's the one who should be in jail," Patrick growled. "I should have let him have it."

"You tried, dear, remember?" Marian nudged his shoulder as she sat on the couch arm next to her husband. "So tell us what happened," she urged Alex.

Alex quickly filled them in on events at the hospital, but wisely kept the details of the linen closet to herself. She had no desire to raise their hopes for something that just wasn't going to happen. While Alex silently admitted she was more than a little attracted to Michael Duffy, she also knew that she wasn't about to make a third mistake. Not after her colossal dud regarding Jason. Luckily she knew she was safe with Michael. With what he'd told her of his past love life, she sensed he was just as wary of any entanglements as she was. Or was he? her brain prodded. After all, look how he acted last night. And today. That wasn't the bland and boring Michael Duffy he claimed to be.

Well, she shrugged inwardly, she would just take it a day at a time.

She pushed herself off the couch and walked into her office. "I've got a lot of work ahead of me." She seated herself at the drawing board, sorting through her colored pens. As she stared at the predrawn black squares, she searched her brain for the idea that had been forming in her brain since her cab ride home with a driver complaining about a crazy plane trip he'd taken recently.

She settled back in the chair, tapping a pen against her teeth. "What if someone flew from Beverly Hills to Burbank on Fly-It-Yourself Airways," she mused. "And a trunk with a man's body was lost during the flight. And now his widow is complaining to Fritzi about the deplorable service and she needs the trunk before they can have the funeral. She should look like an even more macabre version of Morticia Addams." She pushed her chair closer to the drawing board and began rapidly sketching as the ideas flowed from her brain onto the stark white paper. As always, Alex's strip held a touch of whimsy along with dark humor befitting the subject matter.

While some cartoonists hired apprentices to fill in the colors and words after the main artist finished his/her work, Alex preferred to do it all herself because she liked to add a special little puzzle inside the strip that her faithful readers looked forward to solving. This time, the intricate design of the sleeve of the woman's red-and-black cloak would reveal to those who looked for it a grinning skull design. By the time she finished her rough draft she sat back, stretching her aching back and neck muscles as she proudly surveyed her work.

"I thought you had to wear your glasses while you drew," Patrick commented, obviously feeling it was a safe time to come in. He held up a pair of dark-rimmed, oversize glasses.

"I'm supposed to," she admitted ruefully. "I have to use them to combat eye strain. And I usually pay for it when I forget to wear them and work for long periods of time. Thanks for bringing them in. I usually keep them in here." She slipped them on. "And I've got to do the final draft tonight, so I can mail these off first thing in the morning. Thank goodness I'm not behind schedule in spite of all the crazy things that have been going on lately." She gestured to the small stack neatly piled on top of a two-drawer file cabinet. "These aren't due for another three weeks."

"So what are you going to do about the good Dr. Duffy?"

Alex slowly turned her chair around to face her father. "Don't beat around the bush, Dad. Get to the point."

"You saw him at the hospital, didn't you?"

"What makes you think that?" She acted nonchalant, studying her fingernails with an all too casual air.

He began ticking off the reasons on his fingers. "One, the man was on duty today and he works in the emergency room. Two, you were in the emergency room yet you didn't mention seeing him, which you must have since I'm sure he would have made a point to see you. Three, your face was more than a little red when you talked about being there. Not a normal reaction from a woman who was almost arrested for assaulting a man who deserved it. I'd say you did a bit more than run into the good doctor while you were there." His eyes twinkled with broad mischief. "So what happened? Anything remotely decadent?"

"Father!" She pretended shock. "Decadence does not go on in a hospital."

"Wanna bet? Why do you think your mother watched 'General Hospital' all those years? She even insisted on a satellite dish for the RV so she wouldn't miss any episodes while we travelled."

"She was the same way during the years 'Marcus Welby' was on. I think it was more a fixation with doctors than the show," Alex wryly pointed out.

Patrick's grin was a mirror image of his daughter's. "So your mother had a few eccentricities."

"A few? Dad, Mom can't cook worth a damn, but we've never had the nerve to tell her so. She once used hair spray to polish the furniture and she once told a man from that photography studio, Olan Mills, that she didn't need any new carpet!"

"Yes, she does have her moments." His eyes twinkled merrily.

"Yes, she does." Her voice was filled with affection. She sobered. "Dad, as much as I love having this second chance to see you two again, you and Mom can't stay here much longer. It doesn't seem right."

He touched her shoulder. "We have a good reason to be here, kiddo."

"I know you think you do, but—" she waved her hands as she searched for the right words "—you have to look at my side, too. You appeared on the scene to make sure I got married properly because you were worried about me, and that's wonderful. You didn't approve of Jason and he turned out to be a first-class jerk. Can't you settle for fifty-percent success? At least I found out in time."

He shook his head, compassion warming his eyes. "Alex, I know this hasn't been easy for you, but you have to understand this hasn't been easy for us, either. We know sooner or later we'll have to leave you again, and it will be even harder to do it this time. I'm just glad I got to find out that you're doing well. I'm very proud of you, daughter, and sometimes I feel as if I never had the chance to tell you so. You recognized your God-given talent and put it to good use. There's a lot of people out there who wouldn't think of taking the kind of chances you have. I'm glad I was able to come back and see how well you've done." He rested both hands on her shoulders. "I hate to admit it, but deep down I was afraid you might go off the deep end and do something crazy after our deaths. Of course, I should have known better. After all, I'd like to think most of those genes inside you are mine."

Her lips curved. "Something crazy. You mean like come home feeling no pain from my thirtieth birthday party?"

"Don't you mean drunk?"

She shook her head. "No, more like completely anesthetized."

Patrick grinned at the memory. "That you were. You can't carry a tune to begin with and that night you sounded worse than Suzi Q's caterwauling to a full moon."

"It wasn't all that bad," she defended her tin ear.

"You forget, you were too drunk to hear yourself properly. Of course, people who are tone-deaf don't do any better when they're sober."

"Patrick, you're interrupting Alex's work," Marian scolded, walking inside carrying a plate with something that sported a slightly scorched aura and a glass of milk. She set the plate down on the file cabinet next to Alex. "I made you some of my special brownies."

Alex and Patrick exchanged telling looks and slight smiles. "I haven't forgotten your brownies, Mom," she said truthfully.

Marian beamed. "Patrick always tried to tell me they were overdone, but I told him brownies just can't be overcooked."

"Yes, what a shame I can't eat any," Patrick said glibly, earning a warning glance from his daughter. "You enjoy them, Alex." He kissed her on the cheek and sauntered out of the room.

With narrowed eyes, Marian watched her husband leave "Something tells me he was making jokes about my cook ing again," she murmured.

"Nonsense, Mom, we've always loved your cooking," she assured the older woman as she gingerly chose the smalles square from the plate.

Marian wandered around the room, studying the framed animation cels Alex collected. In the place of honor, ove her drawing table, hung her framed first published strip.

"You've done so much this past year," she commented "It's amazing how quickly Fritzi took off."

"Probably because so many people can relate to horror filled trips. Just as the strip depicting life with a new baby brings back memories to parents." Alex bit cautiously grateful she had when she discovered the brownie was rock hard. She was positive her teeth were strong because she had eaten so many of these brownies over the years. She chewed gamely, trying not to let the burned taste attack her palate She silently added prayers of gratitude that her mothe hadn't baked cookies. The boy she'd had a huge crush or when she was fifteen had broken a tooth on one of Mari an's chocolate-chip cookies. Needless to say, he never spoke to her again. After that, Alex kept a supply of store-bough cookies on hand to offer prospective beaux.

Since she hadn't gotten anywhere with her father, she de cided to try her luck with her mother.

"Mom, while it's been wonderful having you here, don' you miss the friends you've made in your new place?" she ventured. "Wherever that may be."

Marian hugged her. "I can always see them, but I only have a limited time with you, darling."

She instantly caught wind of the last words. "How lim ited?"

"Why, until we see you married. I do like Michael. His Aunt Chloe says he was always a well-mannered child."

Alex pressed her fingertips against her forehead. "Mom, you're doing it again."

"Doing what?"

"Talking about people who are . . . are . . ." She threw her hands up. "You know what I mean!"

Marian smoothed the front of her dress. "Alex, darling, I love you dearly, but sometimes you come across just a bit incoherent. You have to understand that some of you children have trouble settling down and we need to come back to lend a hand. To offer you some much-needed advice because we want to see you on the right track."

"I concede that Jason turned out to be a major mistake, and I'm glad I found out before I went any further with him. If you want to see me married again, fine. But what is this obsession of yours about marrying me to another doctor, after what happened the first time?" she demanded, picking up the glass of milk Marian had brought in with the plate of brownies. "Mom, let's face it. Doctors in my life just don't work out."

"Even someone like Michael Duffy?" she asked slyly.

Thoughts of what happened in the hospital linen closet warmed her cheeks. "He's a very nice man, Mom, and any woman in her right mind would adore to have him, but he's *too* nice."

Marian's brow wrinkled in a frown. "How can someone be too nice?"

"Easy, it's a well-known fact I'm a forceful personality, and Michael is the kind of man I could easily walk all over because he's so laid-back. Not that he's a wimp," Alex hastened to add. "He isn't, but he's such a sweet man."

"He was hurt by a forceful woman, Alex. While you've been a human steamroller a few times in your life, you have never hurt anyone the way that woman hurt him."

Alex knew little of Michael's past love life, except wha
he'd told her. She wondered how her mother had learne
about it. "She told him he was boring," she murmured.

"Would you ever say that to a man, even if it was true?'
Marian pressed.

She shook her head. "Never."

"And you are attracted to him, even if another woma
considered him boring."

"One woman's boring man, another woman's excitin
one," she paraphrased. "Mom, I love you, but this isn't
hundred years ago, where you and Dad could choose m
husband for me. Even if I did screw it up the first time.
Michael and I do start seeing each other on a semiregula
basis, I want to know you two won't try any ghostly trick
Please," she pleaded. "I've been through quite enoug
lately without any more surprises."

Marian nodded. "May I at least say that I like your M
chael Duffy?"

"You may," she smiled, "because, you know what, so d
I."

"YOU TIGER, YOU." One nurse winked at Michael as sh
handed him a chart.

He was so engrossed reading the chart it took a mome
for her words to sink in. "What?"

By then she was walking away with a twitch of the hip
and a wicked smile on her peach-glossed lips.

"Ruff!" Dennis clapped Michael on the back. "I had t
admit, old boy, I didn't know you had it in you."

He almost lost his grip on the chart. "Had what?"

Dennis's grin broadened. "Who'd've thought you'd b
the one to topple the high-and-mighty Alex. I'm proud c
you, buddy." Whistling, he headed down the hall.

Michael's brow furrowed. "The high-and-mighty...?'
The light clicked on in his brain. Someone must have see

them either go in or come out of the linen closet. And there was only one person who would truly enjoy spreading the word. Cursing under his breath, his first thought was to go in search of Dr. Craig Sommers and punch his lights out. Then reasoning intruded, as the clipboard in his hand cut into his palm. He'd wait. Cool, calm reasoning had always worked for him before and he would make sure it worked for him this time.

Luckily, Michael didn't have to wait long and his search turned out easier than he hoped.

"And here we thought all the linen closets belonged to ol' Craig," one doctor teased as he passed Michael in the hall. "We might have to set up a schedule around here."

Michael was known to keep his feelings inside and his temper flared up rarely. But when it did, it blew with a vengeance. This was turning out to be one of those times.

After asking a couple of smirking nurses, Michael found Craig in the cafeteria. He headed straight for the corner table, where Craig sat sweet-talking a wide-eyed student nurse.

"Excuse us, please," he said in clipped tones.

The nurse, seeing the darkness in Michael's face, picked up her tray and scurried away.

Craig Sommers was a doctor straight from Central Casting. Blond hair impeccably styled, features that were handsome without threatening other men, and enough charm to entice the most skeptical. His blue-striped shirt with a blue-and-burgundy tie neatly knotted, gray slacks and white lab coat were all neatly pressed. Even his cologne was expensive without being overpowering. Only the smirk on his face marred his perfect features.

"Something wrong, Duffy?" Craig asked amiably, leaning back in his chair, one arm draped along the back.

Michael leaned over, planting his palms on the tabletop. "Let's get something straight, Sommers," he said in a deceptively soft voice. "Your petty sexcapades in this hospital are bad enough, but when you allow an innocent woman's name to be dragged down to your level, it's downright pitiful.''

Craig laughed, not the least bit intimidated. "Alex was never innocent. Besides, if there's a story circulating about the two of you, who says I was the one to spread it?"

"Because this is the kind of story only you would enjoy telling." Michael's eyes glittered with barely contained fury.

Craig leaned back in his chair, curling an arm around the back. "What's wrong, Duffy? Can't stand up to the new reputation? You should be flattered. Most of the single doctors in this place have made a play for Alex at one time or another. Yet you were the only one to get past that ice-cold barrier of hers." His well-sculpted mouth moved in a broad smile. "This is much too good to keep a secret. Alex, my prude of an ex-wife, in a compromising position in the linen closet with our upright, uptight Dr. Duffy. Alex, my dear, I didn't think you had it in you. Think of it, after Alex any woman will be a snap." He flashed the movie-star grin that set Michael's teeth on edge.

Michael leaned over the table further, not caring how threatening he looked. Right about now, it wouldn't take much for his fist to connect with those perfect white teeth, which had probably cost the good doctor a small fortune in dental bills.

"You're scum, Sommers," he gritted. "Why any woman would put herself under your care is beyond me. Let me warn you, if I ever hear anything about Alex Cassidy and myself that's more than *G*-rated, I will rearrange that face of yours so no woman in her right mind will want you. Do I make myself clear?"

Craig shrank back under Michael's intense regard. "Perfectly clear, Doctor."

Michael straightened up. "Just remember, if you want a war, you'll have it."

Craig's face tightened. "I have ears. I can hear perfectly well."

"Too bad you didn't think about it while your mouth was flapping when it should have remained shut." Michael stalked off.

Craig, along with several other interested witnesses, watched Michael walk away.

"Well, what are you all looking at?" Craig said angrily, his face a bright red as he stood up so suddenly his chair fell over backward. Without bothering to put away his tray and dishes, he left the cafeteria with only one thing in mind. Michael Duffy was now his enemy.

Chapter Twelve

"He did *what?*" Alex fumbled for the couch behind her and sank down in the seat as she looked up at Beth who'd just sent her into a state of shock.

"I said, Michael Duffy cornered Craig in the hospital cafeteria and they had a conversation that looked heated and very unfriendly. Neither will talk about it, but you and I both know that for some reason it had to be about you," Beth told her. She had appeared on Alex's doorstep a few moments earlier with news about a showdown at the hospital. The only sorry part was that no one knew the entire story.

"He's someone you could walk all over, huh?" Marian commented, practically smirking in the process.

Alex turned her head in her mother's direction. "Will you please be quiet."

"What?" Beth stared at her as if she'd lost her mind.

Now Alex knew why she didn't like ghosts only one person could see. They made that person look and sound ready for a straitjacket. "Nothing. I can't believe Michael would threaten Craig. This doesn't sound like him." Although he had given her a few surprises. She had a sneaking suspicion what the quarrel could be about. While she and Michael had been cautious in leaving the linen room, it would have been sadly appropriate if Craig had spied them emerging from one of his favorite trysting places.

Beth perched herself on the edge of the couch more than eager to tell all. "I can give you an excellent reason why. Craig let it 'slip'—" she'd held up her fingers indicating quotes "—that he'd seen you and Dr. Duffy sneak out of a linen closet. And everyone already knows he considers them his private domain."

Alex covered her eyes, moaning, "I will never be able to show my face at a softball game again. Dennis, especially, will never let this go. It's the kind of thing he'd make sure was carved on my tombstone. And if he does, I will make sure to come back and make his life absolutely miserable," she vowed.

"How much do you want to bet that Michael threatened Craig with bodily harm if he said anything more about the two of you? Alex, the man was positively primitive when he dealt with Craig." Her eyes shone with delight as she leaned forward, resting her arms on her knees, her fingers laced together. "Michael is the talk of the hospital. There are nurses ready to cut out your heart if it meant they could have a chance at him."

Alex closed her eyes. Between her longtime friendship with Beth and marriage to Craig, she was well aware of a hospital grapevine. And there was never anything known as smothered gossip. "And this is supposed to make me feel better?" She wondered if anyone had ever died of embarrassment.

"The man was ready to fight for your honor, Alex!" she insisted, then sighed. "I wish a man would do that for me. I'm usually happy if they'll open a door for me."

She was afraid to contemplate it. "Perhaps he was worrying about his own reputation. After all, he is still pretty new there."

"Then I would think he'd have cornered Craig in some dark alley instead of confronting him in the cafeteria where the world could see him," she pointed out with exasperation. "Alex, the man is crazy about you." She sighed dramatically. "How come I can't find a man like him?"

"We hardly know each other!" she argued, wide-eyed at the rapid turn of events.

Beth was quick to point out, "You know each other well enough to hide in a linen closet. I mean, it is true, isn't it?" She didn't need to see her friend's bright red face to get her answer.

Alex released a short, sharp scream as she collapsed back on the couch. "I hate logical friends!"

"You hate hearing the truth." Beth picked up Suzi Q and draped her over her shoulder as she rubbed the cat from the top of her head to her tail in slow, soothing strokes that left her purring like a well-tuned engine.

"I'd really like to know what went on in the linen closet," Patrick spoke up, not about to let this lapse.

"I am not going to talk about what happened in the linen closet!" Alex screeched.

"I was afraid you'd say that," Beth mourned, unaware of the reason for Alex's unrest.

Alex pushed herself off the couch and paced the length of the living room, picking up a throw pillow and punching it with her fist. "It's all their fault," she muttered. "They started this mess and I'm the one who has to clean it up. I don't care. I'm telling and I don't want any more tricks. My health insurance can't handle it!" She spun on her heel to face Beth. "They came back on my birthday," she blurted out. "They didn't want to see me marry Jason, so they did something to make sure I'd see him for the creep he was. And then they possessed Michael to become interested in me and did the same to me at the softball game. That's why I didn't act like my usual self when I was flirting with him. They'd fiddled with my mind!''

"Alex, she's not going to believe you," Patrick pointed out with a weary sigh. "You know how logical Beth is. She figured out Santa Claus wasn't real when she was four and she stopped believing in the Easter Bunny when she was three.''

"I don't care, I just want to get it out of my system." She continued her pacing. "It's not fair that I'm the only one who can see them, the only one who can hear them." She tossed the pillow to the floor and stomped on it. "Why couldn't I have had brothers and sisters to share them with? I didn't even believe in ghosts until they showed up!"

"Alex, what are you talking about?" Beth shouted.

"What do you think I'm talking about!" Alex shouted back, throwing up her hands. "My parents have been living here since my birthday. And they refuse to go away!"

She shook her head, a pitying look in her eyes. "Your parents are dead, Alex."

"I know that, you know that. Hell, even *they* know that, but that hasn't stopped them from turning my life upside-down!" She looked wild-eyed. "They're here because they want to see me married off properly, and right now Michael Duffy is their prime candidate. If they have anything to do with it, the man doesn't have a chance." Having run out of steam, she collapsed on the edge of the coffee table.

"Now you've done it," Patrick sighed.

"Honey, your father is right. She'll never believe you," Marian chimed in.

Alex was past listening to reason. "I don't care. I just want to get it off my chest," she argued, grasping her hair in her hands and pulling on it. "I don't care if she calls in the men in white coats, just as long as I can have my say." She turned to her friend. "You think I'm crazy, don't you? Or that this is a repercussion from that time I hit my head.

Well, it isn't. What can I say? My parents came back as ghosts because they wanted to keep me from marrying Jason. And only Suzi Q and I can see them. Why do you think she's always talking to thin air? She's talking to my mother! Who, with my luck, understands everything that crazy cat is saying!'' she shrilled.

Beth looked wary. "Alex, this is serious. You've been under a lot of stress lately. Maybe you need to talk to someone.''

"I am talking about it, I'm talking about it to you. Think about it,'' she implored. "You know my mother as well as I do. Isn't this something she'd do?''

Beth thought about it for a moment, idly chewing on a nail. "My mother would do it,'' she said finally. "She'd come back to see me married off. But, Alex, what you're saying is impossible. There's just no such thing as ghosts.''

"Who says there isn't?'' she challenged. "Lots of things go on that we can't understand. Remember all the times Suzi Q used to carry on conversations with Mom? Who's to say there isn't a way for the deceased to come back and watch over the ones they love? To make sure they're all right?''

"You make a pretty good argument, kiddo,'' Patrick complimented, settling down on the couch. "If I didn't believe in me, I would now.''

She blew out a gust of air. However badly she wanted to speak to her father, she didn't. Beth was having enough trouble taking this in without seeing her best friend talk to the couch.

"Alex, you have to get hold of yourself,'' Beth begged.

"Would it help if I picked up a pillow and let it sort of float around?'' Marian offered bright-eyed, clearly getting into the "spirit'' of things.

"No, Mom. You'd probably only scare her half to death.'' Alex jumped up and began pacing back and forth again.

"If you're talking about me, I'm already scared," Beth told her, warily looking over her shoulder as if fearing a monster with glowing eyes and sharp teeth would jump out and grab her.

"Think about it, Beth. Have I ever done anything this crazy?" Alex reminded her. "I'll be the first to admit I've pulled a few nutty stunts in my lifetime, but have I ever done anything that would be this crass?"

"Crass?" Marian made a face. "Darling, calling us crass is not nice."

"All right, so you're not known to play Halloween early." Beth ran her fingers through her hair, dislodging the tousled waves even more. "Look, Alex, I know you've had a lot of shocks lately, and you've been working too hard because you're so compulsive about delivering your strip way ahead of your deadlines. Maybe if you tried to relax, get some rest and talk to someone." Frank concern showed in her eyes and sounded in her voice. "Sweetie, I'm the first one to know how much you miss your parents, and with the way they were killed—well—it just wasn't fair. But deluding yourself that they've come back from the dead isn't the way to handle it. Especially with everything else that's been going on in your life, what with Jason turning into a major creep and all." She rested her hand on Alex's shoulder. "I want you to remember that I'm always here for you and if you need to talk, well, call, okay? Just, please, don't say any of this to anyone else. They might not understand." She kissed her on the cheek and left.

Alex slumped on the couch, a weary sigh escaping her lips. She grabbed a throw pillow and pressed it against her face to muffle her scream of frustration.

"I'm sorry, honey, but we knew she'd never believe you," Patrick spoke up. "After all, this is the kind of story you see on 'Alfred Hitchcock' or 'Twilight Zone.' Not in real life."

"It isn't right she didn't believe you," Marian fretted. "After all, she's your best friend and has known you for years. Not to mention you've never been a good liar."

"She also knows I had a concussion not all that long ago, and she thinks that and stress have made me lose my mind," Alex had to concede. The light bulb went off over her head. "Of course!" She jumped up and ran into her office. "The brownies." She hurried out, carrying the plate Marian had taken in there earlier.

A confused Marian turned to Patrick. "What do my brownies have to do with anything?"

Patrick grinned. "Your brownie recipe is very special. Beth would recognize it right away."

She was suspicious of his glib reply, but decided to let it rest.

Ten minutes later, Alex was back, looking more dejected than ever. "Why she thinks I'd make brownies like this is beyond me," she muttered, taking the plate into the kitchen.

Patrick walked over and gave her a hug. "There are some things logical-minded people can't understand, Alex. Ghosts are one of them."

"It would have been so much easier if you had haunted Aunt Harriet. Everyone expects her to live with ghosts," she sighed. "After all, she had her dog freeze-dried and set him in his basket."

"Harriet has already had six husbands, she doesn't need our help in finding another." Marian sat on the couch with Suzi Q curled up beside her. "Besides, your father is allergic to dogs, remember?"

Alex's need to be alone while she licked her wounds grew greater with every second.

"Back to work." A weary Alex entered her office and closed her door.

"Things would be so much easier if she and that nice Dr. Duffy would get together," Marian commented. "Chloe's convinced he's very attracted to her. She told me he's her favorite nephew.''

"Chloe also thought that idiot son of hers was a reincarnation of Charles de Gaulle," Patrick pointed out.

"She thought he looked like him around the eyes, dear. That's all.''

"THIS IS CRAZY, DUFFY."

Michael stood outside Alex's apartment building, his hands stuck in his pockets as he stared at the front door.

"All you have to do is go inside and take the elevator upstairs," he told himself. "You've done it before. There's no reason for you to be uneasy about it now." Yes, there was. In the beginning he merely considered Alex a sexy-looking lady, a bit wacky, perhaps, but someone he enjoyed being around. There was the time spent at the mall while she ran from store to store picking out linens, prints for his walls and various accessories to brighten up his apartment because she insisted he needed color in his life. He had to admit he'd enjoyed waking up to such cheerful surroundings in the mornings. She had told him she would add color to his life and she'd done just that. In more ways than one. She had also got under his skin, and he didn't want to see her gone.

Besides, his brain reminded him. She's in your custody, right? Okay, so it was a joke. She knew it and he knew it. But she sure didn't seem to mind the linen closet. His rapidly aroused body hadn't minded it, either.

"So, go up," he ordered himself. "Find out for sure if what happened at the hospital was a fluke or not. Make sure you weren't just trying to prove something to yourself. Andrea may have said you weren't the romantic type, but Alex didn't seem to see it that way. Go on."

Placing one foot in front of the other, he did just that until he stood in front of her door. His hand reached for the doorbell, then was about to reconsider when he felt a gentle but firm pressure on his finger against the buzzer.

Alex's face showed pleased surprise when she opened the door. "Michael, I didn't expect you so early." She took his hand and drew him inside.

"Luck was on our side, it was actually quiet when I left." He eyed her red-and-black tiny-checked oversize shirt and black leggings with frank male appreciation.

Alex slid her arms around his waist. "Well, Doctor, you are most welcome," she murmured, lifting her face. "After all, I did invite you over here after you got off duty, didn't I?"

Michael wasn't about to turn down the invitation. He framed her face with his palms as his mouth lowered to hers. His mouth covered hers with the hunger of a man remembering teasing kisses, which had rapidly warmed to deeper caresses, in a dark closet. His arms circled her body, pulling her closer to him.

"I can't believe she's doing this in front of us," Patrick groused. "Marian, do you see where his hand is!"

"Shut up, dear," Marian beamed as she watched the embracing couple.

"Go away," Alex mumbled, between nibbling kisses as she snuggled up closer to Michael's lean body. His tongue thrust into her mouth, stroking every moist corner with the same kind of hunger he displayed at the hospital. The kind of sincere hunger a red-blooded woman dreams of. Now a part of Alex's dreams had come true.

"Hmm?" Michael wasn't sure he heard right.

"I'm talking to the cat."

"Afraid she'll be corrupted by what she'd see?"

"Corrupted?" Patrick roared. "More like shocked. I can't believe my little girl is doing such things."

"Come on, Patrick, let's give them some privacy," Marian insisted, grabbing hold of his hand, but he resisted her efforts.

"Are you kidding? Who knows what could happen if we leave?"

"Exactly."

Alex didn't have to open her eyes to know her parents had pulled their disappearing act. Considering where Michael's hands were now, it was just as well her mother had taken her father off to never-never land. She sighed with pleasure when the buttons on her shirt were parted and the front clasp to her bra was released. A rush of cool air tightened her nipples just before his warm palms covered them, causing an ache deep inside. His whispered words were dark, the kind spoken between longtime lovers instead of two people who, so far, had shared little in the way of intimate secrets.

Alex, who usually proceeded cautiously, felt as if she'd gone up in flames under Michael's touch. His fingers gently kneaded her aching flesh before trailing down to the elastic waistband, slipping under to draw circles around her navel.

"I'd like to say we're moving too fast," Alex said huskily, tipping her head back and to the side as Michael's mouth found the sensitive skin behind her ear.

"But?" he asked in a rough voice.

"But I have an idea I'm not thinking very clearly where you're concerned." She breathed sharply through her nose when his fingers explored lower.

"Do you want me to stop?"

She seriously thought about tearing his clothing off right where they stood. "Are you kidding? Although I wouldn't mind if we got a bit more comfortable."

"Such as?"

"Such as my bedroom. It has a nice large bed in there, where we could stretch out. It might not have the ambience of the linen closet, but it does have clean sheets and subtle lighting.''

His hand stilled. ''Are you sure? This could get complicated, Alex. Are you ready for that? Ready for what will be said when others realize we're a couple. What Sommers might try to pull? No matter how much I want to drop into that bed with you and make love with you for the next week, I want you to think about what it involves. I don't take things lightly.'' He pressed a butterfly kiss against her closed eyelid as he spoke softly. ''I should have known I was in trouble when you opened your big blue eyes in the emergency room. I was the guy who was going to bury himself in his work, but I was really thrown off the track when you blew into my life.''

''I was unconscious when I first blew into your life,'' she reminded him, tracing lazy patterns across his bare chest. She wasn't fond of men with overly hairy chests nor of men with no hair at all, and the sandy brown hair dusted around the pale brown nipples and arrowing down to his waist to thicken in a coarse darker brown nest was just right for her. It tempted her to draw pictures on his skin.

''It didn't matter. I was still lost to a pair of blue eyes and a lush mouth that knocked my socks off.'' His fingers traced their own patterns across her bare shoulders and down to the tops of her breasts, just missing taut nipples which tightened even further in reaction. ''I just want you to realize what will happen after tonight, because I have a very strong hunch after we make love I won't be able to let you go.''

Alex smiled at Michael's suggestion to stand back and take a breather. Most men would have taken immediate advantage of her weakened condition, but not him.

''Michael,'' she whispered, injecting pure seduction into her voice. ''If you don't finish within the next five minutes what you've already started, I will rip your clothes into shreds and make you my prisoner for the next month.'' She jerked his polo shirt up to his armpits as an example of her intent, then allowed her hands to linger over the pale brown nipples, which stiffened under her light touch.

She could feel his smile against her skin. "Any chance of a parole, warden?" he murmured.

"None."

"Then I plead guilty as charged, and will take my punishment like a man."

She chuckled throatily. "Hallelujah." She backed out of his arms and crooked her finger in a beckoning gesture as she continued to back her way into her bedroom. She was grateful she had made her bed, since she tended to be an active sleeper and her covers were usually tossed every which way in the mornings. She only hoped there was nothing to ruin the seductive image hanging in the bathroom. At the moment, her love-fogged brain couldn't properly function.

Once they reached the bed, Michael paused with a sobering thought. "Alex, I don't have anything with me, if you're not protected."

She smiled. "Everything is taken care of, Doctor."

By now Alex didn't want to talk. She just wanted to be lost within this man for the next year. She hazily wondered if the hospital would miss him if she kept him locked up in her bedroom. Um, the idea had its merits.

Michael's thoughts closely paralleled her own as he wondered how long they could hide away before the world intruded on something this special.

The words they spoke were soft and loving. The touches not at all hesitant, as each learned what the other liked best. Even that wasn't difficult, because each liked whatever the other did. There was no dominant partner as they both shared a magnitude they had never dreamed of. And when their voices rang out in the darkened bedroom, they knew their lives would never be the same again.

It wasn't until Alex opened her eyes and looked around the dark room that she realized she must have fallen asleep. A glance at the clock confirmed her suspicion. She wanted to stretch her arms over her head and purr like a well-satisfied cat, but she resisted the urge. She hated to move a muscle because she didn't want to wake the man sleeping beside her in naked splendor. She carefully rolled over on her side and propped her head on her hand as she studied him.

"Too good to be true," she whispered to herself.

"Believe me, it's true."

Alex lowered her head and brushed her lips across his. "I didn't want to wake you."

Michael opened one eye. "How long did we sleep? This time."

She couldn't hold back the blush tinting her cheeks at his teasing statement. "About an hour. And a half hour before that." She rubbed her nose against his. "You are insatiable, Doctor. What kind of vitamins do you take?"

"I think it has something more to do with the company I keep." He wrapped a hand around her neck and kept her face close to his. His attention was diverted as a pungent odor teased his nostrils. "Are you cooking something?"

Alex's nose twitched just as her face grimaced in horror. "I can't believe this." She disentangled herself from his arms and leaped out of bed, snatching up the first thing her hands discovered and pulling it on over her head. Until the warm, musky scent swirled around her, she didn't realize she was wearing Michael's polo shirt which hit her mid-thigh.

Alex skidded to a halt just inside the kitchen. Marian's French toast sent up tiny spirals of smoke from the electric frying pan.

"How could you?" she screeched, then swiftly lowered her voice. "What do you think you're doing?"

"Luckily, I got to the smoke alarm before it went off," Patrick reassured his daughter.

She stared at him in horror. "And that's supposed to make me feel better? Make this disappear."

"We're ghosts, dear, not magicians. I thought I'd make you breakfast, so you wouldn't have to bother," Marian told her, looking at the pan with a worried frown. "I don't know what happened, dear. My French toast usually comes out so well."

A strangled sob clawed its way up Alex's throat. "You don't understand." She shifted from one foot to the other. "I—ah—I." How was she going to explain she had a man in her bedroom to her parents? While they weren't prudes, she doubted they wanted to visualize their daughter as a "fallen woman" who lured a man into her bed. Hm, the idea wasn't all that bad. She settled for baldly stating, "I'm not alone."

"Darling, we weren't born in the Middle Ages," Marian chided. "We naturally assumed that nice doctor was with you. That's why I'm making you my special French toast. Don't worry."

Alex stared at the burned frying pan and the dark smoke billowing out the open window. "I'm not worried one bit," she lied.

"Hey, everything okay?" A delightfully rumpled Michael appeared in the bedroom doorway, his pants zipped but not snapped. He walked into the kitchen and looked at the smoking pan. "Burning breakfast, are we?"

Marian drew herself up. "You inform that man my breakfasts are famous."

"Infamous is more like it," Patrick muttered before kissing his wife on the cheek by way of apology.

"When I turned the frying pan on I didn't realize there was already something in it," Alex improvised weakly.

Patrick rolled his eyes. "Good going, Alex. He'll really believe that. You would have been better off telling him your dead mother made breakfast."

Alex pasted a brilliant smile on her face and linked her arms around Michael's neck. "I have a wonderful idea. How about if I take you out for breakfast," she said brightly.

He grinned back. "I've got an even better idea." He dipped his head, whispering something in her ear that left her red-faced and short of breath.

"I think I like your idea better," she gasped when he nipped her earlobe. "Just as long as all uninvited guests leave the premises."

"Your cat is still in the living room, so we're safe."

"Is that all he has on his mind," Patrick grumbled, scowling at an unsuspecting Michael. "What's wrong with a little conversation now and then?"

"As if you didn't try anything like that when we were seeing each other," Marian reminded him.

"At least I didn't flaunt it."

"Just be happy it isn't Jason Palmer in her bed."

"If our daughter had been stupid enough to allow what's-'is-name in here, I would have dragged out all the chains and moans any self-respecting ghost could use," he said with a dire frown.

Alex was past hearing. She only knew that Dr. Duffy had the most remarkable hands...and mouth...and teeth...and...

MICHAEL NEEDED SLEEP. Lots of it. Right now his eyelids were so heavy that he doubted even toothpicks could hold them up. It didn't help that he was only an hour into his shift. He prayed it would be a slow night so he could catch up on his sleep in the on-call room.

"You look like something the cat dragged in." Dennis eyed him critically. "Come to think of it, I don't think a cat would bother with you right now."

"Thanks for the compliment," he said wryly.

Dennis scanned the chart in his hands and quickly signed the bottom of the top sheet before handing it to a nurse. "Since the mother doesn't speak much English, get someone who speaks Spanish to explain that if her son's temperature rises again she's got to bring him in right away," he told her. "Make sure she understands these suppositories I've prescribed are not an oral medication," he sighed. "I should have specialized in plastic surgery. There aren't as many headaches."

"I once thought about pathology," Michael admitted.

Dennis nodded in agreement. "Yeah, I could go for that. The patients in the morgue don't talk back."

Macabre humor was a fact of life among the medical profession. For some it was the only way to remain sane in the face of the tragedies they encountered during a typical working day.

"So what's with the bags under the eyes?" Dennis walked with Michael down the hall toward the doctor's lounge. "She keeping you up late?" he laughed at his double-edged joke.

A grateful Michael headed for the coffeepot with its recently brewed contents and poured himself a cup, sighing with relief in between sips of the hot liquid.

"I caught up on the latest medical journals," he evaded, resting his hip against the table.

After hearing about the episode in the cafeteria, Dennis knew better than to push the subject. While no one had heard the exact conversation between Michael and Craig, they all knew it had something to do with Alex. Although he was as curious as everyone else, Dennis wasn't about to ask. Judging by Michael's heavy eyes, there was one good consideration. "Sure it is. Ah, caffeine, drink of the gods," he intoned, flopping back on a patched vinyl couch that had seen better days. "Word has it the so-called budget allowing for extra nurses and doctors has been cut back—again. If I had any brains I'd go into private practice before the double shifts kick in again. If you were smart, you'd do the same thing." He tipped his cup in Michael's direction.

"Trauma medicine isn't exactly a specialty suited for private practice, Dennis," he replied, pouring himself another cup before sitting down.

"No, but you've got surgery or general medicine to think about. Hey, a few refresher courses and you'd be on top of things."

Michael chuckled. "I don't think it's my style."

Dennis leaned forward, resting his arms on his knees. "Last night, I had a kid high on drugs pull a knife on me and if I hadn't been quick I would have been split open like a melon. There's got to be more from life than that. And I want to find it."

Michael hated the idea of losing a talented colleague, even though this wouldn't be the first time it had happened to him over the years. There was too much money in private practice and the hours weren't as crazy. "Then good luck in your search."

Dennis eyed him speculatively. He decided to go for broke. "Will I get my head chopped off if I mention Alex's name?"

Michael raised his head. "Do us both a favor, Dennis, let's not drag Alex into this."

Dennis read his hidden message loud and clear. He also knew what just might be going on between Alex and Michael was the kind of information Craig Sommers would love to capitalize on. Luckily, Dennis liked Michael more than Craig and wasn't the malicious sort. He pasted a look of complete innocence on his face. "Alex who?"

Chapter Thirteen

"Alex, give me a break here. All I'm asking of you is one cocktail party. A couple of hours of your time. No more."

"No."

"Okay, an hour. And then you can leave with a clear conscience, knowing that you've done your duty."

"I already have a clear conscience by not even going. Simon, you know very well how I feel about cocktail parties where everyone stands around and makes inane conversation and sees who can outdrink the other without looking drunk. It isn't my style." Alex's head was downcast as she carefully read each printed page her agent set before her, then affixed her signature to the dotted line. While she trusted him implicitly, she still believed in knowing exactly what she was signing.

The man seated across from her patted his balding head with his handkerchief before carefully folding it and replacing it in his jacket pocket. "Alex, honey, these people pay you a lot of money for your comic strip. Naturally, they want to meet the brains behind Fritzi and 'Chuck-It-All Tours.' It's part of the game."

"Yes, and they're getting a great deal in the bargain. A bargain that does not include me." Her eyes turned icier than ever. "Simon, I told you in the very beginning that I don't play politics nor will I schmooze with the clients whenever they snap their fingers. If they like my work, fine. If there's to be a business dinner, I'm more than willing to attend. But no cocktail parties. I won't put up with some idiot from the main office trying to tell me that the money paid for my strip includes private time with me," she said firmly, handing over the papers which Simon slid into the briefcase lying open on the couch beside him. He'd called her early that morning explaining he was going to be in the area around ten and rather than her having to make a special trip to his office he was willing to bring them by. "If I recall correctly, the first time you brought this up you only mentioned dinner with several syndicate members, nothing about a cocktail party." She speared him with her most intimidating gaze which would have left a lesser man squirming. Luckily Simon was made of tougher stuff. In his business, he had to be.

"They changed their minds," he muttered. "They thought an informal cocktail party would be a better way for people to get together."

She arched a disbelieving eyebrow. "Informal? Simon, for a man who's so astute in business, you're a complete washout when it comes to these matters. All right," she relented when she saw his crestfallen expression. "I'll attend, but I might be bringing someone with me, and don't expect us to stay long," she issued her warning.

He stood up quickly, grabbing his briefcase at the same time. What made him good was that he knew when to move in for the kill and when to back off. This was most definitely the time to back off. "The moment I hear the details about the party I'll pass them on."

"Just be happy that I'm promising to behave." She smiled beatifically.

"Thank heavens," he muttered, walking to the door. "Just no dumping drinks on the money men, okay? The dry-cleaning bill the last time was horrendous."

"If they don't keep their hands to themselves, they deserve it," she said, ushering her agent out.

"Who doesn't keep their hands to themselves?" Patrick asked suspiciously when Alex closed the door after Simon.

"Creepy members of the syndication," she replied. "Luckily it only takes them once to realize they've made a mistake."

Patrick was slightly mollified. "I'm just glad to know you can take care of yourself."

"Patrick, Alex has been on her own for a long time. She knows how to protect herself," Marian reminded him. "And I'm certain she's more than happy you weren't able to do anything about Jason that night."

He looked at her askance. "It wasn't me who threw the cat at that creep."

"A spur-of-the-moment decision that worked beautifully, I might add." She turned to her daughter. "Do I gather you're going to ask Michael to attend the party with you?" she asked with a hopeful air.

She studied her nails which were short, neatly manicured ovals. "If he isn't on duty or can switch with someone that night. It will give him a chance to see what my world is like." She eyed them. "Don't get any ideas about trying to take matters into your own hands again. No offense, but you two have created more than enough chaos the past few weeks."

"Us?"

"Yes, you."

Marian sat on the couch, studying the hem of the dress she detested. "Alex, you know very well that we can't leave the confines of this apartment," she reproached her daughter. "That was part of the terms for our return. Yet you always accuse us of instigating something away from here."

"Part of the terms?" She jumped on the words. "There's more involved with all this hocus-pocus?" She gnashed her

teeth when she saw their expression. "Wait, let me guess. Trade secret?" They nodded. "Why am I not surprised? None of the stunts you two have pulled has been the least bit normal. Why do I expect this to be any different? As for what's happened away from here, deep down I know you had something to do with all of it, and somehow I intend to find out how you managed it."

Patrick was busy switching television channels, looking for a sports game, when his attention was grabbed by CNN. "Well, what do you know," he whooped. "Talk about someone receiving his just deserts. What color do they wear in jail now?"

Alex first glanced at the television screen, then stared wide-eyed when the video camera displayed a business-office doorway where a familiar figure garbed in a well-cut three-piece suit and handcuffs was led away by two police detectives. The moment the prisoner spied the television cameras he brought his bound hands up to his face to use as a shield, but he was too late to hide from the intrusive cameras.

"Jason Palmer of the prestigious investment firm Trainor and Associates in downtown Los Angeles was arrested today on thirty-two counts of fraud and embezzlement and one charge of resisting arrest," the dispassionate announcer's voice intoned. "When confronted in his office by police officers, Palmer shouted they had no right to be there and struck out with his fists, leaving one uniformed officer with a broken nose and a black eye. Until a thorough audit can be performed, there is no idea how many of Palmer's clients have been victimized by his money games."

Alex sat there finding herself not all that surprised at the news. Not after her last confrontation with Jason. No wonder he was desperate to get his hands on her portfolio. He probably needed money to replace what he had stolen from other accounts. She shook her head, saddened that a man with his financial expertise would lower himself to such depths just to get money.

She quickly switched channels to see if any of the other stations had a news item on Jason, then remembered it was too early in the day for the regular evening news. She glanced at her answering machine with its red beeping light winking at her and low-toned beep. She doubted she wanted to hear what it had to say.

"Something tells me I should have the machine pick up my calls tonight," she sighed. "I can't believe Jason would do something so unprofessional, not to mention stupid. He loved his work more than anything. The man wore his professionalism like a uniform. If his checkbook didn't balance to the penny he kept at it until he found that lost penny. This doesn't sound like the work of a man who has all his marbles."

"This is the work of a man craving power through well-heeled clients with an unlimited amount of money to spend," Patrick explained. "He identified money with power, and as time went on he was willing to do anything to get it."

Alex jumped when the phone rang. She waited for the message to play for the caller before the message tape clicked on.

"Ms. Cassidy, this is Lyle Wright with the *L.A. Times.* I'd like to talk to you about Jason Palmer's case and your reaction to today's arrest." He left a phone number and hung up.

It barely clicked off when the phone rang again.

"Alex, this is Michael. Have you seen the news yet?"

She ran for the phone. "Hi, yes, I just saw a report," she said breathlessly. "I'd say he's dug himself a hole he won't be able to climb out of easily."

"Are you all right?" he asked, concern coloring his voice. "All the newspeople are saying they're trying to reach you for a comment."

"Simon was here for a meeting, so I wouldn't be surprised if he returns to his office to find messages from some of them. I just let the machine pick up my calls while he was here and I didn't listen to the messages since the volume was kept low," she explained. "Whether I like it or not, I'll have to say something to someone, but I want to talk to Simon first and see if he has any suggestions. He knows how to handle this kind of situation. Talk about unwanted excitement in my life," she said wryly.

"Perhaps you should think about staying at my place for a while," he suggested. "At least until things die down. If someone is stubborn enough, they could find out where you live and camp on your doorstep."

While the idea sounded wonderful, she knew she had to protest. "It's a generous offer, Michael, but I have work to do. Besides, I doubt this scandal is going to last for more than a few days. By tomorrow something new will turn up. I hope," she murmured under her breath.

"I heard that."

"Um, you've got sharp ears, Doctor."

"It's a good thing I do. Damn, I'm being paged. You know where I am if you need me. I'll come by when I get off duty."

"Michael," she spoke swiftly. "If there's a chance there are reporters downstairs, don't come up. Please. I don't want you involved in all this."

"I'm already involved," he said quietly just before he hung up.

Alex was left holding a receiver connected to dead air. "The man is getting serious," she said to herself, then cursed when she belatedly remembered she had two pair of ears avidly listening to every word. After more than one taste of their trade secrets, she sensed they could hear what Michael said without even bothering to use the bedroom extension!

"If what's-'is-name had to get into trouble, I don't know why he had to drag your name into it," Patrick grumbled.

Alex picked up Suzi Q and settled the cat into her lap, stroking the smooth fur to remain calm. "He didn't. Not deliberately. It just took a reporter some digging to learn we've been dating exclusively for the past couple of years."

This time when the phone rang she wasn't surprised to hear Simon's excited voice on the answering-machine speaker ordering her to pick up the phone.

"Ah, we're playing with our car phone again, aren't we?" she asked playfully, knowing full well why he called. As far as Simon was concerned, the only decent radio stations were those that were all news. "Don't you know talking on a car phone while on the freeway is dangerous?"

"Congratulations on getting involved in a financial swindle, kid," he said crisply.

"That was Jason's department, not mine. I merely attended a few business dinners with him. In fact, I was going to call you later and see how you wanted to handle this. I'm already receiving calls from reporters asking for my reaction to Jason's arrest." She knew that would soothe his fevered brow. Simon loved to feel in control. And she loved to let him handle all the dirty work!

"I'll set something up in my office," he said promptly. "Who's called so far?" He hummed under his breath as he listened. "All right, I'll make the calls and let you know when. It's a good thing he never tried to get his hands on your portfolio. Word is he's left some of his investors in dire straits. If anyone else calls just tell them 'no comment' and refer them to my office."

Alex hung up with a sigh of relief. "I'm glad he's willing to put up with this mess, because I'd probably insult them and only make matters worse." She looked at her parents. "I draw cartoons and live a fairly normal life. How could I get caught up in something like this, even if only on the fringes? I really pick them. An ex-husband who never learned the meaning of fidelity and an ex-boyfriend who's turned out to be a crook."

"I knew he was no good the first time I saw him," Patrick happily inserted.

"Dad, if you dare say I told you so, I will find a way to make eternity miserable for you," Alex said amiably. "And I'm sure Mom will be only too happy to help me out."

Patrick issued a long-suffering sigh that was more dramatic than sincere. "It's a father's prerogative to worry about his little girl."

"Except the little girl is now thirty years old," she reminded him.

"Don't worry dear, he can't do anything," Marian assured her. "Besides, we're only here to see you married, not to advise you on anything else. Even if I would like to see Jason Palmer ground into pâté." Her mother's fierce expression brought laughter bubbling out of Alex.

"I can't believe how bloodthirsty the two of you are." She shook her head. "Okay, I'm going to bury myself in my work until Michael shows up." She headed for her office, but first quickly turned to her mother. "And don't worry about fixing us dinner. I'd like to make something for him."

"Well, if you insist, but I had thought of doing something with that roast you have in your freezer."

Alex thought about the burned roasts she'd consumed during her childhood. She couldn't hold back her shudder. "Honest, Mom, I want to cook," she choked, adding what she knew her mother would love to hear. "Besides, it would make a good impression." The pleased expression on her mother's face told her she'd said just the right thing.

She should have known her day would be full of interruptions, between phone calls and a visit from Beth.

"I want to hear everything," she informed her friend, breezing through the front door. "You've got a gem in Michael, Alex. You better hold on to him tight."

"Yes, but it's playing havoc with both our lives," she sighed, pouring cups of coffee for both of them, handing one of the cups to Beth.

She eyed her speculatively. "Then you've decided to give him a chance."

"Let's just say we're going to see where it leads," Alex murmured, concentrating on her coffee. "We've both been burned and we don't care to go through it again."

"We all make mistakes and we just learn to bounce right back from them," Beth pointed out. "Look at some of the losers I've dated over the years. And if you remember, I dated only two doctors." She ticked them off on her fingers. "There was that landscaping contractor who turned out to be married. And that associate in Simon's office who wanted to tie me to his bed with silk scarves." She grimaced. "My best bet was that cop who fainted at the sight of his own blood, and while the chemistry was fine for me, it wasn't for him. I really hated to give him up," she sighed. "Good men aren't easy to find. But I'd say you've hit the jackpot with Michael."

"I'm afraid of making another mistake," she confessed.

Beth uttered a low-pitched shriek. "Take a chance! You won't know unless you dive in." She looked closer at Alex. "And you have," she whispered. "You and Michael—?" she burst out laughing in joy. "You have!"

"You'll have to repeat yourself, Beth. I don't think the people in the next county heard you. Better yet, post it on the hospital bulletin board," she grumbled.

Beth scrambled off the stool and threw her arms around her friend. "You hardly let Jason stay in this apartment more than five minutes, you finally admitted what you felt for Craig was more lust than love and you and Michael have slept together! I'm happy for you, but I also want you to know that even though you're my best friend I also hate you for snatching up one of the best men around. Find out if he has a brother, even a distant cousin will do.''

''Beth, don't get too excited just yet. We're playing it cautious,'' Alex burst out, stunned by her friend's exuberance. ''I admit I feel more for Michael than I've ever felt for any man, but I want to be sure it's something lasting. Something real. Neither of us cares to be hurt anymore. Although,'' she said slowly, ''as far as I'm concerned, it's very real. And I have a hunch Michael feels the same way.''

''All I ask is one thing. If for some reason the two of you don't work out, you'll put a good word in for me.''

Alex rolled her eyes. If Beth wasn't her best friend, she'd cheerfully hit her. ''Go home, Beth.''

''Friends share, Alex.''

''Go home, now.''

''I'd do the same for you,'' she added magnanimously.

''Beth, home.''

''All right, you don't have to tell me more than once,'' Beth said, amused she had gotten her friend's goat. As she reached the door, her expression sobered and she turned around. ''Alex, you haven't told anyone about seeing your parents, have you?'' she asked delicately.

''My resident ghosts, you mean?''

She winced. ''Alex, please don't do this. Most people just aren't going to understand what you've gone through and they might take it the wrong way.''

Alex couldn't help but feel a little hurt that her closest friend didn't believe her.

''No, Beth, I haven't told anyone else. Only someone who has a ghostly relative living with them could understand what I'm going through. I don't think that's someone I can meet through the personals columns, do you?''

Beth looked uneasy. She knew Alex wasn't one to make jokes like this about her parents, but the idea of them coming back just because there was the chance she might have married Jason and they wanted to see her married to someone else? Still, stranger things had happened. Deciding silence was more than golden on that particular subject right now, she smiled and hugged Alex.

"If you'd like, I'll give you that cop's number," she offered. "He's really cute if you like the Mel Gibson type in a beard."

The tiniest of smiles cracked her face. "Goodbye, Beth."

Afterward, Alex noticed that her parents had also disappeared. And for the first time, she felt more than a little unhappy at not having them around.

"I must be getting used to them," she murmured, hoping this time she would succeed in hiding away in her office. "I wonder if there's a strip in visiting the great scandals of the world."

MICHAEL WAS BONE-TIRED. While he appreciated busy shifts more than slow ones, he ached at the reason behind the increased activity. While a part of him wanted nothing more than to crawl into his apartment bed and sleep for the next week, he knew he wouldn't rest easy until he saw Alex. Funny how important she had become to him in such a short period of time. Where she was concerned, his usually cautious nature was taking a nosedive.

Even now, as he twisted his neck from side to side to relieve the aching muscles, he was climbing out of his car and heading for Alex's apartment building front door instead of his own.

He yawned widely as he leaned on her doorbell.

"You look terrible," was her greeting after she threw open the door.

"Actually, I feel like something a steamroller ran over," he told her. "I hope you looked through the peephole before you opened the door."

"Of course, I don't let just any degenerate inside." She steered him to the couch and with a light pressure on his chest pushed him onto the cushions. "Sit down and relax. I'll fix you something to eat."

He smothered a yawn. "Actually, if you don't mind, what I'd really like is a long, hot shower."

Alex smiled. "The hot water is more than plentiful. But are you sure you can remain awake long enough to take one? You can barely stand now."

His head bobbed once. "Oh, yeah." His first attempt at pushing himself away from the cushions failed.

She swallowed a chuckle. She crossed her arms at the wrist and held them out. "Grab on and I'll pull you up."

With help Michael was able to stand up, swaying only slightly with fatigue.

"There's clean towels," she informed him, steering him through the bedroom. "You're out of luck for clean clothes, though."

"I'm glad to hear that. Unless, of course, they're mine." He walked into the tiled room and started to close the door, then halted, calling Alex's name. She reappeared with a questioning look on her face. "I forgot something." He dipped his head and kissed her about as thoroughly as a very tired man could. "That's better," he murmured, closing the door.

Alex stood at the door, pressing her throbbing lips with her fingertips. "If he knows better, he'll take a cold shower to wake himself up."

After deciding a light meal would be better for Michael, Alex waited about ten minutes, then fixed an omelet and dropped bread in the toaster. When the food was finished, she realized she couldn't hear the shower running anymore and decided it might be a good idea to investigate.

"You didn't drown, did you?" she asked lightly, walking through the bedroom doorway. It only took a second to find the answer to her question. A sound-asleep and naked Michael lay sprawled on his back across her bed with the covers tossed down to the end of the mattress.

She bent over and carefully arranged the sheet and blanket across him. The faint hint of peppermint emanated from his skin. Alex never knew her herbal soap could smell so sexy. As she drew back, she watched Michael mutter something unintelligible and turn over onto his stomach.

"So much for best-laid plans," she laughed softly, closing the bedroom door when she returned to the living room.

MICHAEL'S FACE SCRUNCHED up in a frown as he slowly awakened in the dark room that he hazily recognized as Alex's. He was relieved to know he wasn't so tired he didn't know where he was. Exhaling a sigh, he rolled over and opened one eye. Two bright blue eyes that appeared to glow in the dark stared unwaveringly back at him.

"Hi, cat."

He was unsure whether Suzi Q growled or purred her reply. She remained in her crouched position watching the intruder who dared to use *her* pillow.

"Alex." The word came out husky. He cleared his throat and tried again. "Alex!"

The door opened, allowing a slice of light to streak across the bed. "How was your nap?" She walked in and sat on the end of the bed.

Michael didn't take his eyes off the cat who appeared all too interested in his throat.

"Would you please tell it what a nice guy I am," he requested in a soft voice.

"So that's where you've been, you naughty kitty. I've been looking all over for you," she cooed, picking up the Siamese and draping her over her shoulder. "Don't worry, Suzi Q is perfectly harmless."

"They said the same thing about Cujo and look what happened there." He moved cautiously, even though the cat was restrained by Alex's stroking hand. "You didn't see the way she stared at me as if I was gourmet tuna." He winced at the high-pitched yowl.

"Suzi Q hates tuna," she explained, shifting the cat to her other shoulder. "The word is enough to send her into a kitty tantrum."

Michael sat up, leaning back against the pillow, pushing the other one behind him to add additional bolster. "Sorry I flaked out on you. The shower took what little energy I had left. I barely made it to the bed."

Alex reached out and covered his hand with hers, feeling his body heat radiate upward. "It's natural you'd fall asleep. You looked dead on your feet when you arrived. Do you see me minding?" She accurately guessed the reason. "I'm not her, Michael. Considering your profession, it's understandable there's times when you'll be so tired you'll fall asleep before you can say more than hello." She grinned impishly. "And who says I mind if you fall asleep in my bed?"

He turned his hand over, lacing his fingers through hers. "You're one scary lady, lady."

She arched an eyebrow. *"Moi?"*

His fingers tightened on hers. "You're too understanding."

"Not really." She withdrew her hand and stood up. After depositing Suzi Q outside the bedroom door and closing it securely, she turned around. The dim light in the room only allowed Michael to see Alex's outline.

"I thought you were going to feed me dinner," he said huskily.

"Oh, I will. Eventually." With a cross-armed motion, she pulled her sweater over her head and dropped it to the carpet. Her jeans were unsnapped and the zipper slowly lowered. Shedding them provided Michael with a show of hip action and shimmy he grew to enjoy more by the moment. With a saucy smile on her lips and twitch of her hips, she stepped out of the jeans. Now only wearing a lace-trimmed bra and a narrow lace triangle at her hips that shimmered in the dim light, she stepped forward and placed one knee on the edge of the bed.

"Is..." He coughed to remove the constriction from his throat. "Is this where you begin the seduction?"

"Are you of a mind to be seduced, Doctor Duffy?" Her throaty voice promised untold pleasures as she stalked her way across the bed.

Alex straddled Michael's lap, with a knee on either side, and curled her arms around his neck, giving him an open-mouthed kiss that promised even more dark pleasures. Michael murmured something about having died and gone to heaven. Alex twitched her hips again, feeling his erection push upward.

"Dr. Duffy," she breathed, "when I get finished with you you won't think about dying because the living part will be too much fun." She ran her nails down his arms, which now encircled her waist.

Michael kicked at the restraining sheet and blanket, wanting Alex as close to him as possible. It was sheer agony to have her teasing him like this, but he knew he wouldn't have it any other way.

"Is this another way of showing me what I've been missing?"

"Yes, I guess you could call it that also." She was busy nibbling his ear and trailing her mouth down his neck. "Umm, perfect spot for a hickey."

He closed his eyes, wishing he could find the breath that had been slammed out of his chest when Alex's mouth covered one nipple while she used her tongue to tease it to erection. By the time her mouth drifted its way across his belly, he didn't care if he never breathed again.

Chapter Fourteen

"No more! Give me a break, Alex, I can't handle any more! This is not fair."

"Of course you can, Michael." Her purr vibrated across his nerve endings. "Come on, just one more. For li'l ol' me."

"You're killing me! Besides, I know very well one more won't be enough for you. You'll just keep on asking for more."

"Now don't whine. Come on, darling, for me?"

Michael suspiciously eyed the bowl Alex held in her hands. "I'm already in sugar shock."

She pretended to pout. "You told me you'd help me finish this fudge-ripple ice cream."

"Only because I thought you only had a few spoonfuls left. Not an entire half gallon." He held his stomach and groaned. "I need protein!"

Alex spooned up more of the frozen concoction and carried it to her mouth. She smacked her lips as the rich fudge and creamy vanilla slid over her tongue and tickled her taste buds.

"Now, this is heaven," she cooed, closing her eyes.

"I thought we already discovered that place about an hour ago." Michael took the spoon out of her hand and scooped up some ice cream for himself. "I'm probably sprouting at least ten cavities."

Alex shook her head, chastising him at the same time. "That's a doctor's mentality for you. For once, forget about cholesterol levels and hardening arteries. Think about the moment. About what's so good you're willing to risk anything for it."

He leaned over and brushed a lingering kiss across her lips. "Just as I'm risking my sanity being with you," he murmured.

Her lips parted slightly, inviting a deeper investigation which made them forget about the ice cream. By the time they returned to the present they found only a soupy mess in the bowl. Alex got up to carry it into the kitchen.

"I think you're right—it's time for something a bit more substantial," she said. "How about toasted cheese sandwiches?"

Michael stretched out on the couch, pulling a couple of throw pillows behind his head. "Anything that isn't one-hundred-percent sugar sounds good to me." He yawned. "Want any help?"

She looked over the breakfast bar. "Considering the way you look, I doubt you could stand for more than five seconds. It's as if your nap didn't help."

"Oh the nap helped, all right. It was what happened *after* the nap that took all the starch out of me." His eyes gleamed with devilment.

For a woman who had been so brazen less than an hour before, Alex's cheeks turned a surprisingly bright pink. She ducked out of sight. "Yes, well, it seemed like a good idea at the time."

"Do you hear me complaining?"

Alex pulled the electric frying pan from the cabinet and put out bread, cheese, bacon, mayonnaise and butter on the counter. She quickly assembled the sandwiches and set them in the heated pan.

"I guess it's a good thing we left for a while."

She gasped and spun around, pressing her hand against her heart. "Don't you ever do that again!" she panted, wide-eyed. "You almost scared me to death!"

Marian smiled and eyed the shirt Alex wore. The same shirt Michael had worn when he'd walked into the apartment earlier. "Is it safe to go into the living room? What I mean to say is, is he properly clothed, even if he's without his shirt?"

Alex's eyes grew even wider. "You have to get out of here, right away," she whispered harshly.

"Alex, he can't see us."

"Dad! Oh, my God. Dad will do something horrible, I just know it!" she moaned, pounding the counter with her fists. "Why did I have to turn thirty now? Why did this have to happen?"

"There's a half-naked man in Alex's living room and I won't tell you what the bedroom looks like." Patrick suddenly appeared next to Marian.

In all her agitation Alex didn't notice that her father wasn't as upset as she expected, considering the circumstances.

"I used to have such a normal life!" she wailed.

"Alex, is something wrong?" Michael called out in a sleepy voice.

She muttered a curse under her breath. "No, I usually talk to myself while I cook."

"Your explanations get weaker all the time," Patrick pointed out.

"No thanks to you two."

"Chloe is so happy this is turning out so well." Marian reached behind Alex and flipped the sandwiches. "Dear, you should watch these more carefully. They were ready to burn.''

Alex breathed deeply three times and seriously thought about primal-scream therapy. She wondered if calling Dr. Ruth could give her some answers on how to handle her parents, who just happen to be ghosts, so they don't blow it with the newest man in her life. The idea blossomed. There was no doubt in her mind that she didn't want to lose Michael. The only scary part was that it was happening so quickly and she couldn't help but fear for a relationship that was growing at such a rapid speed. What she'd shared with Craig in the beginning was nothing, compared to what she'd already had with Michael.

Was there something going on that she hadn't figured out yet? A frightening thought kept sneaking in. What if her parents had something to do with all this? What if somehow they had bewitched her and Michael into believing they were falling for each other? Perhaps even falling in love? Wouldn't that be a miserable joke on everyone, after all her high and mighty talk about never falling for another doctor? The idea was enough to leave a bitter taste in her mouth.

''Don't even think it, Alex,'' she ordered herself, feeling the anxiety well up inside. What if that was it? How would she handle knowing all this was nothing more than a ghostly machination that could disappear for good when her parents did?

A pair of arms suddenly snaked themselves around her waist and pulled her back against a warm bare chest. ''Talking to yourself is a sure sign you're losing your marbles,'' he murmured in her ear.

She couldn't help smiling. ''Is that a medical opinion?''

''My usual medical opinion is complete bed rest for that particular ailment. Of course, it does depend on the patient.''

"Is sex all that boy thinks about?" Patrick snorted, watching them.

Alex's eyes snapped open. "Get out!"

Michael's embrace loosened. "Excuse me?"

"No, not you," she babbled, turning in his arms. "Suzi Q was in here and I'm trying not to add to her frustration. Ever since that traumatic trip to the vet when her love life was taken care of once and for all, she hates to see any sign of affection between two human beings."

Michael stared at her as if he couldn't believe what he was hearing. "The cat is in the living room using her scratching post."

She uttered a nervous laugh. "I must have thought I saw her."

He reached behind her and switched off the frying pan. "Alex, what is wrong?" he asked quietly. "Is this going too fast for you? Is it me?"

She knew how hard it must have been for him to ask her that last question. She caressed his cheek with her fingertips, loving the slightly rough texture. "Don't ever think that, Michael. While I do feel, sometimes, that this has happened too fast, I also know that you're the best thing to come along in my life." She injected every ounce of sincerity she had into her voice. She wanted him to realize she was telling the truth.

His features visibly relaxed. "I made myself sound like a fool."

"No, like a man concerned with a budding relationship." She pushed him gently back a pace. "The glasses are in the cabinet to your right. Why don't you get us something to drink while I get our sandwiches ready. I'll take some Coke."

While Alex worked, she glared at her parents several times, sending them silent messages they preferred to ignore. She added potato chips to the plates and set them on the table in the dining area.

While he bit into his sandwich Michael eyed Suzi Q, who now stood near the draperies, looking up at thin air and yowling her little heart out.

"You have a very strange cat," he commented.

Alex saw what he couldn't. That her cat was talking away to Marian. And with her luck, her mother understood cat language.

"The little snitch." She glared at her unsuspecting cat. "She's probably giving her all the gory details."

"So who's she supposed to be talking to?"

"My mother," she said unthinking.

He frowned. "I thought your mother died."

"She did, but that didn't stop her and my father from coming back to change my life around." It wasn't until then that Alex realized just exactly what she'd said.

Surprisingly, Michael didn't bat an eye. "My dad thought for sure that my aunt came back to make his life nuts," he commented. "And if anything could do it, it would be my Aunt Chloe."

Alex snapped to attention at that. "Your Aunt Chloe?"

He nodded. "She was something else. Some would say she was the family oddball. I always viewed her as someone magic who breezed in from foreign lands with colorful stories and African tribal war masks or South American fertility idols that drove my mom nuts. Her husband died early in their marriage, leaving her a wealthy woman. Her first trip was to get away from the memories. After that I think she just plain enjoyed it. She died in an airplane crash in Japan several years ago. I still miss her," he said quietly.

"I don't think you believed us when we said he had an Aunt Chloe," Marian chided her daughter. "Just remember Beth's reaction to your story."

Alex idly tore the crusts from her sandwich. "Michael, do you think that people who die before their time can come back to resolve a family matter?" She hoped her question sounded casual enough.

"As a member of the logical scientific community I would have to say no, but who knows what can happen," he replied, picking up a potato chip and biting into it. "It's a pretty unknown factor. Why?"

"Would you think I'm crazy if I told you that my parents returned the night of my thirtieth birthday, because they died before their time, and they won't leave until they see me properly married?" she asked in a rush.

He studied her long and hard. There was no humor in her voice or face, just a longing to be believed. "And I can't see them?"

She shook her head, quickly pushing back the heavy strand of hair that strayed across her lips. "Just me and Suzi Q, which can make it very strange at times—such as now when she's talking to my mother. The morning when breakfast burned in my kitchen, that was my mother. She always burns the meals. And no matter what they say, I think they had something to do with what happened at the softball field—although they swore up and down they can't leave the apartment."

"I'd like to know what happened at the softball field," Patrick spoke up.

"Not now!" Alex turned on her father. She appealed to Michael. "My father may be dead, but that hasn't stopped him from acting like a heavy-handed father out of a fifties movie."

Michael didn't speak for several moments. "As I said, my dad talked about Aunt Chloe coming back. Her reason was because she didn't feel he was administering her trust properly. She said she was going to stick around until she knew he was being true to her wishes. It sounds as if they come back with the best intentions. Just like your parents. I gather they didn't approve of your investment-banker friend."

She shook her head. "Dad could never remember Jason's name and Mom thought he was a stuffed shirt. They were both ecstatic when he ended up in jail. Jail, oh no! I turned down the volume on my answering machine and Simon probably called about the newspaper interview." She started to get up, but Michael grasped her wrist.

"Considering it's four o'clock in the morning, I don't think he'd appreciate a call," he said dryly. "Finish your sandwich and then we'll talk more about your parents."

She was a bit suspicious. "When I told Beth about them she decided my concussion had done more damage than anyone thought, and she was getting ready to call the men in the white coats to come and take me away. My parents warned me that no one would believe me, but they kept talking about your Aunt Chloe and how she wanted to see you happy." She held her hands out to him. "That's what scares me, Michael. What if they used some kind of ghostly hocus-pocus to make us fall for each other?" There, she finally voiced the fear that had been growing inside of her.

"Honestly, Alex, we're ghosts, not witches," Patrick said with disgust.

Michael took hold of her hands, massaging the cold limbs. "If so, we've got a lot to thank them for."

"Do we? Because if it's true what we have isn't real," she insisted.

"Alex, what are you trying to pull now?" Patrick roared, throwing his arms around in wide circles.

"Are you trying to say that I only think I'm falling in love with you? That it's nothing more than a ghost's trick?" Michael said quietly, too quietly.

There was no mistaking the pain in his voice. "No, never that. It's just that if you knew some of the other stunts they pulled you'd understand why I'm so hesitant." She paused to gather up her thoughts. "All of this started because of them, not me. Michael, I didn't send you those flowers, they did."

A trace of skepticism crossed his face. "How?"

"By using my VISA card!" she screeched. "All right, it sounds so crazy it isn't even funny, but it's true. I ended up in the emergency room because I was starting to tell Beth about them and my father tripped me. That's how I fell and hurt my head." In between words, she tore off tiny pieces of her sandwich and popped them into her mouth. "I'm making it worse, aren't I? Okay, just lock me up in that padded cell. I'll go quietly."

She looked so sad, Michael knew he had to put her out of her misery as soon as possible.

"Are they still here?"

She nodded, a hangdog look on her face.

"And they somehow know my Aunt Chloe?"

Another short nod.

"How can they know her?"

"Any time I ask how something is done all I get is that it's a trade secret. That would be the answer to your question, too," she said softly.

"If Michael wants proof, tell him that his aunt still wears those incredible pink harlequin sunglasses straight from the fifties," Marian told Alex. "And that she told me about the time he was ten and broke his collarbone falling out of a tree where he'd been sitting with a pair of binoculars watching the girl across the street undress in her bedroom."

Alex's misery suddenly disappeared as she burst out laughing. "You sly thing," she chided Michael. "You were a ten-year-old Peeping Tom!"

Now Michael was the shocked one. "What?"

"You broke your collarbone falling out of a tree where you'd been spying on a neighbor of the feminine persua-

sion," she chortled. "I love it! And you tried to tell me you
were bland and boring. Puleeze!"

"Her name was Missy," Marian went on.

Alex nodded. "And her name was Missy."

"This is crazy," he finally announced.

"Now do you believe me?"

"You're making an excellent case for yourself." He
pushed away the rest of his sandwich. His earlier hunger was
gone. There was no way Alex could have known about that
episode. Not when he'd grown up in a different town, much
less a different state, than she had. And no one at the hospital would have known about something he hadn't even
thought of in years. And now Alex, of all people, was the
one to remind him! "And I thought this only happened in
books and movies," he muttered.

"You weren't the one to wake up and find them staring
at you while you were convinced you were dying from a
hangover," she said dryly. "Think how I felt? Actually,
when I first woke up I thought I was dead. After all, my
head felt as if a herd of buffalo had run through it and I
couldn't see very straight except for my parents standing in
front of me. Then I tried to convince myself they were part
of my hangover. Except they refused to go away and they
still do."

"Tell him why," Marian chimed in.

Alex frowned at her mother. "I'd rather not."

Michael looked puzzled. "You'd rather not what?"

She sighed. "I'd rather not remind you that the reason
they're here is to see me properly married off and I'm afraid
they're eyeing you for their next victim, so I'd understand
it if you suddenly decided you had an important appointment elsewhere," her voice trailed off.

A corner of Michael's mouth lifted. "Were they around
last night while we . . . ?"

She looked horrified at the thought. "No! They wouldn't dare do that!" She turned to her mother. "Would you?"

"Of course not. We respect your privacy."

Michael stood up and pulled Alex to her feet. "Are you through destroying that sandwich?"

She nodded, wary of what was coming next.

"Go throw some clothes on, while I clear up in here," he ordered. "We are going out."

"Where can we go at four in the morning?" Now she was confused.

"You said they can't leave the apartment, right?" Michael said, picking up their plates and carrying them into the kitchen.

"That's what they assured me, yes."

He turned around and grinned at her. "Then they can't invade my apartment, can they?"

"Do you mean you believe me?" she asked in a hushed whisper. "That you don't think I'm ready for the funny farm or should be fitted for a size-eight straitjacket?"

Michael hesitated, but he knew he could do no more than give her the truth. She deserved nothing less. "I'm not sure, but I'd like to believe I'm open-minded enough to think it, though. Not to mention you're bringing up a part of my colorful past few people would know about," he said wryly. "Go get dressed so I can have my shirt back, and we'll try a less populated place. That is, if you want to."

Alex fairly flew into her bedroom and returned in five minutes dressed in dark green twill pants and a coordinated print shirt, with Michael's shirt in one hand and her purse in the other. What he noticed most was the glow in her eyes. This was one lady who admitted she wasn't sure if what they shared was real, but she was obviously going to give it her all until they could find out for sure.

"I WAS RIGHT," Alex pronounced, looking around the living room with open satisfaction. "All the color made a big difference." She adjusted the tall vase with silk flowers a fraction of an inch and stood back, gazing at it with a critical eye. "It really should be something a bit more oval," she decided.

"Enough decorating," he ordered, walking up beside her and handing her a glass of wine.

Alex accepted the glass before settling herself on the couch, curling up with her back resting against Michael's chest after he stretched out on top of the cushions with a throw pillow behind his head.

"Considering it's nearly dawn, I should be so tired I can't think straight," she commented, sipping her wine.

"Considering our lack of sleep, we should be unconscious," he said dryly, rubbing her neck with his supple fingers. "Besides, the wine will knock us both out."

Alex closed her eyes and allowed herself to relax under Michael's ministrations.

"You know, I love my parents, but some of the stuff going on now is enough to drive me crazy," she murmured. "Before I had a chance to worry how they did one thing, I'd learn they'd gotten into even more trouble. I still think they were behind the fiasco at the restaurant with Jason. Cherries Jubilee doesn't just slide down a table and end up in a man's lap without some help. And we won't even talk about the spirals of smoke that kept appearing and disappearing around a no-smoking room."

Michael didn't say anything as he continued rubbing the taut muscles along the top of her back. He had his own opinion regarding Alex's ghostly parents, but he didn't want to voice them out loud. Especially when he knew his comments would not be welcome. He admitted he couldn't figure out how Alex knew about his one indiscretion during his tenth year. Not even the shapely fourteen-year-old Missy

Scott ever knew that she was the reason behind his broken collarbone. For now, he'd remain silent and let Alex ramble on. Perhaps if she talked enough, he would figure out where all this came from.

Alex's voice slowed and her body turned boneless until Michael heard nothing but her soft indrawn breaths. He smiled. She'd talked herself to sleep. With a bit of careful maneuvering, he picked her up and carried her into his bedroom. In no time, both were undressed and under the covers with Michael pulling her back into his arms. He couldn't help smiling. He was right the first time, when he sensed things would be vastly different with Alex around. He decided he liked it. And loved her. Now all he had to do was thoroughly convince her that keeping this particular doctor in her life would be the best thing she could do. After all that had happened, he didn't think he'd have all that much trouble. He smiled. Well, if he did, it appeared there were two ghosts on his side, and right now he'd take any assistance he could get.

"MICHAEL, FOR A DOCTOR your eating habits are deplorable." Alex studied the almost bare interior of the refrigerator.

"No use in keeping food here when I'm rarely home," he explained, pouring two cups of coffee. "As long as I have some caffeine to get me going enough to reach the hospital or the nearest fast-food restaurant, I'm happy."

"Fast food? Did you sleep through nutrition classes? Don't you lecture patients on the high amounts of cholesterol, fat and sodium found in those places? Michael, you should be ashamed of yourself," she tsked, shaking her head. "A fine example you're setting."

"Don't forget I've seen your refrigerator. At least I don't keep a cheesecake in the freezer."

"I'm keeping it there for a friend, so she won't be tempted to eat it."

The expression on Michael's face told her what he thought of that explanation.

"Would you believe it's part of my emergency rations for when the big earthquake hits? I don't want to be left without my favorite cheesecake," she asked brightly.

"You're getting better," he admitted, admiring the quick turns her mind navigated.

"It's also a dairy product, which is very important for one's health," Alex added piously.

Michael burst out laughing. He pulled her into his arms for a hug. "That's the best one yet, Alex."

She felt her temperature rise the moment her body brushed against his. Even though they'd made love when they'd woken up, she felt the need again. The need to know they were more one person than two. Funny, she'd never felt that intense need with anyone else, and here this slow-smiling, soft-spoken doctor only had to look at her and her knees buckled! Judging from the glitter in his eyes, he easily read her thoughts.

"Did you mean what you said, about falling in love with me?" she whispered.

Any time for lighthearted words and teasing was past. "Yes."

Her face glowed. "Then you wouldn't be averse to having that love returned."

He had been afraid to hope from the beginning. "Not one bit."

Alex ducked her head. "I'm still nervous about all this. I mean, it's so fast after Jason." She stopped abruptly. "I guess I'm just afraid to trust my own judgment."

He combed his fingers through her hair. "That's understandable, Alex, but I'm not Jason and I don't see you as Andrea. That should be more than enough for us to realize what we share is something very special and what I feel could be lasting, if we're willing to work for it."

She licked her lips. "I'm willing."

He grazed her lips with his. "Then I suggest we should seal the deal."

"Deals are usually sealed with a handshake," she whispered, moving closer into his embrace.

"Yes, but most deals aren't like ours."

Chapter Fifteen

Alex never liked being interviewed, and when the interviewer tried to infer a story that wasn't there, she liked it even less. She was glad Simon was present during the interview as she politely explained that she and Jason Palmer were only good friends. *Why hadn't she allowed him to handle her investment portfolio?* Because she used the same broker her father had dealt with for many years. Fair enough? As if that wasn't bad enough, she arrived home to discover the police had called and asked if she could come down to the station to answer a few questions. Just wanting it all over with, she called and arranged an afternoon appointment with the detective in charge of the case.

"Once upon a time, I had a nice sane life," she sighed, after setting up her appointment at the police station.

"Knew he was a crook the first time I met him," Patrick announced.

They're back! Alex's mind sang out. "Correction, you thought he was wrapped a little too tight," she said out loud. "There's a big difference."

Patrick's eyes narrowed. "Why'd you go over to his place?"

"So Michael wouldn't have to listen to you snore," she told him sweetly.

"I don't snore."

"Yes, you do. Dad, there were nights I wondered if Amtrak was coming through the house."

He pulled himself up. "I don't snore anymore."

She looked interested. "Really?"

"Really."

Marian nodded. "It took death to stop his snoring. Ignore his inquisition, dear. He's just trying to act the part of the heavy-handed father." She looked eager. "Have you and Michael come to any decisions?"

"Mom, it hasn't been all that long since I broke up with Jason! I've only been seeing Michael a few weeks." She could tell right away that they weren't listening.

"If he's done anything improper, he'll have to marry you," Patrick said darkly.

Alex had to laugh. "Sure, Dad, and you'll be right there at the altar carrying a shotgun, won't you?" she teased. "Believe me, he did nothing improper." A streak of wickedness made her add, "Of course, that doesn't mean I wasn't more than a little improper. Who knows, perhaps his father might be coming after me with a shotgun."

Patrick shook his head. "She's *your* daughter," he told Marian.

"Better they find out if they're sexually compatible now than be disappointed later," she replied.

"Whatever happened to the good old days?" he sighed.

"Dad, you're acting like a typical father," Alex said. "And that's part of the good old days I don't mind. Probably because I know he can't see or hear you. I'm going to run some errands before I stop by the police station. Stay out of trouble, okay?" She picked up her purse and slung the strap over her shoulder.

"I knew we did the right thing getting them together," Marian could be heard to say as Alex left.

Her mother's words nagged at her during her drive downtown.

"What did they do to get us together?" she asked herself, pulling into a covered parking structure next to the shopping mall. "The more I say this, the more I don't like it."

All the time Alex did her shopping, picking up some new makeup and skin-cleansing products, the words stayed with her—and the same niggling question. Could her parents have waved a ghostly wand and performed a little magic to cause her to be attracted to Michael? Except attracted was a little too tame a word to describe what she felt for him. She was too uneasy to even think about that four-letter word that began with an *L*. Pushing it firmly out of her mind, she entered one store after another, shopping with mad abandon, something she wasn't known for. By the time she staggered to her car loaded down with packages, she was considerably poorer but no lighter in spirit.

Her afternoon at the police station turned out to be less than pleasant. The detective, a Rob Carson, seemed to believe Alex knew much more than she let on.

"You've said that you've had dinner with Mr. Palmer and some of his clients. Surely you remembered what was discussed," he went on.

"For the twenty-millionth time, I was there to occupy the wife while the men discussed business," she snapped at him coldly. "I did not listen to their conversation."

He doodled on a sheet of paper. "Did Palmer ever leave any papers with you, computer disks, anything he asked you to keep safe?"

She looked him square in the eye. "No, now that I look back on that time, he considered me nothing more than a distraction for the wives."

"You're not making this easy for us, Ms. Cassidy."

"Detective, I came down here of my own free will and am answering your ridiculous questions to the best of my knowledge. If you try to infer I had something to do with Jason's illegal business dealings, then you're not a very good sleuth. And if you continue to act like the 'bad cop' without a 'good cop' around to balance things out, I will insist on having my attorney present during the rest of this questioning,'' she coolly informed him.

The man's face darkened. ''Ms. Cassidy, we've got your boyfriend on a mass of charges that will keep him in jail for a very long time. If there are any accomplices, we want to put them away, too.'' It was clear who he was talking about.

''I will say this once more and that is it. Jason Palmer and I parted company several weeks ago for personal reasons.''

''Ms. Cassidy, in this type of crime personal reasons don't cut it. What happened between the two of you?''

She barely stopped herself from grinding her teeth. She finally decided it wouldn't hurt to tell him. ''I'm sure when you looked through that fancy burgundy leather Day-Runner of his, you not only saw his five-year plan but the names of the people he met with after business hours. He came to me not long ago, insisting he wanted to take over my investment portfolio. I refused and he turned a bit heavy-handed. I threw him out and haven't seen nor heard from him since.''

Detective Carson's brow wrinkled. ''Burgundy Day-Runner? The man had a gray leather Filofax in his brief-case.''

Alex looked puzzled. ''That's strange, because I gave him the DayRunner for his birthday last year and that's what I always saw him use.''

The man slapped the table with his palm. ''That's how he did it!'' He jumped up, then suddenly leaned on the table-top. ''Did he have a safe in his home we would have had trouble finding?''

Alex shrugged, still trying to piece together what was going on. ''I don't know. I've never been in his home.''

He looked incredulous. ''You've been dating the guy for more than two years and you were never in his home?''

"Strange but true. Am I to gather I said something good?"

"Could be." He was back to the "bad cop" syndrome.

She looked at her watch, stunned to see she'd been there for three hours. "Then you're not going to mind if I leave now?"

"You won't mind coming back in to identify the Day-Runner when we find it, will you?"

Taking that as a yes, Alex stood up. "I'll make it easy for you. Jason's name is stamped in gold on the front and in the back you'll find a small card that I gave him when I gave him the book. Thank you for a lovely afternoon, Detective. Have a nice day." She swept out.

He was past hearing her sarcasm since he was too busy talking rapidly into the phone.

Considering the hour, the last thing Alex wanted to do was fight rush-hour traffic home, and she decided to stop by the hospital in case Michael could take a quick coffee break.

Traffic on the surface streets was heavy but moving, so it didn't take her long to reach the hospital. Inside the waiting area she found several people seated in chairs, leafing through magazines or talking quietly. One young girl held a bandaged arm, her face streaked with tears.

"Hi, Alex," Beth greeted her. "Don't tell me you're back here for treatment?"

She shook her head. "I thought Michael might sneak away for a cup of coffee, but I see how busy it is." She started to back her way toward the door.

"Actually it's fairly slow and we've got Dennis here," her friend told her. "I was drafted down here a little while ago when all hell was breaking loose after a school-yard accident brought in a bunch of third-graders. Why don't you go on to the cafeteria and I'll send Michael down in a few minutes."

"Sounds good."

Beth paused. "I saw Jason on the news last night."

Alex smiled. "I think a lot of people did. I don't think he visualized becoming famous that way."

"Things are really turning surprising," she went on with a sly smile. "You breaking up with Jason and ending up with Michael." Her eyes twinkled with laughter. "The man walks around with the sappiest grin at times, but we don't have the heart to tease him. He looks too happy. It's almost like magic," she brightly concluded, then looked beyond Alex as paramedics rushed in. "Back to work. I'll tell Michael you're in the cafeteria," she threw over her shoulder as she ran back to the examination cubicles with the paramedics.

It's almost like magic. The words sounded more and more like a curse to Alex's ears as she took the elevator downstairs.

Yep, a curse, she wearily decided when she almost ran into her ex-husband who was leaving the cafeteria just as she arrived.

"For someone who swore off doctors, you sure did a complete turnaround," he sneered. "Or is it some kind of pity thing, since the guy doesn't have good luck with women?"

"Craig, remember that night I kicked you out?" Her voice was amiable, too amiable.

He stilled. "I *walked* out."

"Your memory is slipping. I kicked you out, just after I kicked you somewhere else because you tried to weasel your way back into bed with me after I confronted you about your affairs. While Michael has threatened to rearrange your face, I'd prefer to damage parts south." She noticed with malicious satisfaction that he had started to back away from her. "Good idea. The more I see you, the more I know that my time with you was most definitely caused by temporary insanity. Do us all a favor, Craig, and grow up. A man of forty-two shouldn't act like this."

"I am not forty-two," he hissed, his handsome features looking ugly under his rage.

"If I say you're forty-two, you're forty-two, and who are people going to believe? You or me?" She bestowed a chilling smile on him and walked off. Alex knew exactly where to strike, and Craig's ego was the most delicate area. The name he called after her was unflattering, but it didn't bother her. After the police detective trying his best to find her guilty of nothing, she considered her run-in with Craig a walk in the park. "Still, the creep deserves more," she murmured, spying a pay telephone on a nearby wall. She quickly snapped her fingers. "Oh yeah, perfect." She rummaged through her wallet for change and quickly thumbed through the telephone book until she found what she was looking for. It didn't take her long to accomplish her task, and when she walked into the cafeteria she had a broad smile on her face.

For a half hour Alex sat in a corner table nursing a cup of coffee and vainly trying to hide her grin of satisfaction.

"Something tells me you've been up to no good." Michael slid into the seat across from her. "Was your interview with the newspaper reporter that bad?" She'd called him earlier to tell him it had been scheduled, and during quiet times he found himself worrying about her.

"He was a bit of a jerk, but no worse than others I've dealt with in the past," she replied, stirring her coffee even though she hadn't put anything in it.

Michael took the stirrer out of her hand and placed it on a napkin. He covered her hand with his. "What's wrong?"

She kept her head down. "Michael, I was a bad girl."

He leaned forward more. "Good-bad or really bad-bad?"

She looked up. There was no disguising the light dancing in her eyes. "About as bad as you can get. I've always wanted to get even with Craig, and I finally came up with the ideal plan."

Michael frowned. "Did he bother you?"

"Not exactly—more like I reminded him of a few things. Such as I know his real age and I know his weakness." She burst into laughter. "Michael, I just ruined his perfect office atmosphere."

He looked confused. "You've lost me."

She looked around to make sure no one overheard her. "Remember I said Craig has a homely nurse in his office because he doesn't want any entanglements there?" She waited for his nod. "Well, in Craig's name I sent her two dozen roses and a five-pound box of candy with a note of appreciation for all the excellent work she'd done for him."

He sat back. "Alex, I don't see how you can think that's funny. What if she has a crush on him? When she says something about the candy and roses he'll say something to hurt her."

She burst out laughing. "No way. You see, Matilda thinks he's the scum of the earth because of the way he treats women. She only stays with him because he pays her so well. When she gets the flowers and candy she'll either flatten him or threaten to quit, and he can't afford the latter, so if nothing else she'll get a huge raise out of this. Unless she blackens his eye or something," she reflected. "I'd sure love to see the fireworks. I just know they're going to be something else. This woman doesn't take anything off anyone. Even Craig is a little scared of her." She giggled.

"Alex Cassidy, you are an evil woman."

She wrinkled her nose at his playful accusation. "Yeah, but it's so much fun."

"And if it backfires in your face?" he pointed out.

"I don't like logical men."

"I just don't want you to be the loser in this."

"I won't be," she assured him. "He's just going to get what's coming to him, that's all. Besides, I didn't come here to talk about Craig. I came here to see you."

He smiled. "The magic words."

"Is that how you see us, magic?" she murmured, tracing the rim of her cup with her fingertip.

He wasn't sure he caught her meaning. "Is there something wrong with that?"

Alex shrugged. "Just that sometimes magic doesn't last and reality creeps in." She looked up. "I just want to know what we have is real."

For a fleeting moment, Michael felt real anger. "After all that's happened, I can't believe you doubt us."

"I married one man who had two separate lives, I almost married another. I don't think I could go through that kind of shock again," she said bluntly.

"Have I ever given you any reason to believe I'm not who you see?" he demanded hotly.

"No, but neither did they." Alex knew she was walking on shaky ground and would have to tread cautiously. "For two people who have been burned badly in the past we seem to be rushing things. I don't want there to be mistakes on either of our sides, Michael."

"What do you want?" he gritted.

"I want both of us to be happy and to feel secure in what we have."

He opened his mouth to speak, only then to curse under his breath when his name was paged with a code number after it.

"As much as I'd like to hash this out now, I'm needed in the ER," he told her in clipped tones. "I'm a fairly sane adult who knows what he wants and that happens to be you. Maybe you better start thinking about whether I'm what you really want." With that, he walked away.

"Damn," Alex whispered. "I sure know how to mess things up."

ALEX NEVER thought of herself as one to indulge in tears at the drop of a hat. The next twenty-four hours taught her differently.

"You've done some stupid things in your life, but this has got to be the craziest!" Patrick stormed. "The man told you he loves you and you make it sound like he didn't know what he was saying!"

"Hey, for all I know you two had something to do with this, since you and his precious Aunt Chloe seem to think we make the perfect couple!" Alex wailed.

He drew an exasperated breath. "Can't you get it through your thick skull that we can't do anything like that! All we wanted you to do was fall in love with a good man! Then, when you do fall in love, you refuse to believe it."

"I never said I was in love with Michael!" Alex argued, even while she hurt inside. She hadn't heard from him in several days and she couldn't lower her pride enough to call him at the hospital or at his apartment.

"You don't have to! In the past twenty-four hours you've gone through three boxes of Kleenex, two rolls of toilet paper and now you're blowing your nose on a paper towel! You didn't even react when the police called you to tell you they found Jason's secret safe with his DayRunner and files incriminating a lot of people." He threw his hands up. "Doesn't that tell you something?"

"It tells me I need to go grocery shopping." she sniffed.

"Both of you calm down," Marian ordered. "And you calm down, Patrick. She's suffering enough without you bellowing at her."

He glowered at his wife. "I don't bellow."

"Yes, you do." Marian headed for the paper towel holder, only to find it empty and no new rolls under the sink. She handed Alex a napkin. "I'm sure Michael is only trying to give you time to come to terms with all that's happened. You've had a lot to deal with lately." She turned to her husband. "Perhaps it's a good thing Alex has had these few days to decide for herself that we didn't have anything to do with their falling in love. Once she realizes that, they can start planning a future together."

"And if Michael changes his mind?" Alex blew her nose on the napkin and grabbed another one. She dreaded to look in the mirror. She was always a sloppy crier who ended up with a bright red nose, swollen eyes and splotchy skin.

"He won't," Marian said with strong confidence. "I've seen the way he looks at you, and he has love written all over his face."

Alex's head snapped up when the doorbell rang. "No, not now!" she wailed, praying and dreading it was Michael.

"Alex, let me in!" Beth shouted.

"Worse." She sighed, sliding off the bar stool.

Beth couldn't hide her shock when she saw her friend. "You look like hell."

"Thanks, I needed that. I suppose you want to come in," she mumbled.

Beth sat on the chair arm. "Alex, what happened between you and Michael?"

She winced. "Blunt, aren't we?"

"He walks around looking like death warmed over, and you look just as bad. We've been so busy lately that a lot of us are working double shifts, Dr. Duffy included. What else can I be but blunt?"

Alex dabbed carefully at her swollen eyes. "He wanted me to take some time and decide how I really felt about him."

"So you're backing away," she predicted. "The idea of falling for another doctor is frightening you."

She shook her head. "No, I just don't want to enter into another doomed relationship. I've had more than my share, and I'm trying to be cautious this time around."

"I'd say, looking at you, that you've already made up your mind." Beth eyed Alex's wrinkled clothes, which looked as if she'd slept in them, which she had, and her hair hanging limply around a face blotchy from all her tears. To be concise, her friend was a royal mess. "Put the two of you out of your misery and call him, Alex."

"What if he's changed his mind?"

Beth sighed at her friend's stubbornness. "I don't think that should worry you. Still, someone better do something soon," she said before leaving.

"I think I'll go to bed," Alex muttered, walking into the bedroom with dragging steps. She missed Michael so much! But how could she, when they hadn't spent a lot of time together? Except what time they had was the kind of quality time most couples could only dream of. They'd never run out of things to say, subjects to discuss. It was more than sex with them, it was a meeting of the minds. From the time she walked in the apartment sobbing she'd made the biggest mistake of her life, Marian had been baking her brownies and Patrick had been ranting about the instability of the female mind. Alex just remained curled up in a chair crying. By now her head was pounding from all her tears and the smell of burned brownies.

"There's got to be a way to get this settled once and for all," Patrick could be heard muttering as she closed the bedroom door for some much needed privacy while she licked her wounds.

MICHAEL WAS plain miserable. Even work didn't ease his pain this time. And being home was even worse because he couldn't get away from reminders of Alex from the sheets on his bed to the silk flower arrangement on his coffee table. Except he didn't want just things here, he wanted the person who'd placed them here. He wanted Alex.

It had been a rough day, and now he sat on the couch cradling his third beer bottle between his hands and thinking about getting good and drunk. But he knew that wouldn't blot out the pain he'd been carrying around for the past forty-eight hours. At this rate he'd be insane by the time the week was up.

"Why are you so afraid, Alex?" he said out loud. "Why can't you just take a chance? You think I'm not scared of what's gone on between us?"

He tipped the bottle upward, allowing the cool liquid to trickle down his throat. When it was empty he resisted the urge to throw it against the mantel.

Images of Alex flew through his mind: cute and saucy on the softball field, warm and womanly that night they went out to dinner and seductive when they made love. There were so many sides to her, he knew it would take years to discover them all and that's exactly what he wanted from her. Those years.

"Is that so much to ask?" he mumbled, setting the bottle to one side and reaching for another on the coffee table. "I should go over there and tell her she's had more than enough time to figure things out." He conveniently forgot it was his suggestion in the first place. "That we're meant to be together."

He quickly downed his beer and headed into the kitchen for another, unaware his gait was more than a little unsteady.

"You really think that's going to help?"

"I sure do." Michael stopped and spun around. A tall silver-haired man in a blue suit stood in the kitchen doorway. While he didn't know the man, he felt there was something familiar about him. "How did you get in here? Not to mention, who are you?"

The man smiled. "Trade secret, Michael. Yes, I know your name and quite a few other things about you and about Alex. She loves you, you know."

"Yeah, I know, I just don't think she wants to admit it. Wait a minute, how do you know about Alex?" he asked suspiciously.

"Could I give you a suggestion?" the older man went on, ignoring Michael's question. "Go over there and tell her that you're ready to plan a wedding."

"She'd tell me it's too soon for a wedding. In fact, I'm a little leery of going that far myself." Suddenly Michael didn't think it odd to speak to a stranger. "I admit I love her, but we haven't known each other very long."

The man continued smiling and shook his head. "Tell the truth, Michael. You want to tie Alex to you in all the ways you can because you don't want to lose her. She's very special and deserves just the right kind of man. And you're that man. The two of you have suffered enough. Don't let her sit there crying and imagining that you've changed your mind about her. She's a stubborn cuss, but I'm sure you can handle her. You two belong together."

"This is crazy. I still don't see how you..." Michael turned to the refrigerator and pulled out another beer, but when he turned back he found the doorway empty. "Three beers and I'm already seeing things. It's time to take that cold shower."

"WHY DON'T YOU TRY a nice hot bath?" Marian suggested, pushing a reluctant Alex into the bathroom. "You'll feel loads better."

"Mom, I know you see a hot bath as the cure for every ill known to man, but I don't think it's going to work here," she told her wearily.

"You won't know until you try. And use those bath salts you like so much." Marian closed the door.

Alex stared at the door, knowing if her mother could have she probably would have locked it, too. She caught a glimpse of herself in the mirror and winced. "Pretty bad, Alex. You look like something even Suzi Q wouldn't drag in."

She twisted the tub faucets, and while the water ran, she decided it might not hurt to wash her hair, too.

"Let's just go all out." Alex slathered her hair with a special mud conditioning pack, twisting the heavy strands on top of her head, then patted a mud mask on her face which left her red and puffy light-colored eyes glowing eerily from the dark greenish brown circles around them. "This almost looks like an improvement."

After an hour soaking in water that turned from steaming hot to a tolerable cool temperature, Alex had to admit she felt better. She'd just climbed out of the tub when she heard something at her front door.

"What on earth?" She hurriedly donned her robe and left the bathroom. What she could hear was the sound of knocking at the door and then, no, it couldn't be! "Oh, no!"

She raced for the living room only to find the door swinging open and Michael stepping inside.

"That door was locked!" she cried.

"I thought you opened it," he told her, looking around to see if she had company.

"Go away!" Alex moaned, turning around. "Please, go away!"

"No." Before she knew it he stood behind her with his hands on her shoulders. "Enough, Alex. We need to get this straightened out between us."

"Not now!" she wailed, wanting nothing more than to do just that but not when she looked like something out of a horror movie. "At least, let me clean up first."

"Yes, now," he said firmly. "If you want to wait in regards to us getting married, fine, but don't think I'm going to let you put me off for too long. All right, it happened fast for us. So what? It just means we'll have more time together. Is that so wrong? Is it so wrong for us to want to be together all the time?"

"Oh, Michael." Her voice carried pain, but this wasn't your usual lost-love pain. "No, it's not wrong at all."

He stared down at what he knew to be rich brown hair that now was matted with thick mud. When he turned her around, he found her face as gunked up as her hair.

"You don't do this a lot, do you?"

Her lower lip trembled. "Mom said a bath would make me feel better. I figured I might as well pamper the rest of me, too. You shouldn't see me like this." She looked as if she was about to cry, and judging from the swollen red eyes she'd already indulged in more tears than most people shed in a lifetime.

Michael tried hard not to smile. "I may as well see you at your worst, as well as at your best."

She looked up a bit warily. "Really?"

"As real as you can get. Besides, I was told by someone to just get over here and talk to you."

"Beth interfered again," she groaned. "When will she stop?"

Michael shook his head. "No, actually, I think he was a figment of my three beers, but he seemed like a nice guy. Silver hair, stocky build, eyes your color..." his voice trailed off when she stared at him.

"Blue suit?" she asked in a small voice.

He nodded.

Alex walked over to a table and picked up a framed photograph. "Is this him?" She held it out to Michael.

He looked as if he wasn't sure he wanted to touch it. When he looked at the likeness he blanched. "It couldn't have been. It doesn't make any sense. He just appeared out of nowhere and started talking about how I should get over here and get all this straightened out. I had no idea how he got in the apartment or who he was. Next thing I knew he was gone."

Alex spied her parents on the other side of the room, looking proudly at the reunited couple. "I thought you couldn't leave this apartment," she accused.

"Special circumstances," Patrick told her. "And you should be glad I did. He wasn't looking too happy, either."

"It couldn't have happened," Michael muttered, shaking his head, too lost in his own thoughts to notice Alex talking to thin air. "The picture probably just stuck in my mind and somehow those three beers I drank on an empty stomach hit me the wrong way." He didn't sound convincing to anyone, most especially himself.

Alex was eager to wash off the conditioning pack and mud mask, but she was also afraid to leave Michael alone. Still, he'd basically proposed, and that meant her parents were gone. She didn't see them around anywhere. She felt sad they had left so abruptly. She would have liked to have said goodbye. "Thank you," she whispered. "You were right. Michael is perfect for me." She turned to Michael. "Come in the bedroom while I take a quick shower," she urged, grabbing on to his hand. "You're right, we do have a lot of talking to do."

Michael muttered to himself as Alex pushed him onto the bed while she disappeared into the bathroom. Five minutes later, she reappeared with her wet hair slicked back from her newly cleaned face.

"So you feel I've straightened it out in my mind?" she said softly, sitting down beside him.

"You better have, because I'm not staying away any longer. I know how I feel and I don't doubt how you feel. Sometimes I think I've known since the first time I saw you, Alex, concussion and all," he replied. "I want us to go the whole way with marriage, a house and kids. I know we can make it work, as long as we talk things over together." He brushed his knuckles across her cheek.

She touched her bottom lip with her tongue. "You have a way with words, Doctor. And I thoroughly agree with your idea. I want us together, as long as you mean all the time."

Some of the tension as he waited for her answer left his body. "If you don't mind having a roommate. While you cheered my apartment up a great deal, I like yours much better."

She looked down at their clasped hands. "My parents are probably very happy they turned out to be right."

Michael chuckled. "Someday we've got to talk about these so-called ghosts of yours."

"You already saw my father, I think that's enough for you," she told him wryly. "I'd still like to know how he got over to your apartment."

Michael lay back against the bed. "Later. Right now, we have other things to discuss."

Her arms went around his neck and pulled his face closer. "But not now."

"No, not now."

Alex had no idea how much time passed when Michael left the bed, muttering about getting something cold to drink from the kitchen. She drowsily asked him to bring her a Coke as she daydreamed about asking Beth if she'd mind being her maid of honor again. Yes, Michael did have a point. Weddings were nice.

"I hope you're happy, Mom and Dad," she said out loud, hoping they could hear her.

"Of course we are, darling," Marian said from the foot of the bed.

Alex smiled. "I thought you two might have already left. After all, Michael and I are getting married and you said that's why you were here."

"True, but we thought about it and decided it might be nice to stay around and see our first grandchild."

She stilled. "Please, no. Michael really doesn't believe in you as it is. There's no way it would work out."

Marian laughed softly. "Alex, my dear, I don't think that will be a problem, because we invited one of his relatives to explain things to him."

The next thing Alex heard was glass breaking in the kitchen and Michael's muttered curse, before his incredulous "Aunt Chloe, is that you? But you're dead!"